To Face a Savage Land

SAVAGE LAND, BOOK 1

TO FACE A SAVAGE LAND

JOHN LEGG

THORNDIKE PRESS

A part of Gale, a Cengage Company

GALE
A Cengage Company

Thorndike Press, a part of Gale, a Cengage Company.

Thorndike Press® Large Print Hardcover Western.
The text of this Large Print edition is unabridged.
Other aspects of the book may vary from the original edition.
Set in 16 pt. Plantin.

LIBRARY OF CONGRESS CIP DATA ON FILE.
CATALOGUING IN PUBLICATION FOR THIS BOOK
IS AVAILABLE FROM THE LIBRARY OF CONGRESS.

ISBN-13: 978-1-4205-2746-9 (hardcover alk. paper)

Published in 2025 by arrangement with Wolfpack Publishing LLC.

Print Number: 1 Print Year: 2025
Printed in Mexico

To Face a Savage Land

One

Hawley Cooper wiped a ragged sleeve over his face, which was red from the heat and merciless sun. He staggered to a stop along the waterfront, weaving a little, and his stomach growled at him.

The moist heat lay over St. Louis like a sodden wool blanket on this late June afternoon, and the city was mostly quiet as people sought out what relief they could from the oppressive weather.

Cooper was barely eighteen years old, had turned such just the month before and he was only just arrived in the rancid, foul-smelling city. He was footsore and hungry. The last real meal he had had was four days ago. He had eaten, he must admit, just the day before yesterday, but that was only a handful of parched corn and several of over-ripe blueberries. His thin homespun cotton shirt was threadbare and soaked through with sweat. His pants of a material similar to that of his shirt were ragged, with a gaping hole in one knee and a smaller one in the seat.

He pulled off his tattered cloth cap and swiped a hand over his soaking head. He plopped the cap back on and slouched off down the street. The smells of the city near the wide river were almost overpowering. First, there was the river itself, foul and algae-coated along the shore, and with a slimy glaze left by the steamships that plowed furrows in the muddy, discolored water; the smoke belching from the stacks of the sternwheelers drifted over him; as did the fetid stench of waste products, both human and animal, which littered the streets and riverbanks. Garbage had been thrown willy-nilly about, adding its odor, as did wood smoke. But one smell overrode them all — cooking food.

Cooper sidestepped a rotting dog carcass, sending a flock of crows squawking unhappily away, only to resettle to their malodorous repast once he was by. Loud, raucous sounds exploded from the foul taverns along his route; children roared their exuberance despite the cloying heat; an occasional dog howled; and birds screeched as they sought prey around the river.

Despite his hunger, and the tiredness that

threatened to overwhelm him, Cooper was wide-eyed. He had never seen anything like this, though he had heard stories of the wild and rowdy town, with its vicious, brawling boatmen, Indians wandering the streets at will, bearded, half-wild trappers and . . .

So intent was Cooper on gawking that he bumped into someone. "Sorry," he muttered, turning. "I . . ."

He stopped at the sight, and swallowed hard, suddenly frightened. The man facing him was not very big, but there was something glittering in the dark, bloodshot eyes that scared Hawley Cooper down to his worn boots.

"Ought to watch where in hell you're goin', boy," the man snarled, his dark face clouding with anger.

"I'm sorry . . . I didn't mean . . ."

"Damn right ye ought to be sorry, boy. Ain't got the sense to stay out of the way of your betters."

The man looked Cooper over carefully, his nearly black eyes piercing. Cooper, at eighteen, was about as tall as he would get, but he had a heap of filling out to do. He was still youthfully awkward, mostly sharp angles and planes. A fine stubble covered his cheeks, chin and upper lip, while equally fine, sandy hair stuck out wildly from beneath the cloth cap. Nervously he wiped at his forehead, and his tongue tentatively darted over dry lips.

"You'd best start bein' more careful, boy," the man said finally. "It ain't often you'll meet up with someone of my forgiven' nature."

"I . . ." Cooper swallowed again. He was not easily frightened, usually, but there was something different about the man facing him, a danger lurking just below the surface, waiting for the right moment to spring forth. The man was a little shorter than Cooper, but had wide, square shoulders, long arms, and large-knuckled, calloused hands. His hair, under a short-crowned, wide-brim hat, was long and greasy. And his face, shaved maybe two weeks ago, was scarred, filthy and had a vicious cast to it.

He wore buckskin pants, fringed along each outer seam. The trousers were caked with grease, blood, dirt and other things upon which Cooper did not want to speculate. His dark-green calico shirt was bespeckled with old vomit, food, grease and other unknown substances. The man smelled of rancid meat, cheap whiskey, tobacco, smoke, blood and sweat. Cooper thought him an old man perhaps fifty, or nearly so but he could be wrong.

"Hungry, boy?"

Cooper nodded, the action making his head hurt.

"Got any specie on ye?"

Cooper shook his head, wary.

"Didn't think ye did." The man shifted the Dickert flintlock rifle in his arm, and he spit tobacco juice. "Ye look like ye got some gumption, boy," he said.

"I do," Cooper said, brightening fractionally, as he glanced at the pistol stuck in the man's wide, brass-tack-studded belt. It matched the rifle. "I'd be willin' to work for my supper."

The man laughed hard and harshly, the sound dribbling off into a hacking cough. "Work," he finally gasped. "Work?" He chuckled a bit, being careful not to choke again. "What can ye do, boy?"

Cooper drew himself up a little straighter. "I'm a blacksmith," he said, pride edging into his voice.

"Ye are, are ye?" The man laughed again, testing the limits of his unhealthy lungs.

"Yes, dammit," Cooper said, a growing anger making him forget, at least temporarily, his fear.

"Ye mean you're a got-damned apprentice, don't ye, boy?" The humor seemed to vanish.

"My apprenticeship was up a while back," Cooper said, suddenly growing wary again, thinking perhaps he had said too much.

The man looked at him and smiled, then laughed loud again, fighting back the coughs. "Ye cut out on your master, didn't ye, boy? Afore your time was up? Ain't that it?"

Cooper started to speak, then clamped his lips shut. The man laughed raucously again. "He put out a reward on ye, boy?" Reward came out in two long syllables. His eyes twinkled almost in benevolence.

Cooper shrugged.

The man grunted, then said, "Name's Josiah Weeks." He squinted up at the sun. Then he looked back at Cooper, his eyes clouded again. "Come on, then, boy, let's go and get your belly filled."

He turned and glided away, Cooper in his wake. As they walked, Cooper noticed the large, bone-handled butcher knife or maybe it was a scalping knife, Cooper thought with a twinge of fear, in the hard, beaded sheath centered on the decorated belt. A tomahawk was stuffed into the belt at the small of Weeks' back, laying diagonally.

Cooper lagged a bit, as he began to worry anew. He desperately wanted food, but he was not sure he wanted to do any work for this man. And why hadn't the man told him what the work was? Fear clutched at his belly.

Weeks had been right. Cooper had fled his apprenticeship with the blacksmith, an overbearing, brutish sort. But other than that, Cooper had never been in any trouble. He worried that Weeks was planning to feed him and then force him into a life of crime to repay him. It certainly could not be that Weeks planned to return him to the blacksmith for the reward, Cooper thought ruefully. The two pennies the blacksmith was offering was no incentive to anyone.

Weeks never looked back, though, and Cooper finally pushed aside the fears. Whatever happened, at least he would have a full belly. If Weeks asked him to do something wrong, he would get out of it somehow.

Cooper hurried, catching up with the trapper. The youth's stomach grumbled in anticipation. Weeks, with Cooper right behind him, turned into a foul-smelling eatery that was placed hard by the river. Cooper had gotten a glimpse of someone from the restaurant tossing a bucket of table scrapings out the back door into the river. He gulped, his hunger quieting momentarily at the sight.

The eatery inside was dim, with dirt floors and a filthy, shabby clientele. Cooper and Weeks sat at a scarred, unclean table. A grizzled, scrawny old man wearing a filthy leather apron shuffled up, and snapped, "What you boys want?"

"Buffalo steaks," Weeks said in like tone. "Keep 'em comin'. And bring some of them prairie turnips, if ye got any. Bread, too. Bring a pitcher of milk for the boy here, and a jug of Lightnin' for me." He set the rifle butt on the ground and rested the weapon against the edge of the table, near to his hand. He spit on the floor at the waiter's feet.

The waiter snarled as he left. Cooper and Weeks sat in silence, Cooper fidgety, embarrassed some by the cacophony erupting from his belly. His senses were assaulted by the sights, smells and sounds of the odious place. Weeks sat calmly, chewing tobacco and occasionally spitting the juice on the floor.

The food finally came, and with it fled Cooper's fears and inhibitions. He waded in, hunger overcoming his natural wariness, blotting out all the questions he still had. Weeks spit out the remains of his chaw and started eating, interspersing bites with large gulps of whiskey from a clear glass bottle.

At last they sat back, pushing their tin plates away. Full, Cooper began to grow more uncomfortable again under Weeks' hawk-like gaze. The trapper took another large swallow of whiskey, draining the bottle. He dropped it on the floor. "Ye got any plans?" he asked.

"Hadn't thought much on it."

"Naw, reckon ye ain't."

"You said somethin' about workin' before," Cooper said boldly. "Now, I'm more than willin' to work hard's I can for you to pay off this here meal. Maybe even extra for a small stake, too. But I'm tellin' you now, mister, I ain't given to bein' a lawbreaker."

Weeks laughed, the sound grating, before saying, "That what ye think, boy? Ye figure I'm gonna have ye stealin' and such for me?"

"The thought passed my mind," Cooper said with a shrug.

"Hmmm." Weeks pulled a twist of tobacco from a pouch at his waist. He tore off a piece, and Cooper noticed several gaps where teeth had once resided. Weeks got the chaw going. "I can use me a camp helper for the beaver season comin' on to us soon."

"What's that?"

Weeks spit, looking disgusted at the

youth's stupidity. He wiped his nose on his sleeve before bellowing across the room, "Bring me another bottle of that got-damned whiskey." He turned back to face Cooper. "A camp helper, boy," he said slowly, voice dripping with sarcasm, "is someone who helps around the camp."

"I know that," Cooper said scornfully. "But what do I have to do, exactly?"

The waiter slammed a bottle on the table and stomped off. Weeks yanked out the cork and tossed it away. He took a long, gurgling swallow. He held the bottle out toward Cooper, who shook his head. Weeks shrugged, took another swig, then said, "You'll set up camp, tend to the horses might even have ye doin' some black-smithin' work, fetch up wood and water, tan the plews I bring in, load and unload the mules, cook, if'n I don't buy me some got-damned squaw somewhere, and do whatever else needs doin'."

Cooper sat in thought for a long while, while Weeks sipped whiskey. Finally the trapper said, "Caution's a virtue, boy, some say, and I can see ye have a heap of it." He spit, then pulled off his hat and tossed it on the table. Scratching his filthy scalp under the greasy hair, he said, "But ye can't set here all the night tryin' to make up your mind, boy."

Cooper smiled wanly, then said, "And what are you to be doin' while I'm doin' all the work for you?"

Weeks' face was dark, but he said mostly civilly, "Settin' my traps and mindin' 'em; makin' balls for the guns; tradin' with the got-damned red stick savages; huntin' and butcherin' the meat; makin' meat for winter; settin' the proper trail; keepin' my eyes peeled for sign . . ."

"Seems I'm gettin' the poor end of this deal," Cooper said quietly.

Weeks shrugged and drank some more. Cooper could see the first signs of drunkenness in Weeks' eyes and face.

"I'd rather be a trapper," Cooper blurted out suddenly.

"You'll start as a got-damned pork eater, same's everybody else, boy," Weeks roared, voice slurring more than a bit. He gulped down another dose of whiskey and became visibly more drunk. "But, hell, I'll even teach ye to shine with a trap, boy. But mind, now, it's only 'cause of my good nature."

"You promise you'll teach me trappin' and such that goes with it?"

"I just said so, didn't I?" There was a malevolent gleam in his dark, drunken eyes. Cooper did not see it.

"Then you got a deal, Mr. Weeks," Cooper said. With a full belly and the prospect of adventuresome work, he was feeling fine. "When do we start?"

"When I get got-damned good and ready. Now leave me in peace, boy." He spit tobacco juice and drank more whiskey, weaving a little in the chair. The bottle was almost empty. "Run along, boy. Ye just hang around town. I'll find your sign when the time comes."

Two

Hawley Cooper's behind was rubbed raw by the time he and Josiah Weeks reached the confluence of the Kansas and Big Blue rivers. The horse Weeks had bought for him to ride was the scrawniest sack of walking crow bait Cooper had ever seen. Its bony back jerked up and down in an annoyingly irregular rhythm.

The saddle didn't help matters. It was little more than a pack saddle, a wide saddle horn of rawhide-covered wood, and then two short boards running lengthwise until they ended in a wood "X" at the back. A space ran between the slats. Cooper had learned that many mountaineers used such saddles. But when they did, they covered the boards and space with a thick haired buffalo hide. It made the seat well-padded. But all Cooper had was a thin two-point blanket Weeks supplied. Cooper not only had to use it for a saddle, he also had to use it as a sleeping roll and as protection against the chill that already tinged the nights.

Cooper also was sore all over. His back, legs and arms ached from the never-ending toil and the mare's jolting ride. His hands were scraped and burned from the jerk of the rope he held to the four pack mules strung out behind his horse. Making it worse were the stomach ills that had plagued him since they left, draining him.

They had been lucky in that the weather had been good so far, but that night, as Cooper made their camp on the Blue River, a few miles north of the Kansas, he could see storm clouds boiling in the west.

"Where's the fire, boy?" Weeks bellowed.

Cooper had been surprised early on to find that Weeks had helped him each night and morning. The trapper had aided in the making and breaking of camp, tended his own horse, and the few extras he brought along, and done some of the other chores. But in the past few days, Weeks had grown steadily surlier, and his help had dwindled to next to nothing.

"I'll get to it," Cooper said politely, unloading a pannier from the last of the four mules.

"Best get to it, boy. I got me an empty belly, and I aim to be fillin' it right off."

“The animals need tendin’.” The youth began to curry a mule.

“Them got-damned animals can wait,” Weeks roared. Cooper turned in surprise to see the older man’s eyes blazing. “I aim to eat straight away, so get to it. Ye can tend them critters after.”

Cooper shrugged. He made sure the horses and mules were well-hobbled, front and rear legs on the same side tied with a short length of rope before gathering up some cottonwood and willow branches.

It took but a few minutes before the fire was blazing under a spreading cottonwood. Cooper had become adept quite quickly at using flint and steel. He speared two hunks of buffalo meat on sharpened sticks and hung them over the fire on an iron support hammered into the ground. The meat was from an old bull Weeks had brought down two days earlier. It was one of the few buffalo they had seen so far, and the meat was tough. But the smell of the sizzling meat set Cooper’s mouth watering.

Cooper pushed himself wearily up and brought a canteen of water from the river. He set the canteen — a hollowed out gourd covered on the outside with rawhide and coated inside and out with beeswax — on the ground near the fire. He went back to the horses. By the time he had finished checking on the animals he figured the meat was ready, so he shuffled back to the fire, stretching his aching muscles.

"That was good eatin'," Weeks said, licking his fingers, grinning unpleasantly. "Not quite enough to satisfy this old coon, though."

"You want more, you cook it," Cooper said tightly. He seethed inside. It was not right, he thought, that he did so much of the work, while Weeks did little and still managed to eat enough for both of them at each sitting.

Despite his hunger, Cooper worked on the animals, rubbing them down with an old brush, and then wads of sweet-smelling grass. He loved animals, and knew their worth, especially out here, where a man afoot was quickly dead, more often than not. So he was very conscientious of this work.

The rain started while he was still working. It was soft at first, with a slight wind, and it felt nice. But by the time he was finished, it was raining steadily, though not yet very hard. The wind had picked up considerably, too, flattening the grass, and making the nearby willows bend. He put both hands in the small of his back and stretched backward, loosening the muscles. He gathered up more firewood, and then made certain his whole supply was covered with a piece of canvas. He also made sure there was tinder under the cover for the morning.

He grabbed two more pieces of meat and set them over the fire. As he flopped down, thankful that he had built the fire under the protective covering of the tree, no matter how meager it might be, Weeks looked at him in annoyance, but said nothing.

"My horse and one of the mules need reshoeing," Cooper said. "We ought to do it here, so we don't have no trouble up the trail."

"Ain't got the time for it, boy," Weeks said sternly. "I want to make the Pawnee villages soon. 'Sides, there's no buffalo hereabout. Ye keep eatin' so much, we'll run out of what we got soon enough."

Cooper shrugged, annoyed. Weeks had never been a pleasant man, but at least he had been civil at first. However, the past several days left Cooper wondering what lay ahead for him . . .

Still, he could not contain his curiosity. "You said we'd be goin' to Pawnee villages?" he asked.

"Yep. I'll trade for some plews, maybe a

bit of corn and such for winterin'. Might even look for a woman to do the cookin' and for other doin's. Winters do get cold and long up in them Stony Mountains, boy." He grinned, but there was no humor in it, nor warmth.

"You like Pawnee women?"

Weeks scowled and spit out the last of his tobacco. "Bah," he muttered. He stood and unrolled his six-point blanket and turned in, pulling a heavy, thick buffalo robe over him.

Cooper sat in thought, worried. He ate the meat and drank from the canteen, since Weeks had drained the pot of harsh boiled coffee. With mind ill at ease, Cooper finally turned in, pulling his meager blanket around him and over his head, trying to keep out the drizzle.

He awoke in a sea of mud, with the rain thundering down on him. "Damn," he mumbled, shivering as the wind blew through the thin blanket and chilled him. Weeks snored loudly, head burrowed under his almost waterproof wool blanket and the thick buffalo robe.

Cooper stood and stumbled through the mud to where he had neatly stacked the trade goods under a canvas covering. Working with trembling fingers, he got one pack open and pulled out a piece of canvas, another two-point blanket and then a plush six-point one. It was pitch black out, with no stars to be seen under the canopy of angry clouds, and the moon was not visible. He sloshed to a spot minutely higher than the one in which he had first made his bed and spread out the canvas. On that he put the thick blanket, and then the new thin one. He lay down in the middle of it all and pulled as much of it around him as he could, digging his head into the pile. He shuddered, still cold from the wet clothing. But he soon warmed, and with the rain beating a calming rhythm on his "nest," he fell asleep again.

The storm had passed on when Weeks roughly kicked Cooper awake in the morning. The sun was shining. "Get your lazy, do-nothin' ass up, boy, and set the fire to goin'. It's gone out, and there's no coffee to help me open my eyes."

Cooper, feeling a little guilty, threw off the blankets. "I'm sorry . . ." he started, standing hurriedly.

Weeks cut him off by roaring, "What'n hell ye doin' with them blankets, boy?" His dark eyes were aflame.

"It was cold, and I was soaked through. I . . ."

"Don't give me no sass, boy. Them blankets cost me good specie back to St. Louis. Now I can't sell 'em."

"I'll pay for 'em," Cooper said stiffly.

"You're got-damn right you'll pay for 'em, boy. Ye can be got-damned sure I'll take the price out of your wages first off."

"If I ever get paid," Cooper muttered under his breath.

"What'd you say to me, boy?"

"Nothin'," Cooper replied innocently.

Weeks glared at him, then said, "Well don't just stand there, boy. Ye a tree or somethin'? Go on and get to workin'."

Cooper cleared away the soaking ashes of yesterday's fire, giving thanks that he had kept wood and tinder protected from the storm. He gathered up what he needed and soon had a good fire going, coffee on, and meat cooking.

He hung his blankets on lower branches of a cottonwood to dry, and then did the same with Weeks's blanket and buffalo robe. He checked the packs of trade goods and supplies, pleased that nothing had gotten wet. He saw Weeks set to the fire and fill his tin mug with coffee, then reach for some seared meat. Cooper marched over to the fire and sat, taking the other piece of meat and pouring himself some coffee.

Weeks scowled but bent to pouring sugar into his coffee. Cooper was disgusted at the amount of it. He took none himself, usually, though he occasionally liked some honey in his coffee. Well, it was none of his doing, and Weeks would run out of it soon enough the way he was using it. He shrugged inwardly and tore into a piece of half-raw, not-very-tender meat.

Cooper was done first, but Weeks managed to get the last of the coffee. When Weeks was done, Cooper rinsed out the trapper's mug and the coffee pot. Then his own cup. The pot, and Weeks's mug were packed away, but Cooper tied his own mug to his cheap belt with a thong of rawhide. It was his cup, one of the few things he owned, and he was determined not to lose it.

The rest of his paltry personal belongings were in a possible sack he had made for himself from a discarded scrap of four-point blanket he had found. It had a long strap to let it hang over his shoulder, diagonally across chest and back, on his left side. His shooting bag with balls, extra flints, patch material, knapping tool, screwdriver and other small tools and such needed for his rifle hung the other way, so it was near his right hand.

The possible sack did not have much in

it, but it held all Cooper's possessions: a folding pen knife, small straight razor and wad of soap in a kit; two bandannas, one red, one blue, and both well used; several pennies; an awl; some sinew coiled around a small stick; a bit of deer antler he had found and thought he might find a use for; his flint and steel kit; tinder box; a whetstone; a worn clay pipe and small twist of tobacco; a few beads he had found; a few rawhide thongs; two bone needles; and a deck of playing cards.

He took pride in the things in his possible sack and the cup that dangled near it. During the weeks he had been in St. Louis waiting for Weeks to leave, he had found several odd jobs. He saved his pennies and occasional other small coins. With the money, he bought the jackknife and few other things, all of them used. But the cup he bought new. It was of real pewter, well-made and held a pint. It had a picture of an elk engraved on one side, and he cherished it. It was the first time he had ever owned anything so fancy.

Cooper began packing the mules, one at a time, panniers neat, weight distributed evenly so as not to burden the animals. He was used to the routine now, but he still took his time with it, so it was done right.

All the while, Weeks chaffed, but finally, seeing that Cooper was almost done, Weeks saddled his horse and rode out.

Cooper smiled. Weeks wanted to show his displeasure, and to frighten Cooper. But the youth knew better. Weeks would not ride too far without Cooper; not when Cooper had all the supplies. Cooper knew the trapper would be waiting a half-mile or so up the trail.

For just an instant, Cooper thought that maybe he would not follow; would take the supplies and trade goods and mules and head off in another direction. Trap on his own maybe. He could find a way west. Or he could just ride south until he cut the Santa Fe Trail; maybe head into the Spanish lands, sell the supplies there and try to hook up with another trapper to teach him.

He shook his head as he tightened the cinch on his saddle. No, he probably would die before he found anyone to help him or before he got to Santa Fe. He had heard of the fierce Comanches and Navajos and Kiowas and Cheyennes and Apaches he would have to ride through to get there.

He smiled again, despite the gloom he felt, as he tossed the thicker blanket across the slats of his saddle. Riding would not be so bad now, he thought. He climbed up and slid his rifle — a cheap trade fusil of the kind usually traded to Indians — into the rawhide loop near his saddle horn. The rifle would sit crossways across the saddle in front of him, ready for use, but leaving his hands free. He gathered up his reins in one hand and the thick rope leading to the pack mules in the other. "Come on, old girl," he said to the bony horse. "We'd best get to ridin'."

It was a brilliant day, the sky and air scrubbed clean by the rainstorm of the night before. A few high clouds, little more than puffs of shimmering white, floated across the vast expanse of bright blue. A soft breeze blew, ruffling the tall grass, and keeping the temperature down. Cooper grinned with the pleasure of the fine day.

Within a half-hour he caught up with Weeks, and even the sight of the foul trapper could not dampen Cooper's spirits.

He felt even better when, midway through the day, Weeks downed a large, fat buffalo cow. There would be good eating that night, Cooper knew; and he would be sure to cook enough to sate both of them.

Three

Hawley Cooper was bright with excitement, forgetting even his anger at Josiah Weeks and the aches and pains that weighed on his body. He was about to get to see his first Indians, real Indians, not the wretched creatures who populated the St. Louis waterfront. Weeks had said just a few minutes ago that they would be in a Pawnee village within the hour. By midday certainly. Indeed, Cooper could even hear the yapping of their dogs.

It was a week since they had picked up the Big Blue River and Cooper had told Weeks the one mule and one horse needed reshoeing. They would have been in the village by now had Weeks listened to the youth then, but he had not, and two days after they left that spot Cooper's horse threw the left foreleg shoe.

"Got-damned horse," Weeks snapped. "Got-dammit, you'll ride that got-damned horse even if she has tossed a shoe, boy."

Cooper dismounted. "I ain't goin' a step farther," he said adamantly.

"Got-dammit, boy, get movin'," Weeks bellowed, his voice hollow in the wide-open emptiness of the Plains. Spittle flew from his mouth.

"I ride this horse anymore without shoein' her and she'll not be fit for nothin' but baiting coyotes," Cooper said calmly. He knew horses, and he knew their limitations. He was not one to abuse an animal needlessly. "If I'm afoot, I ain't gonna be of no use to you. You want to ride on ahead, you go on. I'll keep my horse and that one ailing' mule and the tools. Once I get 'em fixed up, I'll catch up."

Weeks sputtered and fumed, then relented. "All right, boy," he said tersely. "We'll take the time. But we can't stay here for it."

"Why not?"

He waved a hand around. "What're ye gonna use for a fire, boy?" Weeks asked as if Cooper had lost his mind. "There ain't no trees hereabouts. Leastways, I don't see none." He shaded his eyes with his hand and looked around with an exaggerated motion.

"How far then?"

" 'Bout two mile on there's a spot with

good water and plenty of timber," Weeks said after a few moment's thought.

"All right, then." Cooper took his horse's reins in hand and started walking, leading the horse and the pack animals behind him. Weeks looked at him in disgust, but Cooper ignored him.

After a mile, the grass grew so tall, interspersed with giant, colorful sunflowers, that Cooper was lost in it. Reluctantly he remounted the mare and walked the animal as easily as he could.

Finally they were there. There was a wide stand of cottonwoods spreading out on each side of the river. White puffs of cottonwood seeds drifted toward them as they made their way along, making it look like it was snowing.

Cooper dismounted at the grove, but Weeks still sat his horse. "I'm goin' out to make meat," the trapper said. He leaned his forearms on the pommel of his saddle and said, steel in his voice, "I expect ye to have camp set when I get back."

"What about the two animals?"

"Their time will come, got-dammit, boy." He sat up and swung the horse's head around hard.

Cooper felt anger surge, but he forced it back. Weeks was becoming insufferable.

What would he be like once they reached the mountains, Cooper wondered. Perhaps he should have left the trapper down at the Kansas. But no. He was inexperienced, and did not know his way in this vast, trackless waste.

Slowly he pulled his animals into the trees. The sun was shining brightly, but there was an ominous look to the northwest, and Cooper thought he heard a distant rumble of thunder. He hobbled the animals, unloaded the mules and set about making the camp.

First, he put up Weeks' tent. He figured they would be here a few days, while he worked on the animals, and Weeks probably would want his comforts. So would Cooper, especially if another storm was on its way. But he would have to do without, as he had all along. He sighed, looking at the flight of a hawk. Then he gathered up firewood, enough just for a cook fire right now. Later he would have to lay in a good supply for his "forge."

He went back to the animals, rubbing them down, keeping an eye out for Weeks. He finally spotted the trapper just as he was finishing with the animals. Quickly he bent to making his fire. He snapped the flint against steel, sending showers of sparks at the charred cloth and flaky tinder. A curl of smoke popped up, and Cooper bent and blew gently until a small flame burst forth. Cooper hurriedly stacked on twigs. When they caught, he added larger twigs, then branches. As Weeks rode into the camp, Cooper was just adding two good-size logs.

Weeks tossed him a bloody bundle and then dismounted, leading his horse away toward the others. Cooper opened the piece of buffalo hide that was tied with a rawhide thong. Inside were the tongue, fleece and some of the ribs of the buffalo, along with the kidneys. There was no liver, which most men out this way considered a delicacy. Cooper supposed Weeks had eaten it while butchering the buffalo.

Cooper threw the tongue on the coals to bake, while he propped up the ribs, watching briefly as they began to sizzle. He hurried to the packs and pulled out some cornmeal. With deftness built of practice, he made up some cornpone and laid the cakes on hot stones.

Before long they were eating. Weeks, for the first time since they had left, pulled out a jug of whiskey, carefully wrapped in buffalo hide. He uncorked it and drank deeply as he reached with his knife for the tongue in the fire. He did not offer Cooper a drink.

Cooper pulled one of the long ribs covered with rich meat from the fire and gingerly tossed it from hand to hand until it was cool enough to eat. When it was, he ripped into it. He just loved the taste of buffalo meat, and already preferred it to anything else he might be able to get. It also had done wonders to curing his stomach ills.

He threw Weeks a few corn cakes. Weeks grunted thanks and ate them, but with far less enthusiasm than Cooper did. Cooper drank water. Weeks sipped or, most often, gulped from his jug.

"How long's it gonna take ye to get your work done, boy?" Weeks asked, mouth full of meat.

"Couple of days, I expect."

"Got-dammit, can't ye hurry it up none?"

"I can, but we'd only run into the problem again down the trail. Might's well get it all done now."

"Got-dammit," Weeks sputtered, tearing at some of the fleece. He had not taken long to demolish the tongue. "Them animals should've been shod right back to St. Louis."

"Most likely. But you should have made certain before we left."

"That's your job, boy."

"You never give me a chance."

"I were too busy."

"You're always too busy," Cooper said bravely. He was still mighty sore and very tired. He never seemed to get enough sleep or food for all the work he was doing. It made him cranky, and sometimes, like now, he forgot himself. "Or in a hurry. Now we got to spend time puttin' things to rights."

"Don't ye go lecturin' me, boy," Weeks snapped. He drew his large knife. Cooper had seen Weeks use it for butchering, and if Weeks was to be believed he also used it for scalping. If he was as good with it in a fight as he was in butchering, he was quite adept with it, Cooper knew, and had no desire to tangle with the man and his blade.

Cooper gulped, a sliver of fear spreading across his belly. "I ain't lecturin' you," he said hastily.

"Ye callin' me a liar then?" Weeks turned the knife so that it caught orange glints from the fire and from the sunlight that filtered down through the cottonwoods.

"Why now, Mr. Weeks," Cooper said, feeling quite queasy. "It's just that I . . . I . . ."

Weeks broke into his wild, coarse laughter, and managed to get through it without coughing. The sound still grated on Cooper.

After eating, Cooper cleaned up, and then sought out armful after armful of firewood. By dark, he thought he had enough. Before turning in, he made sure the wood was well-covered.

Cooper awoke in the night to the soft pattering of rain. He burrowed into his blankets and drifted back to sleep, and when he awoke again, the sky was clear. He made a breakfast of bacon with cornpone, and the two men washed it down with hot coffee. "That's the last of the bacon," Cooper said as he cleaned up after the meal. "And we're low on cornmeal."

Weeks nodded, not much interested.

Cooper shook his head and began building up the fire to generate as much heat as possible. Then he got his tools. They had not brought many, but there were enough for him to do his work: a small anvil; some iron bars; half a dozen files; a small pair of calipers; a shoeing knife; small sledgehammer; shoeing hammer; a pair of tongs; several punches; a craser; a fuller; a pritchel; oil stone; and a can of sperm oil. It was more than most beaver men would have brought along, but since Cooper was trained, Weeks thought they might pick up some extra pelts by having Cooper do some work for the various tribes.

Cooper retrieved a long-handled ax and chopped down a moderate size cottonwood near the fire. With a small adze, he made the stump mostly level. It would do for his workbench. He put the anvil on it, then filled a buffalo paunch with river water and set it nearby.

All that day he heated iron and hammered it, crimped it, bent it. Frequently he would have to toss more wood on the fire. He sweated heavily, perspiration dripping from his bare chest and arms, from his forehead and chin. Twice the heat made him dizzy, and he staggered off to the river and plunged in, thankful for the blessed coolness.

By evening he thought he had enough shoes made. He was bone weary from the constant hammering and from the draining heat. But still he managed to cook some of the buffalo meat Weeks had brought in fresh that day. Within minutes of finishing his meal, he was asleep.

The next day he was stiff and sore. But he forced himself to work, ignoring, for the most part, Weeks's grumbling. He spent the day actually working on the animals, cleaning shoes, replacing some, filing hooves, whatever needed doing. By late afternoon he was done and began repacking his tools into the wood crate.

"Took ye long enough, boy," Weeks said. The trapper, whose age Cooper had revised down by some ten or twelve years, had gone hunting in the morning, coming back with some deer meat and the best cuts of a young buffalo cow. Then he spent the rest of the day napping or eating, while Cooper worked, sweating in the hot sun.

Cooper grunted as he heaved the small anvil off the stump. He made a great effort to ignore Weeks.

"I'm talkin' to ye, boy," Weeks said sullenly.

"Go to hell," Cooper said without thinking. He set the anvil down and then turned back toward the crate of tools.

"What'd ye say to me, boy?" Weeks asked tightly.

"You heard me," Cooper griped, exhaustion overcoming common sense. He turned with the crate in hand, and Weeks hit him. Cooper staggered back a few steps before falling on his behind, the crate of heavy tools crashing down onto his shins.

"Damn," Cooper mumbled. He reached a hand up and pulled it away from his lip coated with blood. He shoved the box of tools away. "What in hell did you do that for?" he asked incredulously.

"You'd best learn to respect your betters, boy," Weeks said, his face ruddy with anger.

"Don't ever hit me again," the youth said through clenched teeth. His head, jaw and legs hurt, but he would not let Weeks see him giving in to it.

"And if'n I do?" Weeks asked with a sneer.

"You'll see," Cooper said, standing. He reached for the box and Weeks hit him again, knocking him back down.

"Don't ye threaten me, boy, less'n ye can back it up. I've killed better men than ye for a heap less."

Cooper stood shakily. He was torn between anger and a growing fear. He was strong, but Weeks had handled him easily, though he was not really paying attention when Weeks had hit him. Still, Weeks had the kick of a mule in his fist. He shook his head and winced as it began to pound. Gritting his teeth, he picked up the box and shoved past Weeks, fear still gnawing at him. When he finished his work, he ate in silence, and then rolled into his blankets before dark.

His head and face still hurt in the morning, and his face was discolored. His left eye twinged every once in a while, but they were not so bad. He avoided Weeks as much as possible. Weeks said little to him, but he did begin singing badly to be sure as they rode off.

Cooper was not much of one to hold a grudge, and his anger began to dissipate in the afternoon sun. So did his fears. He passed the day in looking at the tall grass, various wildflowers, and animals that drifted near them. He saw at least a dozen grizzly bears snuffling around, and Weeks steered them clear of one grizzly sow with two cubs. Antelope and deer were plentiful, and they saw many buffalo.

The storm Cooper had thought he had seen building several days earlier had not materialized, for which he was grateful. But another one swept down on them the next day, bringing hellacious winds and driving sheets of hard rain. The temperature plunged, and Cooper shivered in his worn cotton clothes, until his teeth chattered. Finally he pulled out his six-point blanket and wrapped it around himself. He sighed in blissful relief as it warmed him considerably.

The storm passed within several hours, but it left behind an ocean of clinging mud, slowing their progress. They pushed on, making a poor camp that night. The clear skies and warm temperatures of the next two days dried the ground, at last, until their riding produced a cloud of dust.

That night Weeks said, "We'll be in one of the villages soon. Most likely tomorrow."

"How can you tell?"

Weeks pointed almost due north. "Oh," Cooper said, feeling foolish, for there, in the distance, he could see a number of columns of smoke.

FOUR

Hawley Cooper gazed in amazement as he rode into the Pawnee village behind Josiah Weeks and a cavorting phalanx of Pawnee warriors, who had escorted the two white men for the last half-mile.

The warriors were not tall, generally, but they rode arrogantly. "They're near about the worst horse Injuns ye ever saw," Weeks had told Cooper when they first saw the warriors. " 'Bout the only ones worse is the Utes."

But still they were proud of themselves. Most of the men wore only a breechcloth and moccasins; and in the village sometimes not even that. Most had large earrings that looped and swirled around the entire rim of the ear. And most were shaven headed except for a strip of hair from front to back in the center, often built up into a roach with grease and animal hair.

Cooper's jaw dropped as they entered the

village. Never in all his days had he seen . . . Why some of the women were bare-breasted! Come to think of it, the majority was. Most of the women over the age of thirteen or so wore a simple kilt-like dress from the waist down, but absolutely no clothing above. The very young ones and the boys, too wore nothing at all. The women were not the slightest ashamed of their nakedness. Indeed, many stood and boldly watched the white men enter the village.

Cooper and Weeks rode past the mud and stick homes, each with smoke drifting from the hole at top. Naked children ran yelling in their games. Dogs ran helter-skelter, barking and snapping. Meat racks abounded, each with long, thin strips of buffalo or deer hanging over them, drying in the sun. Women were constantly vigilant lest one of the pesky mongrels snatch a prized piece of meat.

Some women worked at various stages of tanning buffalo hides, scraping or washing, working brains into the hides, pulling the big, heavy hides over rawhide ropes. Cooper could see still others off to the other side of the village, either working in the small fields of corn or gathering the berries that grew in profusion. Some worked on making clothes or grinding corn or . . .

The place was such a bustle that Cooper could not take it all in at once. Finally Weeks stopped ahead of him, and they dismounted, leaving their horses and mules. Weeks sat, cross-legged, next to an old, wrinkled Indian with long, thick, graying hair. Suddenly ill at ease, Cooper flopped down next to Weeks.

There was a tension in the air, Cooper thought, and he was afraid of the unknown, of what foolishness Weeks might try to pull.

Only yesterday Cooper had asked Weeks about the Indians and learned just how much Weeks hated the red men.

"They're nothin' but got-damned murderin' savages, boy," Weeks had said, his face suddenly condensed in fury. "All of 'em. Each and every last man jack of 'em. No better'n animals, are they. Even the best of 'em, if there is such a thing. The men're all struttin' got-damn peacocks, and the women all got-damn disease-spreadin' whores, boy. Do ye hear me now, boy, and what I'm sayin' to ye?" Spittle dribbled from his chin, and Cooper began to grow worried, and frightened, at the mad gleam in Weeks's eyes.

"Then why do you have any truck with

’em?” Cooper asked. His mouth had gone dry.

“Got to, boy. Can’t get along in these parts without doin’ so. Need their plews, their good will.” The last was said with loathing.

“But . . .”

“Don’t ye but me, boy,” Weeks screeched. He stopped his horse and swung it around so he could face Cooper. “Didn’t ye learn anything the last time ye sassed me? Eh? Don’t go flappin’ your got-damn gums on things ye don’t know nothin’ about, boy.”

He calmed fractionally. “Injuns don’t give a good got-damn about no white man. They’re just like snakes, or grizzlies. Animals. Foul smellin’, dog-eatin’ bastards.”

Cooper opened his mouth but caught himself and snapped it shut before any words came out. He just nodded as Weeks turned his horse and rode on. Cooper wondered what some Indians could have done to Weeks for him to have such a black heart toward all Indians.

Could it be that Weeks was right? Cooper wondered. He had heard the talk about the Comanches and the Blackfoot and others, and how they tortured a man beyond endurance. Maybe the stories were true. Maybe Weeks was right.

But that couldn't be, he thought. No, he had seen and heard of too many white men who had gone off to live with the Indians of their own accord. Men who married into the tribe and fathered children of those people. They could not all be bad. Could they?

Now he sat in the Pawnee village, watching the vain warriors and slim, sometimes pretty women, and he wondered anew. These people certainly didn't seem to have murder in their hearts, but one could never tell. Until they had been on the trail a week or so, Weeks had seemed almost an amiable, if irascible, fellow. But slowly he had turned more and more evil, the farther they got from civilization. And yesterday's outburst had left Cooper reeling. Would Weeks do something stupid to get them both killed?

He sat and tried to relax, sweeping his gaze over the rank of warriors opposite them. Weeks smoked a pipe with the old Pawnee, and then food was brought. Cooper dug in, not knowing what was in the bowl, and not much caring. It was tasty, and he wolfed it down.

After they had eaten, Weeks and the old Indian talked. Cooper sat, fascinated for a while, unable to understand more than an occasional word as the two men chatted in a quick-paced amalgam of Pawnee, French, English, Spanish and sign language.

Finally he could sit no more. Steeling himself, Cooper stood and moved off, wandering through the village. He felt curious eyes on him, but he was not sure whether it was fact, or his imagination. A number of warriors had left the discussion and were scattered about the village, totally at ease. They gambled or napped, worked or relaxed. More than once a burst of laughter startled Cooper.

Most of the women were back at their tasks, too, as the newness of the visitors wore off. White men were nothing new to this village. Several of the younger women smiled at Cooper, and he smiled back, beginning to feel deep stirrings within him. He had been with a woman before, but only once, and his young blood ran hot with desire now.

Fear kept him alone, at least for a while. Fear of this new place; fear of what Weeks might do; fear that at any moment he would hear a screaming horde of Pawnees coming after him, ready to tie him to a stake and do unspeakable things to him.

He shivered and took a deep breath, clutching his used trade rifle tighter, and reaching his other hand for the cheap pistol stuck in the tattered belt. It reassured him only a little.

Then he saw a girl — well, woman actually, that was obvious — and his fears fled, replaced by a burning lust. She was maybe fourteen or fifteen and possessed of creamy skin and an ample bosom. She looked up from where she had been grinding corn. The work made her naked breasts sway seductively. She smiled, dazzling him, and sat back, wiping a forearm across her forehead. Sweat glistened on her face and in the valley between her breasts.

She said something to him, but he shook his head. "I don't understand," he said, his mouth suddenly arid. "Do you speak English?"

"Little."

"It's more than the Pawnee I speak," he said, smiling, though there was a knot in his belly. He squatted next to her. "Will you talk with me a while?" he asked in a whisper.

She grinned at him, making his heart pound. "Yes."

"What's your name?" he asked.

She rattled off something in Pawnee, and he looked blankly at her. "It means," she added, "Corn Flower."

He almost chuckled but caught himself as

she stared at him in wonder. "It's a pretty name," he said finally. "You speak pretty good English, Corn Flower. Where'd you learn?"

She shrugged, the action jiggling her breasts. Cooper caught his breath. "From trappers. Traders come live here sometimes."

He nodded, thinking hard, almost not hearing her. He knew what he wanted, what his loins told him he must have. But he was too frightened and too uncertain to ask. So they sat and chatted as best they could about the land, and the weather, and the animals, until finally they fell silent. Cooper stood, his legs shaky as desire rampaged inside him. "I better go," he croaked, unhappy with himself.

"Why?"

He waved a hand vaguely around. "I don't know. Go find my partner, maybe, or . . ." His voice trailed off.

"Stay."

"I'd like that, Corn Flower. I . . ."

She stood and took his hand in her tiny, warm one. Her touch and nearness almost overpowered him. She tugged him toward the lodge behind them. He resisted a little. "Don't I need to give you something? Or maybe your father?"

"You give me present, not father. Now come." She tugged a little harder, and he could not resist.

They entered the dark, musty lodge, and Corn Flower quickly dropped her single garment. Cooper was a bit disturbed by her brazenness, but his loins burned, and he shoved the disturbing feelings aside. In seconds he was next to her on the buffalo robe bed.

It was over much too quickly for them both. But with their youth and resilience, they were ready for each other again before long.

As they lay next to each other, trying to catch up on their labored breathing, Corn Flower said, "We can't stay here no longer, Hawwy." She had trouble with his name.

"You want me to leave?" he asked, worried. He never wanted to go.

"No. We stay together. Good, huh? But not here."

"Where're we gonna go?"

"Outside. You have blankets?" She looked at him questioningly, her dark eyes almost luminous in the gloom broken only by the coals.

" 'Course I got blankets."

"Good. Come." She stood, holding out her hands to him. He took them and let her pull him up. She replaced her skirt, and he adjusted his clothing; he had never quite gotten around to removing most of it. They stepped out of the lodge into the beautiful, moon-lit night. Cooper had not realized they had been in the lodge so long. A soft breeze was blowing away from them, taking the village odors with it.

In the firelight near the counsel lodge, Cooper and Corn Flower could see dancing, and Cooper could feel the drumming right down to the worn soles of his boots. Cooper saw that Weeks, who still sat across from the Pawnee leader, looked quite drunk, as did the chief.

The young couple strolled to where Cooper had left the animals. They were gone, with all the supplies, and Cooper began to panic.

"I know where they are," Corn Flower said. She led Cooper to another lodge. "This lodge is for you and your friend," she said, leading him inside. All his and Weeks' supplies were there.

Cooper nodded, got his bedding and followed Corn Flower.

The young woman brought him near the river, with its symphony of sounds from crickets, cicadas and frogs. In the protection of a small circle of cottonwoods, he spread his blankets, and they made love again, hurriedly, with the impetuosity of youth.

After a while, Cooper said, "Damn, I'm hungry. I ain't had nothin' but that stuff at the council fire since mornin'."

"Stay here," Corn Flower said. "I will bring food."

She was gone a long time or so Cooper thought. Then she was back, breathing hard from hurrying, with some recently boiled buffalo and a dish of boiled corn. It wasn't that good, but Cooper didn't care. He ate it down. It seemed he never quite got filled up.

They made love again, and then fell asleep, entwined in each other's bodies. It was not quite dawn when they awoke and made love once more. Then Corn Flower said, "I must go."

"Will I see you again?" Cooper asked, aching.

"I'd like."

"I'll see what I can do." He was downcast, knowing he would be riding out of the village within a few hours at most. Suddenly he brightened. "Maybe I can take you with me." It was as much a question as a statement.

She smiled. "Good."

He rose and rolled up his blankets. "Reckon you'd better go first," he said, still excited by her presence, but trying to impress her with his common sense.

"Good." She stroked his cheek, and then flitted off, silently.

Cooper watched until she was gone behind a screen of trees. He lifted his blankets and walked off, whistling a tune his father had often hummed while working when Cooper was just a boy.

He heard retching and coughing near the river. Cautiously he peered around a tree trunk, and saw Josiah Weeks bent over. Cooper grinned and strolled off. He put his blankets in the lodge and got some buffalo meat. Building up the fire just outside the lodge, he put the coffee pot on, then hung several pieces of meat on his ramrod and held it over the fire.

Cooper was just finishing his meal when Weeks showed up. He was badly hungover, and in a foul mood. He slumped down with a groan next to the fire. He went through another spate of coughing. "Got-dammit," he finally wheezed.

"Want somethin' to eat?" Cooper asked cheerily.

"Ye set food in front of me now, boy, and I'll gut ye." He moaned.

"Coffee?"

"Yep."

It took several hours and several cups of strong, black coffee before Weeks started to think he might live another day. Cooper sat, waiting patiently on the outside, but fidgeting inwardly in anticipation. There was something he had to ask Weeks; something tremendously important. But Weeks had to be in a good mood or in as good a mood as he ever got.

"Where'd ye get yourself off to last night?" Weeks finally asked, almost pleasantly, shortly before the sun reached its zenith.

Cooper grinned. Now was his chance.

Five

Hawley Cooper's grin threatened to split his face.

"You found yourself a woman?" Josiah Weeks asked suspiciously. "For all night?" Weeks' voice rose with the question.

"Yep."

"Got-damn, boy, I never knew ye had that kind of sand in ye. That shines, it does."

Cooper could not believe it. Weeks was treating him almost like an equal. Now was the time. His grin dribbled away, replaced by a somber look. "She's somethin', Josiah . . ." He gulped at the use of Weeks' first name, but the trapper paid it no mind. "She really is. As fine a woman as I ever seen. She . . . She . . . She shines. Yep, that's the way of it." He was proud of himself.

Weeks looked surprised but said nothing as Cooper continued. "Anyway, I took a shine to her, Josiah" still no reaction "and I'd like you to . . . I mean . . . I don't have . . . But you . . .”

“Spit it out, boy,” Weeks said before belching. He looked as if he had just swallowed something sour.

“Well, Josiah, as you know, I ain’t got no money.”

“That’s right, boy.”

“But I been workin’ hard for you, and maybe you could let me have some of my wages now . . .”

“What for?” Weeks raised an eyebrow in question, though he thought he already knew.

“So’s I can offer Corn Flower’s pa it for her.”

Weeks broke into laughter, which changed quickly into coughing. He stopped both, finally, and sat wheezing, holding his head in both hands. When he looked back up at Cooper, his eyes were bloodshot through, and his chest heaved.

“What’s so damned funny?” Cooper demanded, growing angry.

“Couple things. First off, I ain’t got that kind of specie on me. Second, her pa, whoever he is, ain’t gonna want no money for her. He wants horses, boy, and a heap of ’em. And maybe some guns.”

“Where am I gonna get horses?” Cooper almost groaned. Then his eyes widened.

"You said guns? We got some guns we can . . ."

Weeks' look froze him. "Them guns is for tradin' for plews and other such plunder as we need to survive, boy," Weeks said harshly. "They ain't for buyin' ye a warm winter's bed."

"I heard that's what you done," Cooper said stubbornly.

"Where'd ye hear such a thing?"

"It's all over the village. You went and bought yourself some old squaw for a rifle, a pistol and some powder and ball."

"That's different, boy. That's my plunder, and I'll do with it what I see fit. Ye hear me?" His eyes burned.

"That ain't fair," Cooper said, taken slightly aback by the hatred and anger in Weeks' eyes. He was close to tears, so angry was he, and his breath came in fits and starts.

"Who in hell ever said anything about fair, boy?" Weeks snapped, his face mottled with anger.

Cooper leaped up. His fists were bunched as rage tore through him. He started walking away.

"Where'n hell ye goin', boy?"

Cooper stopped and turned slowly, fighting to control the anger. "I aim to find that girl's pa," he said deliberately. "And see if I can make a deal with him. Come next season, I'll have my own possibles, and I can come back and pay him off." He spun on his heel.

"Got-dammit, come back here," Weeks bellowed. "Ye go on over there and you'll like as not get us both killed."

Cooper craned his neck around. "You gonna help me?"

"Yes, yes, got-dammit. Now get on back over here." When Cooper sat back down, Weeks said, "Ye just let me handle this, boy. Ye got no sense in these matters. I've dealt with these murderous savages before. Now, what did ye say this girl's name was?"

"Corn Flower. She lives in a lodge over yonder." He pointed.

When Weeks came back a little more than an hour later, Cooper was waiting expectantly. His brightness dimmed when he saw the look on Weeks' face. "What's wrong?" he asked, anxiously.

"Ye are some, boy, I'll say that for ye," Weeks said, his face fluctuating between bemusement and anger. "Got-damn, ye are some."

"What? What did I do?"

"Your little Corn Flower is married, got-dammit. To an older warrior named Iron

Bow. I know the bastard some. He's one of the most murderous of these heathens and has a heap of respect 'round here."

"Oh," Cooper gulped.

"I suggest we mount up and get our asses out of here."

"But why? If Corn Flower likes me, what's so wrong?" Cooper asked, not wanting to face the reality of it.

"Iron Bow give that girl's pa more'n two dozen ponies for that adulterous squaw. Ye got that kind of plunder to give him? And to Iron Bow for the loss of that bitch's affections?"

"Well . . ."

"Of course ye ain't. Besides, once Iron Bow hears of all this, he's gonna be one mean son of a bitch." Weeks blew his nose into the air and then wiped the residue off his face with his sleeve.

"But . . ."

"But what, boy?" Weeks scratched his crotch, then his chest, oblivious to the lice that crawled all over him. "Ye think since she spread herself for ye so willingly last night she wants to spend her life with ye? And ye with her?"

He laughed stridently, surprising both of them when he did not fall into a spate of coughing. "That's it, ain't it?" He cackled some more. "Mayhap it's true she wants ye, boy. She ain't but a girl, barely past the time of becomin' a woman. Or so I reckon from the glimpse I got. And Iron Bow ain't as spry as he used to be. But these savage bastards got their own ways. Iron Bow ain't gonna give that woman up so easy. Leastways not to the likes of ye. Maybe if'n ye hadn't already lain with her, ye might've been able to dicker. But not now. He'll lose respect, or at least he'll think he will."

Weeks squinted into the sun, looking around the shabby camp. He hawked up some phlegm and spit in the dirt. The two men were still standing, and Weeks set the butt of his flintlock into the dirt and leaned on the muzzle. "The main thing for ye to remember, boy, is that you're a bit too late. So get your got-damned mind off her." He laughed again, the harsh sound bitter and not at all humorous.

"We need to leave in a hurry?"

"Well, boy, Iron Bow is a mean, spiteful, unforgivin' bastard with a murderous intent to any white man. He finds out some young white buck's been layin' with his youngest wife, he ain't gonna be in the most humorous of spirits." Anger grew again in the bloodshot eyes. "And, got-dammit, since I talked to ol' Crooked Leg that girl's pa I'm in it now, too."

"Then let's go." Cooper cast fearful glances about.

Weeks laughed at the fright. "Ain't that much of a hurry, boy. Iron Bow's out somewhere in Sioux country tryin' to raise hair. Leastways, so I been told."

Cooper almost grinned, thinking of the possibilities. "When's he gonna be back?"

Weeks shrugged and straightened, keeping both hands folded over the muzzle of the rifle. "Could be today, maybe next month. If Crooked Leg thinks there's anything in it for him, he'll send someone out to find Iron Bow and tell him. He's been gone a spell anyway, I hear, and most likely'll be back soon."

Cooper nodded, crestfallen. "Reckon I'll start gettin' ready." He turned away, then suddenly spun back, eyes glittering with excitement. "Let's take her with us," he said, breathing hard.

"Corn Flower?"

"Yep." Cooper almost bounced with effervescence. "It won't take long to pack and be ready to leave. We'll be all set. Soon's dark comes, I'll fetch Corn Flower and we can ride out. By the time anyone realizes she's gone, we'll be miles away."

Weeks spit again, giving himself time to

control his temper. "Ye are the got-damnedest, stupidest, most got-awful foolish son of a bitch I ever met, boy."

Cooper's face froze and then turned sour.

"Why don't ye think, for just one time in your life, boy. Did your ma raise ye to be this got-damned stupid, or have ye been followin' its sign on your own?" He snorted in disgust. "Never mind."

"What's wrong with my idea?" Cooper demanded, angry.

"I told ye afore, boy, Injuns ain't no better than animals. It don't take much to set their hearts against ye. Sometimes nothin' at all." He struggled to control his rising anger. "We pull this scheme and we'll have every got-damned Pawnee on the Plains followin' our trail set to raise hair. Can't ye see that, got-dammit?"

He stopped and drew in a ragged breath, then said, no more calmly, "That what ye aimin' for, boy? Ye plan on havin' a pack of yellin', bloodthirsty savages doggin' our trail?"

The last was nearly screamed, and both men suddenly looked around, nervous, afraid that Weeks might have been overheard and understood. But if anyone had understood, they gave no sign of it.

" 'Course I don't want that," Cooper said

in a whisper.

"Well, that's just what you'd get us, boy. Got-dammit, listen to me. I know these red devils. Ye don't. I've seen these critters at their devilish work. They are the spawn of Satan himself, boy, with no souls to be saved, and so none to keep their base instincts in check. Once their blood passions is raised, there's no stoppin' 'em 'til their blood lust is slaked."

Cooper stood in wonder as Weeks breathed heavily from his ranting. There was a murderous gleam in Weeks' eyes, and he absentmindedly toyed with the butt of his pistol. A shiver slid down Cooper's spine as he watched the trapper, and once again he wished he had left Weeks long ago. But he could not now; not here in a Pawnee camp, with at least one warrior out for his blood or would be soon.

With sagging shoulders, Cooper turned and began pulling their supplies out of the lodge and stacking them outside.

"Don't rush like somebody's chasin' ye, boy," Weeks said from behind him. "But don't dally, neither. I'll be back in a spell."

Cooper kept to his work. Before long, several Pawnee boys came up leading his and Weeks' horses and mules. Cooper nodded his thanks and began packing the supplies on the mules.

Soon after he caught a glimpse of Corn Flower heading out of camp on foot with some of the other women. Like her companions, she carried a basket on her hip. Cooper took a step in her direction. Then he stopped, remembering where he was, and who she was. He felt a block of ice in his belly at the thought of Iron Bow, Crooked Leg and a dozen other warriors hunting him down, lances and bows and guns ready. The fear deepened when he thought they might not kill him at first.

He shivered and went back to his work with renewed fervor. He forced himself to slow down, trying to look natural. All the while his eyes scanned around, keeping watch for a returning party of warriors. If he saw them, he wanted to be ready to leave in a hurry. He touched his pistol frequently, and glanced at his rifle nearby, trying to reassure himself.

He finally finished and sat in the dirt near the fire he had built that morning. The day was hot and muggy, but Cooper still felt chilled inside. He waited for Weeks a while, then shrugged and roasted himself some buffalo meat. He was still eating when Weeks returned, an Indian woman in tow. She held the rope to half a dozen horses.

"Ye near ready to leave, boy?" Weeks asked. Cooper noticed the anger was gone from Weeks' face and eyes, but the trapper's voice held no hint of friendliness.

"Anytime you are."

"We got time to eat first, I reckon," Weeks said, sitting. He said something to the woman in Pawnee. She put the horses with the others, then took off some pots from one of them. Soon food was cooking. Weeks said nothing, only sat with his rifle on his crossed legs. He ate without hurry and without manners, as was his custom.

When he was done, he tossed the bowl into the dirt. The Indian woman retrieved it, cleaned it and the pots and put everything away in a parfleche, which she tied on a horse.

"Let's go," Weeks said, rising.

"If she's comin' with us," Cooper said, rancor evident in his voice, "maybe you ought to tell me her name." He looked longingly toward where he had last seen Corn Flower.

"Tall Grass," Weeks said after a long pause. "Now let's go."

Six

Hawley Cooper pulled up alongside Josiah Weeks and said, "I think someone's on our trail." He whispered, not wanting to alarm Tall Grass.

"Yep."

"Why didn't you say anything?" Cooper asked peevishly. His situation had not improved, and it was wearing on him.

"I was waitin' for ye to find out on your own, boy," Weeks said, glaring at him. "Took ye long enough, too."

"How long's he been there?"

"Three, maybe four days."

Cooper hung his head, deeply ashamed. He was disgusted that he had not known it sooner. Of course, Weeks had not seen fit to teach him anything, but still . . . He wiped a trembling hand over his sweating face. Though Tall Grass now did all the cooking and some of the other camp chores, Cooper still had more than enough to keep him busy, and he was always tired. Tired of the riding; tired of the monotonous, undulating ground with its short, browned grass and dying wildflowers; tired of the tension that grew daily between him and Weeks.

They had left the Pawnee village ten days ago, taking their time following the Big Blue northward. Late the next day they had made camp near the river's confluence with its west branch. They forded the fast-running river carefully the next morning, and they took off at a faster pace, following that branch of the river westward to its end. After that there was a day's waterless ride across open, scrubby ground before the Platte spread out before them, wide and shallow. They camped there that night and then rode on westward the next morning along the Platte's south bank. The usually shallow river was split frequently by many small islands and the big Grand Island that grew with thickets of brown, often thorny brush and stunted, forlorn cottonwoods. An occasional willow grew up from the mud.

Cooper and Weeks talked little these days, as they meandered along. Weeks began to set his traps each night or nearly each. He caught beaver steadily, though they were of rather poor quality. Still, Weeks had Tall Grass show Cooper how to tan the beaver skins to make them as glossy and plush as possible.

Sandstone abounded, with round ridges of the rock all about. There were no buffalo, and little other game, so Cooper got his first taste of beaver tail. Weeks hung several of the tails over the fire, letting them dangle in the flames until they were done. Cooper was surprised at the taste. It wasn't buffalo, but it was a sight better than some things he had eaten, and a heap better than going hungry.

Cooper wasn't sure just what it was that had made him think there was someone following them. It was just a sensation at first, the prickling of the hair on the nape of the neck, an uneasy feeling. He looked behind him often, eyes scanning the bleak, brown horizon behind them. Nothing. Time and time again he searched. Nothing.

Then he saw something. Or thought he did. He wasn't sure what it was, if it was there. He just knew there was something or someone following them. He kept a more wary eye on their back trail then, since he was bringing up the rear, like he always did.

"Is it an Indian?" Cooper asked, finally.

"Yep. Pawnee."

"You sure?"

Weeks ignored the question. Then Cooper

asked, "Do you know who it is?" He thought he did and did not like the feeling it left in him.

"I don't know all them savages real well, mind ye, boy," Weeks said with the hint of a malicious grin. "And I never had me no truck with Iron Bow, but I do believe that'll be him."

Cooper felt sick as fear twisted his entrails. He must have shown it, for Weeks burst into his awful laugh. "It's nothin' to make light of," Cooper said weakly. "Think he's after us?"

"Most likely it's ye he's after, boy. I ain't done nothin' against that black-hearted bastard. But you . . ." He drifted off into another gale of laughter.

"You don't think he could just be out huntin', do you?" Cooper asked without much hope.

"I doubt it, boy. I ain't had a real close look at him, ye understand, but from what I seen, he's painted and set to raise hair. 'Sides, there ain't no buffler 'round here, less ye seen some I ain't."

"What're we gonna do?"

"I ain't gonna do a damn thing, 'cept keep my eyes open, follow my trail, and watch my topknot."

"What should I do?" Cooper cast fearful

eyes back. He could see the Indian clearly now, and even at this distance he could see the roached hair, long lance, and the rifle across the saddle. He shivered.

"Take that got-damn old musket of yours there and drop him," Weeks said harshly.

"From here?"

"Sure." There was a glint in Weeks' eyes.

"With this?" Cooper held the trade rifle toward Weeks accusingly.

Weeks shrugged. "Shit, if that won't work for ye, then go on out there and face him, boy, or wait till he comes up on us, and then do it." He grinned with his lips only.

Cooper thought for a moment, then said with fear coloring his voice, "He ain't gonna come close enough for me to shoot him, is he?" He did not wait for an answer. "He's gonna wait till it's dark, and then come slinkin' into camp and take my hair. Ain't he?" Cooper's face was white as chalk, and his breathing was ragged.

"Reckon he will," Weeks said, excitement barely suppressed.

"He won't let me get close enough to him, either, will he?" Cooper asked with a gulp.

"Reckon not. Maybe you'll have to keep awake for the night, be ready to face him. Ye ain't got but two got-damn choices, far's I can see, boy. Set your mind to facin' him.

Or just climb off that horse here and now, take off your cap and wait till he rides on down to fetch your hair." The excitement died, replaced by loathing at Cooper's cowardice.

"How about we head across the river?" Cooper asked. He was on the verge of desperation.

Weeks snorted in disgust. "Got-damn, I swear ye get more addle-pated every day. Look at that got-damned river, boy. It's maybe a hundred yards across and maybe one deep. Ye really think that's gonna stop Iron Bow?"

"No," Cooper mumbled.

"Got-damned right it won't. And worse, you'll probably get us all killed. This here area along the river's full of quicksand. We try'n cross here and Iron Bow mostly likely won't have to kill ye. The river'll do it for him. Your bones, and mine, will be rottin' at the bottom of that got-damn river."

Cooper nodded glumly, a knot of fear constricting his chest, making it hard to breath, or to talk. Finally, though, he managed to ask, "Where're you plannin' on makin' camp?"

" 'Nother mile or so."

Cooped nodded again, mind nearly blank from the fright. But he fell into line as Weeks rode off, followed by Tall Grass, who held the rope to half the horses and pack animals. The other animals trailed Cooper. Every few minutes Cooper would glance over his shoulder. Iron Bow no longer made any effort to conceal himself; he just followed along a mile or so behind the two white men and the Indian woman. Occasionally he was hidden by one of the sandstone hills, and Cooper would feel a momentary glimmer of hope. But the next time he would look back, Iron Bow would be there.

They finally stopped near a pair of cottonwoods along the banks of the Platte. Cooper had trouble setting up the camp. The terror ate at him, and his hands were clumsy as he tried to work.

Weeks startled him when he said, "I'll be back after a spell, boy. Ye see to things here." He paused, then said, "And don't ye fret too much." He laughed his hoarse, mocking laughter.

"Where you goin'?" Cooper asked, the fear lodged, seemingly permanently, in his belly.

"Huntin'." The loathsome peals of laughter came again.

Had the fear not been so deeply imbedded in Cooper by now, he would have realized there was little game here. They had seen nothing larger than a rabbit for two days. But he could not think straight; he had enough trouble trying to concentrate on his simple chores.

As the afternoon began to wane, the terror began to grow inside Cooper, feeding on itself, until the youth could do little more than sit and stare at the small fire Tall Grass had made. Sometime before full dark, in the gray of twilight, he was vaguely conscious of hearing a shot. Dimly he was aware of trying to find a reason for it. Weeks could have shot some game, or tried to; Weeks could even have shot Iron Bow, as he had proposed Cooper do; or, and this was the most frightening, Iron Bow could have shot Weeks, leaving Cooper and the woman alone and virtually defenseless.

Terror filled Cooper's mind with giant warriors riding gigantic horses. Various tortures stole into his mind and poisoned it, reducing him to a shell of the vigorous youth he had been. Nothing in his short, boring life had prepared him for this moment; he had never killed anyone, never even had the desire to do so. All he had was second-, third-, and fourth-hand stories about the ferocity of the Indians out here in the West. He had never quite believed them, but after seeing the strutting bronze warriors, seeing their ease with weapons, and the many scalps fluttering gently from lances and lodge poles, and from hearing Weeks' loathing for all Indians, he was no longer sure.

Cooper caught his breath sharply at the sound of a wolf howling in the dark close by, and slowly his mind began to accept his surroundings again. The fear began to dribble away, as he realized it had turned into night, and Iron Bow had not come for him.

There was a sudden, renewed stab of fright. Weeks had not returned either. His heart sank. Iron Bow had killed Weeks, he was certain, and would be coming for him any time. He would wait until the moment was right, and then come charging into the camp, lance ready . . .

Cooper shook his head. No, dammit! he swore silently. He would not let himself be taken like a baited bear. He made sure his rifle was at hand, primed. Then he self-consciously checked his pistol, stuffing it back into his belt. By God, he thought, forcing himself to stay calm, if he must die, then he would damn sure put up a fight before going under.

He built up the fire some and got a small brief smile of thanks from Tall Grass, who moved closer to the blaze. Though it was still August, the nights were cool, and the fire welcome. Suddenly Cooper heard the soft snicker of a horse, and he tensed, the fear building again, threatening to choke him. Be he battled it down, though his breathing stayed fast and ragged. He moved back a little from the fire.

"Tall Grass," he hissed, trying to keep his voice from cracking. "Move back. Go on, get away from the fire." He did not know if she understood. He had never heard her speak English. She and Weeks talked either in Pawnee, or in a combination of Pawnee, Spanish and French.

The woman did not move. She simply ignored him. But the horse was close now, and Cooper tried to steady his shaking hands as he raised his rifle and aimed it at the spot he thought the horse would appear. Then he heard, "Ye plannin' on shootin' me, boy?"

Weeks rode into the circle of firelight, and Cooper sighed deeply. He was surprised to find that his hands were still shaking. He shuffled away from the cottonwood trunk he had used to steady himself. "I thought Iron Bow had killed you," Cooper said, a rush of friendliness surging through him.

Weeks laughed, the sound more vile than

ever. "Old Iron Bow ain't gonna bother ye, boy, nor anybody else in this lifetime."

Cooper looked up at him perplexed.

Weeks laughed harder, the sound screeching out across the sandstone. Weeks tossed something on the ground at Cooper's feet.

Cooper bent. It was mostly white, with black fur, and it was wet with something, and . . . *Oh, God,* Cooper thought sickly, *it's a scalp.* He felt the bile begin to flume upward, but he clenched his teeth and forced it back. He knelt and with a finger touched the balled-up piece of skin surrounding the thin black scalp lock. The top slowly began to flap open, as if of its own accord. Cooper gently helped it along, a strange sensation creeping up his spine. There was something inside the scalp, which had been rolled up and the edges stuck loosely together with the blood. It did not take much to peel open.

Cooper knelt there, staring for some seconds. There was something awfully familiar about the things inside, something . . .

He stumbled up and backward, gasping in horror. He spun, retching, emptying the contents of his stomach on the ground as Weeks' debased laughter rang out, echoing eerily back at them.

Finally the heaving of his empty belly stopped, and the aftershocks quieted. Weeks still sat on his horse, watching, roaring with hideous laughter, wiping joyous tears from his eyes. The sound was chilling and sickening to Cooper.

"Well ain't ye gonna keep them prizes I brung ye?" Weeks asked, choking on the coughs that bubbled in and out of the laughter.

"No," Cooper mumbled. "No. Take them . . . it . . . all of it . . . away." He staggered off, away from the frightful sight of the scalp lock and the bloody, severed sexual organs of a Pawnee warrior.

The enormity of what he had seen grew on Cooper, and he thought he would be sick again. But he managed to keep his gorge down. His brain wrestled with it all. How could a man, any man, do what Weeks had done? And then to sit there and laugh about it . . . it was inhuman, ghastly. Maybe Weeks was not a man after all, but a beast.

"Oh, dear God," Cooper muttered in almost silent prayer, "what have I done? What have I gotten myself into?" He knew now, though, what he had suspected for a long time, that he would never be able to trust Weeks. He would never turn his back on the depraved trapper again. Never.

He thought briefly again of leaving, running off into the night once Weeks was asleep. But reason caught up to him. He was several hundred miles, as best he could reckon, from any sort of town or fort, and he was surrounded by hostile Indians, who would kill him without a qualm, and most likely with great joy.

No, he must stick it out, praying that he would live long enough to get back to St. Louis and there somehow anyway he could find his freedom.

Seven

Hawley Cooper made sure he was up before Josiah Weeks and Tall Grass. It was not difficult, since he had slept only a little, and poorly at that.

He had been pleased though he was not sure that was the right word to see that Weeks had removed the offending objects by the time he had wandered back to the fire the night before. He was chilled, and glad for the blaze. Weeks was in a jovial mood, and soon was off to his tent, which Tall Grass had put up at Weeks' late insistence after Cooper had wandered off.

Cooper tried to sleep, but his disgust, and the animal-like sounds of Weeks' lovemaking drifting from the tent made it difficult. As did the self-loathing that infected Cooper. He was not proud of having been so incapacitated with fright; and his reaction at Weeks' mocking laughter worsened the feeling.

Weeks was still in a jolly mood in the morning when he stepped from his tent, breathing in the clean, fresh morning air.

"This here day shines, boy, it does," Weeks said cheerfully. "Hell, there ain't nothin' like killin' some got-damn redskin bastard to make a man feel like he's done right."

Tall Grass stepped out of the tent and began fixing a meal while Weeks sat, waiting, and Cooper set about packing the mules for the day's journey. As he did, he surreptitiously watched Tall Grass. As usual, her wide, bland face showed no emotion. Her eyes were as dull as always, but Cooper thought he could detect a sagging of her shoulders that had not been there only a few days ago.

He shrugged and kept working. It was only after he had finished his chores that he went to the fire and took some meat. He sat and ate a little before filling his pewter mug with coffee. Warily he watched Weeks, who had more animation in his face than Cooper had ever seen there before.

Eventually he steeled himself and asked diffidently, "Why'd you do that to Iron Bow?"

"Do what?" Weeks asked, with a malicious gleam in his eyes. "Kill him? It were either him or us, boy."

"Not kill him," Cooper said. "I can understand that. But . . . the other . . ." He felt sick and could not bring himself to say it.

"Scalpin's common as grass out here, boy. There's nothin' to it. Ye just grab ahold of the hair, and ye take your old skinnin' knife" he pulled his "then ye slice around the forehead like this . . ." he demonstrated in the air. "Ye make a complete circle," he added, gleeful at the look of revulsion on Cooper's face. "Then ye wipe your blade off, put it away, stand on that old coon's shoulders and tug. It'll make a most satisfying poppin' sound if ye do it just right." The laughter exploded out of him, ugly and defiant.

Cooper shook his head with displeasure, nausea welling up.

Weeks stopped laughing, and said with a wheeze, "I reckon that ain't what ye was talkin' about neither, was it, boy? Eh?"

"No," Cooper mumbled.

The joviality dropped from Weeks' face. "As to the other, boy, ye best learn not to get so got-damn sick bellied over such doin's. All I was doin' was payin' back in kind."

"Payin' back?" Cooper asked incredulously. "That Pawnee never done nothin' to you."

Weeks shrugged with disinterest. "Maybe not, boy. But others of his kind has done such things to white men afore. Good white men. And to other savages, if that means anything. I told ye, boy, they're wild, savage bastards. They'll do that to an enemy every chance they get. Has something to do with their Godless, heathen religion. So's the dead buck won't get to the Happy Huntin' Ground, or some such got-damn foolishness."

"But you don't have to be like them," Cooper protested. "If they're beastly creatures, like you say, why act like 'em?"

" 'Cause it's the only got-damn thing they understand, boy. Don't ye ever forget that. Ever. Ye act soft toward any Injuns and you'll be a gone beaver soon enough. I ain't had truck with Injuns all these years and lived to tell of it by treatin' 'em like I would a white man."

"That ain't the way you were back in their village. You treated 'em well back there."

" 'Course I did, ye got-damn fool. I was by myself in a village of devil-spawned savages just waitin' to take my hair. But them boys know me. They know I'll kill 'em quick's I would a serpent, given the chance."

"Why didn't they kill you first. Years ago?"

"They're scared of me," Weeks said with a

hoarse chuckle. He pinched Tall Grass on her flat bottom. "Ain't that right, woman?" She gave him a weak smile before shuffling off about her work. "And they know I'll trade with 'em. Bring 'em rifles and powder and other such plunder. Most other folks trade 'em beads and geegaws and foofaraw. Ain't too many'll bring 'em guns regular."

Cooper sat in thought a while, sipping coffee. "Why treat with 'em at all," he finally asked, "if you hate 'em so much?"

"Got to, boy. I need their plews. And their jerky and pemmican and corn and such." He wiped his runny nose on his sleeve. "And ye ain't gonna make it from St. Louis to the Stony Mountains without havin' truck with at least some Injuns."

"But why rifles and such?"

He didn't say that he secretly hoped that by arming the various tribes he thought they might all kill each other off, though that was what was in his heart. Instead, he said, "It buys more good will with 'em than tradin' 'em useless foofaraw." He snorted.

"They ain't really people, ye know," Weeks said, taking a bite of beaver and chewing slowly. "Not like you and me. They got the notion they own this land, even if they don't have no use for it. But they still think it belongs to them. Hell, everybody knows it was bought and paid for by old Tom Jefferson back in ought-three, when he were still the president. Paid a heap of specie for it, too, Mr. Jefferson did. Paid the Frenchies far more'n it were worth. But these got-damn savages still think they got title to it. Hell, they got no more claim to this land than them got-damn greasers down south."

He paused to eat a bit more and pour the last of the coffee into his mug, ignoring the fact that this was his fourth mug and Cooper had only had one. "Still, they do have that foolish idea in their heads, and there's too got-damn many of 'em to just run 'em off. But ye wait, boy. One of these days some of the mountaineers are gonna get got-awful tired of payin' tribute to these horse-stealin', murderous savages. Then the kettle'll boil over for sure. Give me fifty good mountaineers, like some of them boys General Ashley brung out a few years back the ones that took on all them Rees and I'll ride through every got-damn tribe from the Missouri River to the Stony Mountains themselves. And maybe beyond. And, by God, then I'd turn south and send them got-damn greasers packin', too."

Cooper was certain now that Weeks' mind was diseased. He must have suffered brain fever once, Cooper thought, but that did not make him feel any kindlier toward the trapper. Still, there was a fascination with the man's thinking and strange behavior.

"Why do you hate Indians so much?" Cooper asked softly, not wanting to set Weeks off on another rampage. "I mean, you're travelin' with a squaw; you've lived in Indian villages; traded with 'em and such . . ." He trailed off.

Weeks' eyes grew dim, then brightened with hate at what he had seen in a brief flash to his past. "You shouldn't go askin' such questions, boy," the trapper said through a tight throat.

Cooper sat quietly and watched Weeks as he drained his pewter mug. Tall Grass came by and took the coffee pot. A few minutes later she came back with it filled and set it on the coals to heat. Neither Weeks nor Cooper had said anything in the interval.

Weeks closed off his right nostril with a finger and, with a loud snort, explosively expelled mucous onto the ground through the open nostril. He repeated the process on the other side before wiping the slimy residue on his sleeve.

"I come out West back in ought-eight, from St. Louis with Manuel Lisa's boys. Got-damn, it don't seem like nigh onto twenty year. Up the Missouri River we went, by keelboat and canoe. Lisa had built hisself a fort where the Yellowstone and Missouri meet, the year before. Called it Fort Raymond, after his son, but most of the boys called it Lisa's Fort or Fort Manuel. When we got there, we was sent out in small groups to trap. Or, since it were still warm, to build up the trade with the Injuns as there was in the area."

Weeks pulled out his twist of tobacco and sliced off a sizable hunk and began chewing it. As Weeks worked it, Cooper poured himself some of the new coffee Tall Grass had made, burning a finger as he did. "Dammit," he muttered, sucking on his right index finger to ease the pain. Weeks did not laugh, as he usually would have, and Cooper could see by the trapper's eyes that Weeks was leaving old Fort Raymond, pack loaded and heavy on his back.

"I set out with half a dozen other boys: a Scottie, an Irishman, two boys from back in Kentuck', and two got-damn Frogs. Worst jabberers ye ever saw, them Frogs. We set out on foot, carryin' our rifles, backpacks with such supplies as we'd need and some plunder for tradin'. Old John Colter — ye ever heard of him, boy?"

When Cooper shook his head, Weeks said, "He were the first of the mountaineers, really, though some of the Frenchies and even a couple American boys, as well as some of the got-damn Nor'westers had been out here afore him. Anyway, ol' Colter, he had wrapped up the Crow trade some earlier. Leastways as best as could be done at the time. And some of the other boys was sent westward, where we heard was some Snakes and other peaceable critters. So me and my boys was sent north, to try'n open trade with whatever redskins we found that away."

Cooper rarely smoked, but an occasional pipe was a treat. He thought this would be a good time. He pulled out his small clay pipe and filled it, lighting the tobacco with a burning twig. Surprisingly, Weeks waited until he was done before continuing:

"We found us Injuns to the north all right, boy. Run smack into a heap of red-angry Blackfoot that had got themselves done up good by a bunch of Crows Colter was with. Old Colter killed hisself one of them Blackfoot bucks, or so everyone said. Them Blackfeet was some unhappy with whites since Lewis, or mayhap it were Clark, had killed a couple Blackfeet. Colter's killin' another one of 'em only solidified their hate of the whites. We didn't know none of this at the time and got-damn if we didn't walk right on into their village, peaceable as could be, lookin' to make friends.

"They treated us well, and not knowin' them critters like I do now, we didn't think none the worst of it. They fed us good, listened as a couple of us made speeches and such, using just signs and some English and French."

Weeks' voice turned bitter, and his eyes glassed over with hatred. "That night, though, whilst we were sleepin' amongst 'em, feelin' like we'd done old man Lisa and his partners some good, them bastards set upon us."

He spit into the fire and sat silent for some moments. Then: "I weren't where they thought I'd be. Unbeknownst to 'em I'd made me a deal with this pretty little squaw, and that lodge they give us was a heap too crowded for such doin's. So me'n her was sharin' a robe off under some trees. I had drifted off to sleep, highly pleasured, when I was awoke by this most got-damnedest commotion.

"Right off I knew what was up, so I lodge-poled that bitch there in the robes with my fusil, grabbed up my few possibles and such and stole off toward the Blackfoot horse herd. I looked back and seen them got-damn howlin' bastards draggin' five of my amigos out of the lodge. I wondered where the other one was but figured he was rubbed out when them Blackfoot set on them in the lodge.

"I got to the herd, which weren't bein' watched too well, since most of the savages was more interested in the doin's in the village. I cut the throat of one of Bug's Boys, stole me a pony, and grabbed up another 'un just in case. Then I saw somebody mountin' not far away. I threw my rifle up and was set to put out the bastard's lights when I realized it were one of my own kind.

"When I got to him, Tom Ridley it were, one of the Kentuck' boys, he told me he had been outside the lodge pissin' when the ruckus started. He just lit out, without his shirt, and without his rifle. He had his pistol, but none of his other possibles, not even extra powder and ball. We high-tailed it up into the timber, figuring them Blackfeet would be out after us right quick. But they must've been satisfied with them five they got, since it were a while before they did."

Rage began to color Weeks' face, and he fought to control it. "Me'n Ridley dug in behind some brush on this hill lookin' down on the village. Figured we might be able to save the other boys. But there was no way we could.

"Them savages did things to them five boys that ye never . . ." He paused, breathing hard. There were no tears in his eyes, just an indelible rage that contorted his features.

Weeks drew in several deep breaths, and spit twice, as if he could hurt his enemies with his spittle. "For four days Bug's Boys kept our amigos alive, torturin' 'em all the day and most of the night. It were the cruelest thing ye could ever see. And after four days, with them boys hardly humans anymore, the warriors got tired of their sportin' and gave 'em over to the women. The squaws weren't as creative as the bucks, maybe, but they was some more direct."

He looked sharply at Cooper, anger emanating from him like musk. It relieved Cooper of any duty he might have felt to be sympathetic. "That's why I pay Injuns back in kind, boy. Get my meanin'?"

Cooped nodded, gulping, as he felt his groin tighten.

"We thought of tryin' to put them boys out of their misery," Weeks said more calmly. "But we could never get close enough for a shot. Half a dozen times me'n Tom thought to flee, but every time our path was blocked by some got-damn Blackfeet, who was lookin' for us. They give that up, though, soon after they was done workin' over our amigos, and me'n Tom was able to make our way back to the fort. First chance we got, we took us a boat back down the Missouri. Tom were never the same after. He went back East, and I heard he went plumb loco one day and had to be shot."

"And you?" Cooper asked.

"I made up my mind the day I saw them devilish bastards start workin' on my friends that I'd come back and make as many Injuns as possible pay for what they done. I've had me a shinin' time doin' so, too," Weeks said, some of the joy returning. "It gives me a heap of pleasure to set things right with any Injun. Understand, boy?"

Cooper didn't. Not really. What had happened was horrible beyond description, but Weeks' never-ending and perverted retaliation was as bad. But he nodded just the same, unwilling to argue over it.

Eight

Hawley Cooper fought his horse, and the tug of the animals behind him, across the treacherous, shifting bottom sand of the Platte River. Josiah Weeks and Tall Grass were already on the north bank and riding westward, but that suited Cooper.

It was midway through the day after they had left the camp where Weeks had slain Iron Bow. After their conversation of that next morning, Cooper had said fewer than a dozen words to the grizzled Weeks. Cooper just followed Tall Grass and her animals, eating dust, content to keep a watchful eye on Weeks and to study the land passing by his curious eyes.

They had entered an even rougher country, with short, brown grass and heaving sandstone hills punched up all around. Much of the stone was barren, and game was rarely seen. They had made a poor camp last night, which quickly soured

Weeks' buoyant mood. But Cooper ignored him, even when he heard Tall Grass being beaten inside the tent.

Cooper wondered about the woman, and why she should stay with such a man or why she had come along with him in the first place. She was not so young that her father could sell her off for a few horses or a gun; nor was she so old that she could not find a husband.

Tall Grass was not a beautiful woman, but she was far from ugly. She was rather tall for a Pawnee woman, and thinner, too, with an angular face; long, pointed nose; high, prominent cheekbones; and wide, sloping forehead. Her behind was mostly flat and her breasts rather small, but, like many Indian women in the summer, she often went about with only a buckskin skirt, and she was pleasing enough to look at, though Cooper thought she was far too old for him.

She cooked more than middling, too, Cooper thought, keeping his eyes fixed on Tall Grass' bare back as she rode along some yards ahead. And she seemed pleasant enough. She should have had no trouble finding herself a husband. Instead, she was stuck with Weeks.

Cooper finally realized that she stayed with Weeks for the same reason he did —

she did not know where she was, really, and had not the means of escape, nor the means to get back to her people if she did flee. He still did not understand, though, why she had come with Weeks in the first place. He could not see that Weeks had given her enough foofaraw to make her do it.

He shook his head, wondering, not knowing that she had had three husbands. But she was unable to conceive, and so she was not wanted by any of them any longer. It also meant her prospects for another marriage were slim. So her last husband sold her to Weeks for a gun and some powder. If he had known, he might have had more sympathy. As it was, he felt sorry for her, but figured she had brought it on herself by choosing to go with the crusty trapper.

However, Cooper thought mostly of his own survival. He could not worry about anyone but himself. If, when the time came, he could help her, he would try. But if he could not, then so be it. He must live and grow strong. He must learn the ways of the mountains and the Plains, and do it on his own, since it was obvious Weeks was not going to teach him anything except to hate.

Cooper felt a confidence growing in him; a confidence that had not been there only two days ago. He was powerfully ashamed of himself for allowing the fear of Iron Bow to overwhelm him, changing him back into a helpless infant, a baby that had to be cared for and protected by Weeks. The trapper had had to solve Cooper's problem for him, though it probably was more to assuage his hatred than to save Cooper.

Still, it pained Cooper deeply to learn that he had been laid useless by fear, and he vowed it would never happen again. Never.

"Goddammit, horse," he said sharply as the bony nag shied to the right after stepping in a patch of shifting sand. "Come on, get movin'." He steadied the animal and forced her forward. The water was not deep, but the bottom sands were tricky, and the horse unwilling to deal with it, so Cooper had to fight all the way.

But finally the horse stood on the north bank, breathing heavily. Cooper let her rest for a few minutes, watching as Weeks and Tall Grass dwindled on the horizon. He looked around, eyeing the barren hills that stretched as far as he could see to the north and west. It was a desolate place, and the wind blew constantly, though with varying strength. He usually liked the wind, but for some reason it gave him an eerie feeling here.

The horse munched scattered strands of

grass on the riverbank as Cooper watched a hawk soaring overhead. He wished he knew what kind of hawk it was that glided so gracefully on the updrafts.

He heard a snuffling snort and glanced down river. "Damn," he muttered at the sight of the grizzly, which stood on hind legs, sniffing, trying to find the source of what had disturbed its feeding.

"Come on, old girl," Cooper said, urging the horse forward. He did not want the horse to trot, only to walk away calmly. The horse had not smelled the bruin, and so was content to walk slowly. Cooper kept a watch behind, but soon the grizzly dropped down on all fours and shuffled away eastward.

They made another poor camp that night, with little wood for fires, and little food to cook anyway. They went to their bedrolls early, and Cooper lay agonizingly thinking of the delights offered him by Corn Flower. His groin ached with the thought, the feeling compounded from the sounds emanating from Weeks' robes.

It was a long night for Cooper, and mostly sleepless. He was glad when the morning birds stirred him from his dozing. He built up the fire, putting the coffee pot on with a handful of beans. He dunked his head in the river, gasping at its cold bite.

Before long they were packed, mounted, and on the trail again. They were hungry as they moved through more rough, scrubby country. But by afternoon they began to find more grass, though the barren sand hills still dominated the northern horizon. They were in luck this day, as they spotted several deer and two antelope at the river.

Weeks signed to Cooper that he should shoot. Cooper did not like having his rifle unloaded, while Weeks' was primed. But he had no choice. He fired and brought down an antelope not far away. Weeks fired as Cooper reloaded. A good-sized mule deer dropped.

They ate well that night, though Cooper found he preferred the deer meat to that of the antelope. The antelope meat reminded him too much of the goat meat he had eaten upon occasion when his father had butchered one on the farm.

The next several days were much the same. Slow travel through sandy, rough, mostly stark country, broken only by patches of sage or short bunch grass. Even cottonwoods, those hardy trees, were few in number. But Cooper began to notice they were rising ever so slightly, the ground inclining fractionally in anticipation of becoming the Rocky Mountains still several hundred miles to the west.

The land began imperceptibly improving, too, as the sand gave way to a more fertile soil, and the grasses began growing in more profusion. The wildflowers were gone, burned away by the heat of the summer; and much of the grass was withered. But still there was plenty of grass, and trees grew in more abundance. Cold, fresh streams cut the land more frequently, too.

Then Cooper saw them for the first time, really. He had heard stories of the vast buffalo herds that darkened miles upon miles of the prairie with their constantly shifting mass of hundreds of thousands of bodies. But he had been skeptical. It seemed to him that everyone had a different story to tell about the wonders of this land. And they couldn't all be true, could they?

But stretched out before him were so many buffalo he could not hope to count their numbers. So many were there, that the three travelers had to stop a mile or so before actually reaching the herd, and make camp, for safety.

"Got-damn, I hope they move soon," Weeks muttered, stalking.

Tall Grass said something softly to him in Pawnee. "Got-dammit, woman, don't tell me what to do," Weeks snapped, backhanding her. It was the first time Weeks had ever hit the woman in front of Cooper. The youth started forward but stopped when Weeks glared at him. "Ye got somethin' to say, boy?" the trapper demanded.

Cooper stood, calculating his chances. He had felt the power of the older man's fists before, and it had hurt considerably. Though he could stand the pain, he wanted to weigh his chances of success carefully. He did not think they were very good. There would come a time, he knew, when he would have to confront Weeks. It would come to that. But this was not that time. He shook his head and turned away.

Cooper unpacked the mules and rubbed them down. When he was done, Weeks came up and said, without preliminary, "Come with me, boy, and bring a couple of them mules."

"Why?"

" 'Cause I just told ye," Weeks said in annoyance. He turned and stomped away. Mounting his horse, he sat and waited. A few moments later Tall Grass joined him, and then Cooper. Without another word, Weeks rode off toward the buffalo herd.

When they were within a hundred yards of the fringes of the herd, Weeks stopped and dismounted, "Get down," he said.

When Cooper and Tall Grass had done so, he handed his horse's reins to the woman, then said to Cooper, "I aim to shoot me some buffler, boy. Since we might be here a spell, we might's well make some meat. Once I get through shootin', Tall Grass is gonna show ye how to butcher buffler proper. Then ye can help her with the others."

"While you go back to camp and set?" Cooper asked. He was tired and grouchy, from too little sleep and too much tension.

"Can ye drop a half-dozen of them buffler from here, boy? And do it without scaring off the others?"

Cooper shrugged.

"I don't reckon ye can. So I'll have done my part." He turned and knelt nearby. He laid out his necessities: powder horn, roll of greased patch material, a pile of balls on the open flap of his shooting bag, ramrod, and patch knife. He primed his rifle and set himself, left elbow anchored on left knee; right knee on the ground. He fired, the explosion of the rifle rocking his shoulder back. A buffalo dropped, and lay kicking. A few looked at the strange antics, but then went back to foraging.

Without hurry, Weeks loaded the Dickert again, then primed the pan from the small horn of fine-grained powder, snapped the frizzen shut and fired again. Another buffalo fell.

In all, Weeks fired seven times, missing only once. And that was not a complete miss. He winged a large cow that had moved just as he fired. But there were six dead buffalo, all fat cows.

Weeks stood, picked up his things and put them back into place. "Now, ye best listen to Tall Grass, boy," he said. "She shines when it comes to butchering fat cow. I expect ye to do the same soon." He stuck a booted foot in the stirrup, and the sunlight glinted off the sharp rowels of his Spanish spurs. Then he was in the saddle and riding off, back toward their camp amongst the cottonwoods and willows.

Cooper smiled at Tall Grass, trying to make her feel a little more comfortable. But her black eyes stared back at him from her bland face without expression or seemingly life. "Do you speak English?" Cooper asked.

Still she stared at him, saying nothing. Cooper shrugged. "Well, lead on, my lady," he said, sweeping his hand and arm out before him in a grand gesture.

She turned and walked, leading her horse. Cooper followed, leading his. A rope led from the pommel of his saddle to the first mule; another from the first to the second; and another to the third.

Tall Grass sliced open the belly cavity of the first buffalo with her large knife. Straining, she began peeling back the hide. Cooper leaped to help, and she looked almost grateful. Normally she would have had many women helping her, and she would be able to chat and laugh and sing. But not here.

She held up her hand for Cooper to stop, which he did, his breathing strained from the exertion. He looked around nervously at the vast mass of buffalo still close enough to almost touch. Tall Grass got a rope and attached it to the hide. She dallied the other end around the high pommel of her saddle, and then pulled her horse forward. The hide peeled off the side with a great sucking sound.

Tall Grass tied another rope around the buffalo's "upper" legs and then to Cooper's horse. The animal strained forward, pulling as hard as she could, but could not roll the massive buffalo over.

With infinite patience, and while Cooper kept an anxious eye on the herd, Tall Grass moved the first rope from the hide to the buffalo's legs, and then had both horses heave together. Slowly the beast rolled, and with the horses' help, the hide was pulled free. With her people to help, it would have been easier, the Pawnee woman thought. The buffalo would have been propped up on stiff legs, the hide slit along the hump, and each side pulled off easily. But the only help she had was that of this soft-spoken, shy young white man.

Quickly and silently she showed him how to butcher; which were the best cuts; and which were the poorer cuts, that still could be used for pemmican, boudin sausages and jerky.

Deftly she cut out the livers and kidneys. She eyed them longingly, but shrugged. Cooper understood after a few moments, and smiled at her. "Go on," he urged her softly. "Take one."

She shook her head, and Cooper knew she at least understood the language. "Go on," he said again. "Josiah says anything, I'll tell him I ate it." He smiled again.

She grinned for the first time and bit into a raw liver. She offered it to him, and he took a mouthful. Happily they shared the treat as they worked.

At last they had plenty of the meat rolled in bloody buffalo hides and packed on the mules. Tall Grass took a stone hammer from a beaded saddlebag. With all her might, she smashed it down on the weakest point of one buffalo's skull. After three tries, Cooper took the tool. With his greater strength, he punched a wide hole in the skull. Tall Grass got a rawhide bucket and scooped buffalo brains into it.

Satisfied, Tall Grass nodded to Cooper. The two mounted and rode back toward the camp. Tall Grass had not said one word to Cooper.

Nine

Hawley Cooper pulled up sharply when he saw the Indians ahead. There were six of them that he could see, but there might be more, for all he knew, hidden by the ridge upon which the six sat.

Cooper was near the crest of another ridge, just starting down into the gully, behind Josiah Weeks and Tall Grass, who were in the shallow coulee. To Cooper's left, the Platte made its now boisterous way; to his right was the undulating prairie with its humped, grass-covered ridges cut by washes, buffalo wallows and small valleys. Buffalo sign was everywhere.

Cooper kicked his bony horse, who had shown signs of covering her ribs with some meat now that grass and tender cottonwood shoots were available. But she still looked like a sack of skin-covered bones. The horse moved a little faster. Cooper wanted to catch up to Weeks. He was still keeping his distance from the trapper, but this was not the time to be stand-offish.

Weeks stopped and waited, watching as the six Indians began their slow, stiff-legged walk on their horses down the grassy ridge. Cooper trotted up to Weeks. "What are they?" he asked, fear beginning to numb his arms and legs. He gritted his teeth, determined not to let it affect him.

"Sioux. One of the most murderous of the got-damned savage tribes. Crows'll most likely just steal your horses or anything else ye got to hand. But these got-damned buffalo-humpin' bastards live for war. Ye never can tell just what they'll do."

"They a war party or hunters?"

"Could be either. Got-damned Sioux got no morals that way. They could be huntin' buffalo and decide to spend a few days slaughterin' innocent folks. But this bunch looks like they set out to raise hair. Them bucks is painted and well-armed."

The Sioux began trotting down the hill. "Oh, my God," Cooper muttered. "They're gonna attack!" He began scrabbling to get his rifle from the loop on the saddle. Fear built up in him, but his adrenaline burned through his veins, making him want to take action.

"Leave it, boy," Weeks said through tight lips.

"But, Josiah, they're gonna kill us. I ain't givin' up so easy. I'm gonna fight . . ."

He had the rifle free at last, but so excited was he that he fumbled with it, trying to prime it. The rifle tumbled from his hands, falling to the ground. "Oh, damn," he said, fear striking coldly in him. As he dismounted, he heard a strange sound.

He looked over to see Weeks laughing hoarsely, like he always did. The trapper sat loose in his saddle, tears of joy in his eyes.

Cooper, his face a mask of fright, glanced up. The Indians were very close now, splitting to surge around the two white men and the Pawnee woman. But they had little heart for an attack now, since they also were laughing at the foolish antics of this young pup of a white-eye. They swung around, circling, and then headed back up the hill where they had started. They stopped about halfway up and shouted.

"What're they yellin'?" Cooper asked, retrieving his rifle.

"Insults. Most of 'em's directed at ye, boy. Seems like they never seen anybody handle a rifle afore quite like ye do." He laughed again. "They also had some rather unseemly things to say about your sire and dam."

Cooper's cheeks burned from the humiliation and shame of his clumsiness. Making it worse was knowing that under his still-new beard his face was pink. It angered him all the more and added to the self-loathing in which he was wallowing.

Dammit, why did it always have to be so, he wondered. He had always been clumsy. He had always tried to do what was right, but it always seemed to blow up in his face. He just never . . .

He shook his head in self-aversion. He should have gone out to meet and fight Iron Bow. He would have died, he knew, but it would have been an honorable death. And he would have been out of his misery, without regret.

Cooper sighed, the weight of his despondency heavy on him. He did not want to bear it any longer. Still afoot, he slid the rifle into the loop on the saddle. He patted the horse, of whom he had grown rather fond, on the nose. Then he spun and walked forward. Weeks said nothing, only watched with bright eyes. Tall Grass gasped.

Cooper stopped about fifty yards in front of Weeks and Tall Grass. Standing with hands on hips, he roared, "Well, come on, dammit. Come and do your worst."

He waited a few moments, then yelled,

"Well, what in hell are you waitin' for? What are you, a bunch of old women?"

He watched with a detached feeling as the six warriors started their ponies running at him. The small, wiry animals gathered speed quickly. Cooper waited patiently, wondering at his sudden lack of fear. Maybe it was that he had chosen to die. Without the fear of death, there was little else to dread.

He also was surprised at how clearly he could see the rushing warriors. All wore only breechcloth and moccasins. The first was broad and gave the impression of being short. He had a great hooked nose and Cooper thought he could even see that he had bad teeth, as the Indian's mouth split in a howl. The second was rather handsome, Cooper thought stupidly, though his skin was much darker than that of the others. He was a big, burly man, with streaks of lightning painted on his chest and cheeks. On his head was a wolf skin, with the head intact. The third wore a buffalo-horn headdress and had a badly scarred face, which he tried to hide under a heavy coat of war paint.

Cooper was aware of the other three, but all six were nearly upon him, and he could no longer register particular sights, though his eyes remained open. The first Sioux raised his coup stick though Cooper did not know what it was and whacked Cooper on the shoulder. The youth grunted at the pain but kept his eyes straight ahead.

The second Sioux struck Cooper across the chest with a trade rifle as he thundered past, whooping. Cooper staggered under the impact, thinking he would be dead soon. The third roared by at that moment and swatted Cooper with a hard riding quirt, knocking him flat.

The other three Indians swooped by as he struggled to rise. His shoulder hurt, and his chest felt as if it was on fire. There was blood and a stinging pain over the right eye where the quirt had struck.

The Indians circled and weaved their ponies, when suddenly another darted forward as Cooper managed to stand. This Indian rode so close that Cooper could smell the bear grease on the man's body as he roared past, smacking Cooper on the head with his bare hand. When he was past, he pulled up his horse in a flurry and yipped, announcing his bravery. He was a young warrior, not many times on the war path.

The fifth, also a young warrior and not to be outdone, rode close and jammed his horse to a stop. He leaped down and charged Cooper. The white youth braced himself as the Indian barreled into him, flattening him again. The warrior yelled and whipped out his knife.

Well, Cooper mused, this is it. But he kept his eyes full on those of the young Sioux. The Indian almost grinned as he grabbed Cooper's hair. Oh, no, he thought in horror, he's gonna scalp me and leave me that way.

The knife flashed once in the sunlight, and then the Indian was gone. Cooper sat up, wondering. There was no pain. He reached his hand up and gingerly touched his head. He gulped, then looked at his hand. No blood. He sighed with relief, as he realized that all the Sioux had done was to cut off a small lock of his hair.

Cooper stood and picked up his cap. Fear began to rise in him again, as he realized he really did want to live. He battled the fear and turned to face the sixth Sioux. He would not show this son of a bitch any fear, no matter how deeply he felt it.

But the Indian just sat there on his pony. He was an older man, his long, braided hair touched with gray. The top half of his face was painted red; the bottom half yellow. Dots of yellow paint speckled his wide chest and several feathers fluttered from his hair.

His horse was a short, powerful mustang, with at least a dozen hands painted on the front flanks.

The Indian rode slowly a little closer, stopping about ten feet away. He almost smiled, and then nodded his head, as if in approval. He said something in a language Cooper guessed was Sioux. The Indian talked solemnly for several minutes before smiling again. He touched the side of his right fist against the left side of his chest, then swung the arm outward, with the fist opening so the palm faced the ground.

With a few sharp words, the warrior, whom Cooper figured was a chief, wheeled his horse and called his men to him. They rode off fast, toward a herd of buffalo Cooper had seen earlier in the day grazing on another ridge several miles north.

Cooper realized he was shaking as Weeks and Tall Grass rode up to him. Weeks looked enraged, and he raised the .54-caliber Dickert to take a shot at the rapidly disappearing Sioux. Cooper spotted him and stepped forward, bumping into the trapper's horse just as he fired. The shot went well wide.

Weeks spat a curse and swung the rifle barrel at Cooper, who ducked out of the way. His hands shot out and he grabbed the weapon. He yanked, but not very hard, and stared up into Weeks' eyes. Both men knew it would have been easy for Cooper to pull Weeks off his horse.

They stayed that way for some seconds, both breathing hard from the tension, though neither said a word. Then Cooper released the gun barrel and turned away. Gathering up the reins to his horse he sprang into the saddle in one bound. He sat waiting, back straight and proud, as Weeks reloaded, angrily ramming the rod down into the barrel. Cooper thought Weeks might snap the hickory rod. And he fully expected the trapper to shoot him, so he pulled his pistol as he waited.

But Weeks finished, and with face marred by his anger, he rode off. Cooper closed his eyes and took several deep breaths. He had been close to death several times within the past few minutes, and it left him shaken. But he was also happy, proud in knowing that he had faced death and done it bravely. He would be able to do so again, if he chose.

They rode a long way that day, stopping only after dark. Cooper set about making camp, but did so at his own pace, and even made his own small fire when he had taken care of the animals. He had no coffee pot, but he could cook his own meat, and he would drink water.

The sky was ablaze with stars as Cooper wearily rolled out his blankets. He had a momentary attack of panic when he thought of Weeks, sitting by his own fire, brooding for what reason only he knew. It would be like Weeks to wait until Cooper was asleep and then attack him.

"Humph," Cooper muttered, angry at himself. He shifted to get more comfortable in the covers, thinking, The hell with it, if Weeks comes after me, he'll come after me. There's nothing I can do about it now. Within minutes he was asleep.

Weeks' mood showed no sign of brightening the next day, but Cooper had resolved not to let such things worry him. He would do whatever was necessary to survive, and he would guard against Weeks as best he could. That was all he could do now.

Just before midday a storm boiled up. It came in hard and fast, dumping heavy rain on them. Jagged flashes of lightning rent the gloomy sky, and angry bursts of thunder coughed overhead. Cooper pulled his blanket around him and over his head, hating the rain, and the flash floods, swollen streams and slick mud it brought. It never let up the rest of the day, and when they made camp, Cooper could not see the massive spire of Chimney Rock across the Platte from where they camped.

It was still raining the next morning, though not nearly as hard, and they broke camp early. It was a miserable day's ride, with the horses and mules slipping and straining in the often fetlock-deep mud. Lightning still crackled and spat regularly. That night they spent huddled against the bulge of a tall, white, barren bluff.

The rain came intermittently for the next two days as they continued their weary, wretched way west through cold downpours, slopping through mud, fighting across shallow, fast streams bordered by slick, steep banks. Cooper's horse lost her footing twice and dumped him once into the water of a wash, another time into a pond of mud. Once one of the mules went down to its knees, squealing and braying. The animal was balky for a long time after that, too.

But at long last, the sun burst through the clouds, and the day became warmer and brighter. By nightfall, the sky was clear. They camped at the juncture of the Platte and Laramie rivers. The next morning Weeks was almost jovial, and Cooper was coming to expect these widely varying moods that seem to have no cause. "We'll rest here a few days," Weeks said as Cooper walked up and knelt, reaching for the coffee pot.

"There any reason?" Cooper asked non-committally.

"A couple. First we need to dry out. I am plumb got-damn weary of all that rain, boy. I need to let my old bones soak in the sunshine a spell. Second, we got to start makin' meat for the winter. There's a heap of buffler hereabout; plenty of wood for fires for dryin' the meat; good grass for the horses. This here's a prime spot. If it weren't for the got-damned wind a blowin' all the got-damned time, and them mean-as-hell winters, this'd be a heap like the Garden of Eden."

Cooper nodded, and, after hesitating, sat. He took a sip of coffee and asked, "Why didn't those Sioux kill me the other day?"

"They was countin' coup, boy," Weeks said, a little angry.

"What's that?"

"They touch you with a hand or weapon or somethin'. Shows how brave they are, that they can get close enough to an enemy to touch him without gettin' killed. Plain got-damned foolishment to my thinkin'. Should've just killed ye straight off." He stared hard at Cooper for a few seconds.

"It's what I would've done."

Cooper grinned insolently. "Why didn't the last one do it?"

"Only so many can count coup on one enemy."

"Do you know what he said to me?"

Weeks looked at him with distaste. "Some buffalo shit about ye being so brave to just stand there like that." He stood, spit into the fire and stalked off.

Ten

Hawley Cooper, much to Weeks' annoyance, shot a buffalo for the first time when they stopped early one afternoon to make meat. Cooper had been somewhat lucky. He was a good shot, but the trade rifle Weeks had given him was not very accurate at more than seventy-five yards. Already the nights were colder, so Cooper took the buffalo's hide and with Tall Grass' help when Weeks was not paying attention, tanned it to use as a sleeping robe.

More than once they had been forced away from the river by rough country and short, bald hills bunched close to the riverbank. There was little game most days, but by riding a few miles north, where the grass was plentiful, they could find their fill of buffalo, as well as elk, deer and antelope.

One night they spent near the humped bulk of a hill. After Cooper had finished making camp, helped butcher buffalo for the evening meal and done his chores, he climbed up the massive hump. "Good Lord," he breathed when he reached the top. He could see for miles in any direction. The land rolled and swayed but was mostly treeless. Only a few stunted cedars and pines struggled to survive. To the north he could see the Rattlesnake Hills all puffed up; and he could see moving brown masses of buffalo. Northwest, dimly on the horizon, he thought he could see a range of snow-covered mountains, but he was not sure of his eyesight. If there were mountains there, they were obscured by the great distance, and the gathering of clouds.

As Cooper picked his way carefully down the hill face, he noticed several names scratched into the rock. With a mischievous grin, he pulled his knife and began hacking away, until, after a long time, he managed to carve his name alongside the others. He was proud of doing it, since his name was one of the few things he could write. He had not learned much reading and writing, but he had a prodigious memory for the spoken word.

They spent several days near the imposing rock making meat. Once the meat was butchered, Tall Grass would cut it into thin strips and set it out on racks Cooper made.

There the meat would dry in the sun and arid air. Or she would build smoky fires and set the meat over it to slowly smoke to hardness. Most of the meat was made into jerky, but the rest was made with the addition of plenty of melted buffalo fat and whatever berries could be found nearby into pemmican. The concoction was ladled into parfleches and left to harden. It would last seemingly forever and was a nourishing meal for winter.

Finally they had enough meat to load down all their pack mules and extra horses. "Still ain't enough," Weeks said in irritation. "Got-damn Pawnees should've sold me more horses, but they wouldn't, damn their thievin' hides."

"What're we gonna do?" Cooper asked.

Weeks shrugged. He had grown more morose, and rarely spoke to Cooper. The youth did not mind, except he wanted to learn, and Weeks would not — could not — teach him if he did not converse. Weeks also had taken to beating Tall Grass with more regularity, until Cooper tried to put a stop to it the first full day at Independence Rock.

Cooper was sitting near the fire, listening to the sounds of Weeks hitting the Indian woman, and then the trapper's grunting lovemaking, if that's what one could call it.

Weeks came out of his tent and sat at the fire looking smug and satisfied. He took a cup of coffee and shouted in Pawnee back over his shoulder toward the tent. A few moments later, Tall Grass stepped into the overcast day. Her left eye was discolored and puffed almost shut. Blood trickled from one nostril and seeped from a corner of her mouth. When she bent over the fire to get some meat and hand it to Weeks, she winced with pain. She moved stiffly but said nothing.

When she left, Cooper glared at Weeks, who smiled distastefully. "Nothin' like a shinin' robe session with a willin' squaw to start the day," Weeks said in a voice that made Cooper's flesh crawl.

Cooper continued staring, though he remained silent. However, he touched the pistol in his belt lightly, his hand not even lingering, just brushing the weapon's butt. Weeks saw it, though, and the smirk dropped from his face. Scowling, the trapper finished his meal and stomped away.

But it helped, as Cooper became aware that Tall Grass suffered far-less-frequent beatings after that. The woman acknowledged it only once. Several days later, her hand touched Cooper's for a fraction of a second while they were butchering a buffalo cow. Cooper looked at her, startled, and she stared deep into his eyes for a moment before glancing back to her work.

After several days near Independence Rock, they moved on, slowly because the animals were loaded. Early that day they wound through a strange pass along the Sweetwater River, with towering cliffs on each side crowding the river. Here the water churned turbulently as it roared through the canyon. It was another sight to awe Cooper, and if he had been a chattering type of man, he would have been silenced.

Once through the canyon, they picked up a little speed, as much as the animals would allow. The ground rose steadily, though imperceptibly to the travelers, and the land was barren.

Three days after they passed Devil's Gate, four Indians boiled out from behind a small stand of cottonwoods along the riverbank. They covered ground fast, screeching war cries.

Cooper's heart pounded, and he was not sure what to do. Perhaps they were just going to count coup, like the Sioux had done. But to Cooper's eyes and ears these Indians seemed bent on killing them.

Cooper looked at Weeks. The trapper doubled back, screaming profanely at Cooper to help him control the pack animals. Since they had left Independence Rock, Weeks did not trust Cooper to keep even half the animals, so now Tall Grass struggled with them all.

The woman was fighting the rope to the first animal as the beasts snorted and bucked and pulled, their nostrils flared and their eyes wide in their fright, whinnying or braying. Suddenly Tall Grass was yanked off her horse onto the ground. Cooper, his heart in his throat, kicked his horse, trying to get it to move faster.

The horse responded slowly, frightened by the screaming warriors who were within a few yards of them now. Cooper lost sight of Tall Grass in the cloud of choking dust churned up by the horses' hooves. He gulped, figuring she was dead already. No one could live in that stomping melee of flashing horse and mule hooves.

He also lost sight of Weeks, who was on the other side of the cloud, but he could not worry about that now. He managed to grab one of the ropes about midway through the bucking line of animals, just as the line snapped. But he got a good enough grip, and, using mostly his strength, rode along with the animals, dallying the rope around his saddle horn as he did.

He let the horses and mules slow of their own accord, while working them in a small circle back toward Weeks. He heard a rifle shot and looked up sharply. He could see nothing but a swirling knot of warriors and horses. Suddenly Weeks burst from the dust cloud, tugging hard at the pack animals.

Cooper grinned as he watched all four Indians count coup on Weeks, each whack harder than the last, almost knocking the trapper from his horse. But the trapper held on to his saddle horn, and Cooper could hear his bellowing imprecations even where he was.

The warriors swarmed around Weeks, grabbing at the pack animals. Weeks swore and lashed out with his rifle, hitting one Indian across the nose. Weeks kicked his horse, forcing it to move, and dragged the other animals with him. The Indians spotted Cooper and broke off their attack on Weeks to head for the youth.

Cooper panicked, but fought the feeling, noticing that the Indians had Tall Grass' horse and one of the pack horses loaded with meat, which they had managed to cut loose. He sat waiting, since there was nowhere to run, and he prayed they were only going to count coup on him, too. He sang out some words, trying to calm the animals again.

Cooper saw that Weeks had dropped the rope to the pack animals and was rushing after the Indians. He was only a little surprised at that, but more so when he saw Tall Grass standing in the midst of the diminishing cloud of dust, picking up the rope to the horses.

The Indians howled as they rushed Cooper, and he winced with every blow as each Indian charged past and swatted him with coup stick or bow. He concentrated on staying seated in the saddle and keeping control over the nervous pack animals.

Each warrior made a grab for the rope to the pack animals, but Cooper held fast, hoping no bones had been broken by the blows.

Then the warriors were racing off to the northwest. Cooper dropped the rope to his pack animals and charged after Weeks and the Indians. The trapper was gaining on the warriors, and suddenly he jerked his horse to a stop in a burst of dust and foam. He brought his rifle up and fired. Cooper saw one of the Indians fall before he heard the report of the rifle drift back to him. The three remaining Indians turned in a sharp circle and headed back.

Cooper swore softly, yanking out his own rifle. He did not fumble with it this time, but it was useless, he realized, at this distance. He would only waste powder and ball if he fired now. He saw Weeks calmly stuff the rifle back into the loop on his saddle and reach for one of the two .54-caliber pistols set in holsters on his saddle.

"Oh, God," Cooper muttered, as he saw one of the Indians break off and head toward him. Cooper stopped his horse and dropped the reins. He threw his rifle up and fired, but the shot was wide, and the Indian did not slow.

Cooper saw one of the other warriors fire three arrows at Weeks, but none seemed to hit the trapper. Then Weeks was veiled by dust, and Cooper's attention snapped back to the Indian who was almost atop him.

Cooper breathed deep once and stuffed the rifle back into the loop. He heard the thudding boom of one of Weeks' pistols, and it made him grab for his own pistol. He cocked it, but by then the Indian was on him and the mare shied. The warrior lashed out with a metal tomahawk. The blade bit into Cooper's arm to the bone, just as he fired. The shot was wild, as Cooper yelled with pain. But the mare took him away from the Indian. Had it not been for the horse shying, the tomahawk would have split his skull rather than his arm.

Cooper managed to grab the flopping reins and slow his old horse and bring her around. But the warrior was nearly on him again. Ignoring the throbbing in his arm and the blood that poured freely down it, Cooper snatched out his rifle again. As the Indian charged up, Cooper used the rifle as a club, smacking the surprised Indian across the chest, while ducking the flashing tomahawk.

The warrior grunted and toppled in a backward somersault over the horse's rump, landing on his back. He lay there, conscious, but stunned, unable to move. Cooper stopped his horse and rushed back. He slid off the animal just as the Indian, still struggling for breath, tried to get up. With a yell, Cooper jumped on the Indian, pinning him.

Then he had a sudden, frightening thought: *Now that I have him, what do I do with him?* The Indian bucked and writhed, trying to throw him off. Cooper held on desperately, but the warrior managed to free his left arm, the one held down by Cooper's damaged arm. He punched Cooper in the nose, rocking Cooper's head back, though he had not been able to get all his power behind it. Cooper gasped, realizing just how big and how strong this warrior was.

The Indian tried to hit him again, but

Cooper shifted his body so the blow landed on the meaty part of his shoulder. It stung a bit, but it pumped him up as adrenaline pulsed through him. He forgot his fear in the heat of it.

With a deep breath, he raised up his left arm, freeing the top half of the Indian, and he punched the warrior as hard as he could. The Indian grunted softly as the fist cracked into his cheekbone. But he reached up and grabbed Cooper by the throat and squeezed.

Cooper gagged and made sputtering noises. He clutched frantically at the warrior's powerful hands and tried to yank them away. But it was to no avail. The Indian's thumbs sank into Cooper's neck, closing the artery to the brain, cutting off the oxygen.

Cooper scratched and clawed at the hands, forgetting completely the jagged, bloody wound in his arm. There was no fear in him; just a wild desperation. Spots appeared before his eyes, and the Indian's face two feet from his began to swim before him. *This is the end,* he thought. He gave up, letting his hands fall limply to his sides.

His right hand brushed the hilt of his knife, and his eyes widened. As the blackness began to sweep over him, he wrenched the knife from its cheap sheath and slashed out blindly with it. Two, three, four times. Then he lost count.

The world was gray and dim, but he was still conscious. He felt the hands on his throat fall away, and Cooper sank onto his hands, face nearly on the Indian's. His head pounded and dark spots still swam in his vision. He gasped, drawing in ragged breaths as fast as he could, making hoarse, gurgling sounds.

Through the haziness, he heard, "Gotdammit, ye done it, boy. I never thought ye had it in ye."

He ignored the voice, and whatever else Weeks had to say at the moment. He concentrated instead on his breathing, staying there, kneeling on shins atop the warrior's stomach, balanced on his hands, one on each side of the Indian's torso.

It seemed like hours before he pushed up off his hands and rolled onto his buttocks. His head fell back, and he sucked in more deep breaths. His throat hurt and his arm ached, but finally he was breathing almost normally. He looked down into the sightless eyes of the warrior, and realized he was sitting on a dead man.

He vomited once at the sight of all the blood covering the warrior's chest and face. But he bit back the bile, and stood slowly, wiping his knife absentmindedly on his pants before putting it away.

ELEVEN

Hawley Cooper was quite fascinated by the activity in and around the small Crow village.

Warriors rode off beyond the fringes of the camp, practicing their already superb horsemanship. Women toiled on huge buffalo hides or sat working industriously at the beadwork that was unsurpassed by any tribe. So exquisite was the beadwork of the Crow women, that tribes from all over would trade for such decorated clothing. Even their enemies.

Other women worked at making meat, and at the same time were busy shooing the many yapping mongrels away from the meat. Some played games, or carted firewood, or hauled up buffalo-paunch buckets of water from the river nearby. Whatever they were doing, they did it in small groups, from which emanated much talking and laughing.

Warriors squatted outside their beautifully painted lodges making or fixing weapons; or they sat in serious and animated discussion, or in raucously humorous talks. Some slept, and more than a few were gambling, mostly at the hand game. Several openly appraised with their eyes the quality of the white men's horses. Nearly all the warriors, Cooper noticed, wore their hair extremely long, usually past their waists, and a few even past their knees.

These were handsome Indians, Cooper noted, tall and regal. Many were naked, or nearly so, in the warmth of the afternoon. Even — especially, in Cooper's eyes — the women, who were, for the most part, quite pretty. They ogled Cooper — and even Weeks — and the youth willingly stared back, though the women's brazen glances made him a little uncomfortable.

Children ran willy-nilly, laughing and shouting; only rarely crying. They circled lodges, always mindful of the warriors' weapons racks outside, and careful about the many fires scattered around. Some stopped briefly in their play to stare at the two pale-faced men with the hair all over their faces.

It was nearly a week since Weeks and Cooper had battled the four warriors. Kaws, they were, Cooper had learned right after the fighting and Cooper had mostly recovered. His arm was still quite painful, but it did not hinder him in his chores. Tall Grass had applied some poultices to it, and no poison had infected the arm.

The youth was also feeling considerably better about himself. He felt himself more of a man now — stronger, braver, somehow even older. And more than once he touched the scalp that dangled from his saddle horn. It was still a wonder to him that he had it.

When he had managed to gain his feet after killing the warrior, Weeks said roughly to him, "Take his hair, boy."

"Scalp him?" Cooper asked, voice rising in pitch. The thought sickened him anew.

"Do it, boy," Weeks said harshly.

"No!" The word came out raspy. Cooper cleared his throat and tried again. "No!" The voice was more normal this time.

"Best do as I say, boy."

"Why?" Cooper asked, trying to hide his loathing for this man and the subject of their terse conversation. "It ain't gonna do him no good — nor me."

"Wrong, boy. It might do ye a heap of good. Ye take that got-damn buck's hair now, and ye just might have yourself a bit less trouble with some other black-hearted savages ridin' hard on your ass fixin' to raise your own got-damn hair. They see ye've took a scalp, and they might not be so hellbent on raisin' your topknot."

He took the time to blow snot out of his nose and wipe the residue away. Then he spit. "And when ye got to be dealin' with some son-of-a-bitchin' Injuns supposed to be friendly, they'll know you're a warrior, got-dammit. A man blooded in battle. A man with some balls. It'll earn ye respect, boy, and that counts a heap with these got-damn heathens."

Cooper was weary, and his body ached in several places. The surging of adrenaline was wearing off, and it left him drained. He was in no mood, or position, to argue with Weeks. Steeling himself, he pulled his knife, and under Weeks' gleefully gruesome directions, Cooper took his first scalp.

He had regretted it while doing it, and for a time after. But in a few days, the remorse dwindled, and that bothered him, too. He thought that perhaps he was turning savage. However, the Crows had looked at him with respect when he rode into the village.

They sat at a council fire with some of the Crow warriors. Using signs, English and French, Weeks "spoke" to the Indians, telling, at their insistence, of his and Cooper's battle with the Kaws.

Weeks embellished the story, telling of the overwhelming odds the two had faced, and how he and his young companion had fought with gun and knife, tooth and nail, fist and tomahawk, until they had overcome the vastly superior force.

After that particular narrative, Cooper leaned over and asked Weeks in a whisper, "How long we gonna be here?"

Weeks looked at him surprised. "Few hours, I reckon," he said with a shrug. "Why?"

"I got business," Cooper said, embarrassed.

"Eh?"

Cooper nodded his chin in the direction of two young, nubile Crow women, maybe fifteen years old. The two sat working with several older women. The girls stared boldly at him and giggled frequently.

Weeks looked. When he turned back, his face was mottled. "Ain't ye had yourself enough got-damn trouble with squaws, boy?" he asked, voice little more than a hiss.

Cooper's face hardened. "You got yourself a goddamn woman you can bed regular. I ain't had but that one time since we left St. Louis. And now I aim to take advantage of it."

"Got-damn it, boy, stop thinkin' with that miserly pizzle 'tween your legs and start usin' your head. We ain't gonna run afoul of these red-skinned bastards just so's ye can bed some got-damn Crow."

"It ain't your concern, Josiah," Cooper said firmly. "All I need from you is to know when we'll be pullin' out."

"When I'm got-damn good and ready is when, boy. Ye ain't ready, I'll leave ye here to the tender mercies of these bastards."

Cooper shrugged, then said flatly, "It'd be a heap better'n spendin' more time with you."

He started to stand, but Weeks grabbed his arm, oblivious to the questioning, startled glances the Crows gave them. His face was blotchy with anger as he hauled Cooper back down. "Now ye listen to me, boy," he snapped. "These Injuns might be a pretty people, but they're nearabout the dirtiest folks ever lived. Chances're good them two little gigglers over yonder already bedded a heap of bucks. Most likely they got themselves the French disease, which they'll be happy to pass onto ye. Ye want your pizzle to rot and fall off, boy?"

Cooper shrugged, growing adamant. "I'll take my chances."

"What're ye gonna use for foofaraw, boy?

Can ye answer me that? Neither of them girls is gonna bed ye just 'cause ye got a pretty face and have raised hair."

"I'll think of somethin'."

"Ye touch my trade goods, boy, and I'll rip your guts out right here in front of everyone."

Cooper gulped, but then realized he had nothing to fear. "You gonna tell me when we're leavin'?" he asked.

Weeks scowled, then snapped, "No more'n three hours. And ye better be ready, boy."

"I will be." Cooper stood and left, walking past the two girls, and around a lodge. He had glanced their way as he passed and now his heart pounded. He hoped he had not misread their glances and giggles.

He had not. A few minutes later one of the girls joined him, carrying a blanket, which she spread out beneath a cottonwood. Cooper's blood ran hot, and he reached out hungrily for her.

The girl could speak little English, and he no Crow, but they got along quite well. He did learn that her name was Falling Leaf, after they had made love the first time. They had tried to talk then, using the few English words Falling Leaf knew; the little French they both could handle; and the bit of sign language Cooper had picked up from watching Weeks.

Falling Leaf giggled as she played with Cooper's beard. Such a thing on a man would offend most of her elders, but she thought it funny that a man should walk around with the lower half of his face covered with hair.

She laughed at his clothes, too, and he was embarrassed at their poor condition. The shirt was so thin that it was virtually transparent, and his pants were nearly worn through at the seat and inner legs. His boots, old when he arrived in St. Louis, were full of holes and the soles flapped loosely at the fronts.

He tried to explain that he had no other garments but Falling Leaf did not seem to understand. Finally he shrugged and pulled her close to kiss her long and deeply.

Cooper worried that they might be heard and that someone would come to investigate. The screen of brush around the cottonwood was not that dense. Falling Leaf was enthusiastic in her lovemaking, and let it show vocally. Very vocally.

But he found that he suddenly no longer cared. And, later, he did not care either.

Then he was scrambling into his clothes. The sun had moved enough that his three hours must be up or nearly so. He reached into his possible sack and withdrew the small handful of beads he had stashed away, and the piece of antler. He gave them to Falling Leaf, then grabbed his rifle and ran.

Cooper slowed as he rounded the lodge, not wanting to seem in too much of a hurry. But Weeks was still at the fire, though he was standing and looking over horses with a practiced eye.

Cooper strolled up and asked, "You near ready to go?"

Weeks gave him a withering look before going back to work.

"Want me to help?"

Weeks ignored him. Cooper shook his head. As a blacksmith and farrier, Cooper had become an excellent judge of horseflesh. He could have saved Weeks a lot of work. Even though it was evident that Weeks knew well what he was doing in checking the horses, splitting the work would have made it go much faster. Cooper considered trying to find Falling Leaf again but decided against it.

Weeks took almost another half-hour looking at ponies. When it was done, he passed over several cheap trade fusils, with the necessary accouterments. Then all involved sat and smoked a final calumet to seal the deal.

As everyone stood after the pipe was smoked, Weeks said to Cooper, "Rope all them horses together, boy."

Cooper got a length of rawhide rope from one of the pack mules, and then went to the new horses without saying a word. He looped an end over the first horse's head. He measured out some of the rope — enough to give the next horse some room, but not enough to let it stray, and made another loop. He repeated the process until he was done. Then he walked along, working the loops over the horses' heads.

He was rather surprised at the number. He thought Weeks might procure a few more. But he had taken fourteen. It would be unwieldy, especially if they faced more hostiles, but there was nothing he could do about it.

There was a tap on his shoulder as he finished up the last of the horses, a docile looking pinto. He turned to see Falling Leaf and her companion smiling up at him. He smiled back, and said, hoping Falling Leaf would understand, "I got to be going soon."

The two young women looked at each other and giggled. Finally Falling Leaf held out two buckskin-wrapped packages tied with rawhide thongs. "What's this?" he asked, and both girls started jabbering at him in Crow.

"I don't understand," he said meekly.

"They're gifts for you."

Cooper spun, shocked to hear English. He saw a youth a little younger than he standing nearby and grinning. He looked like a Crow, with his dark skin and long hair. And he was dressed like a Crow, too. But he had blue eyes and spoke Cooper's language.

The dark youth held out his hand. "I'm Gray Mountain," he said in a pleasant voice. "I was out huntin', and just got back when I saw we had visitors."

"You speak English well," Cooper said stupidly, shaking Gray Mountain's hand.

Gray Mountain smiled again. "My father was a white trapper. Came upriver with the Missouri River Fur Company back in eighteen-nine. Met him a friendly Crow woman named Coyote, and a while later I came along. I was brought up with the Absaroka — Crows."

"Are we that close to the Missouri River?" Cooper asked. "I figured we was some distance away."

"We are. My band here has been down in Snake country, tradin'. We do it occasional, though we're usually at war with those foolish bastards." He smiled once more. "You'd best take your gifts before Falling Leaf changes her mind. Young 'uns like that can be notional, and I've heard that said of all women."

Cooper chuckled. "Me, too." For the first time since he left St. Louis he felt like a person, with someone he could talk to. He took the packages and asked, "What are they?"

Gray Mountain translated the question to the girls, listened to Falling Leaf answer, then said, "Clothes." He grinned and waved a hand at Cooper's shabby apparel. "Seems Falling Leaf thinks a man of your talents should be dressed some better'n you are."

Cooper smiled, then grew sad. "I'm sorry," he said, holding the packages out. "I can't take 'em. I have nothing to pay with."

Once more Gray Mountain went through the process of translating. Then he said, "They're gifts. And Falling Leaf says," he laughed, "you do not have to pay since you pleasured her so well. And letting her play with your beard was payment enough for some old clothes."

Cooper laughed, too, and the girls joined in. Weeks called to Cooper, who said, "Tell her I said thank you." Cooper mounted his horse and tied the bundles to the saddle. Weeks called out again, more angrily. Cooper waved to the two young women and to Gray Mountain as he rode out.

Twelve

Hawley Cooper stepped self-consciously from behind the screen of trees and bushes. He was dressed in the buckskins Falling Leaf had given him. The clothes were not new, and Cooper figured they probably had been taken from Falling Leaf's brother or father.

The pants, and he was rather surprised they were pants and not just leggings, were about the right length, but the waist was somewhat large, and he had to tie them up with a length of rawhide.

The hunting shirt was long, with a ragged bottom and long-fringed sleeves. It had been made for someone with a much larger chest and stomach. But Cooper figured he had room to grow into it. He was used to such things. With three older brothers, he had always worn hand-me-downs that often were too big for him when he got them.

The moccasins were too large, too, and he

did not know what to do about them. His boots were next to useless, and these were fine, well-made, warm moccasins, with hard leather soles. He would like to wear them but could not the way they were.

Tall Grass looked at him, and then away. Cooper thought she might have smiled at him, but he was not sure. Josiah Weeks looked up from running his ramrod through the old Dickert flintlock, cleaning it. He scowled, and asked, "Where'd ye get them clothes, boy?"

Cooper was not so afraid of Weeks anymore. He had fought an Indian warrior hand to hand and won. He had even raised hair. He knew Weeks could best him in a knife fight; and, with the accurate Dickert, outshoot him. But face to face, in a fair fight, Cooper was not worried now. Of course he was still concerned that Weeks being the type of man he was might shoot him in the back. So he would continue to be cautious, but still, he thought more of himself now, and would not be spoken to in such a manner.

"I got 'em from some friends. But I reckon you wouldn't understand that, since I figure you got none."

"I got friends, ye Injun-humpin' bastard," Weeks said with a smile. "Did them girls give 'em to ye? Or did ye buy 'em? Eh? Maybe with some of my trade goods? Did ye steal some of my plunder to pay for 'em?"

"I wouldn't touch your goddamn possibles, old man," Cooper said sharply. "Not even was my life hangin' in the balance. I owe you for the possibles you bought me back in St. Louis and the extra blanket I took. That's all I'm ever gonna owe you too, you thievin' old coot."

"Ye owe me a heap more'n that, boy," Weeks said, furiously jamming the wiping stick into the dirt. The wind kicked up, making the loose end of a piece of canvas covering some trade goods snap angrily. "It were me who took ye up off the streets of St. Louis and give ye work. It were me who saved your miserable hide when Iron Bow came a huntin' for ye. You've ate more'n your share of the meat I've killed for ye."

"Meat I butchered," Cooper snapped. "You ain't ever give me nothin', you peckerless son of a bitch, but a life of trouble. I've worked, and goddamn hard, too, for all I got, and all I ate." He was breathing heavily as anger coursed through him, and his fists balled.

Weeks seemed not to have heard him. "And what about them Kaws we fought, eh? You'd be dead now it weren't for me."

"The hell I would. They was content to count coup. Just like them Sioux earlier. But no, you had to go'n get your feathers ruffled 'cause they counted coup on you . . ."

"And stole one of my horses."

". . . so that you went and shot one of 'em, in the back." He was outraged.

"Don't ever give an Injun — any Injun — a chance, boy. They'll not be so kind to ye given the opportunity. Got-damn savages ain't worthy of consideration. It ain't like they was real people, ye know. How many times I got to tell ye that, afore ye learn, boy?" His eyes had that wild glow in them.

"You're just a sour-hearted old man," Cooper said, more in annoyance now than in anger. He sat and began honing his knife, just for something to do.

Weeks spit tobacco juice, barely missing Cooper's left leg, and went back to cleaning his gun. "Well, now that you've done paradin' in your fancy new finery, boy, best set to puttin' up my tent."

"We're stayin' here?" Cooper asked, surprised.

They had ridden hard after leaving the Crow village, and Cooper had wondered why. They did not stop that night, and by morning were mostly through South Pass, though Cooper did not know it. They stopped and had a hurried meal. Cooper, always curious, asked, "Why the hurry?"

"Because," Weeks snapped in tired annoyance, "the got-damn Crows is the worst horse-stealin' bastards north of the devilish, black-hearted Comanches, that's why. Just 'cause we bought some horses from 'em don't mean they plan on lettin' us keep them critters for long. I want to outrun 'em."

"You think they'd come after us just to steal our horses?"

"Got-damn right they would, thievin' sons a bitches."

"One of 'em told me they was on their way back from tradin' with the Snakes. They got women and kids with 'em. A whole village of 'em. They ain't likely to come after us."

"When in hell did ye get to be so knowin' of the ways of Injuns, boy? Ye think havin' some women and kids along'd stop a half-dozen bucks from comin' after us? Huh? 'Specially some of the younger ones, boys lookin' for honors, tryin' to put a cavvy of horses together to get a wife."

"Oh," Cooper said, crestfallen.

"Just mind you don't go sassin' your betters, and don't go talkin' of things ye don't know nothin' of. Like Injuns."

"But I . . ."

"But, hell, boy. You seem to have got the notion that since you've dallied with a couple Injun girls all to a sudden ye know what goes on in those critters' minds. Well ye don't, I can tell ye. So mind your manners, and your tongue."

Weeks angrily mounted up, and the crusty trapper kept the three of them in the saddle until well after dark. They were back on the trail before first light, too. Now they had stopped again, and Weeks had originally indicated they would be leaving in the morning.

"So why are we stayin'?" Cooper persisted.

" 'Cause I said so, got-dammit." With an effort Weeks calmed himself. "We been pushing the animals hard, boy, ye should know that."

"I tried to tell you that yesterday."

"And now that we got more horses, we can make more meat. Right here along the river the huntin's poor, but up over them ridges" he pointed "toward them Wind River Mountains ye can see to the north there, there's plenty of buffler. We'll stake our camp here."

"All right." Cooper took a final look at his blade, satisfied with its sharpness. He slid it away, and then dropped the whetstone in his possible sack.

"Them mocs look a mite large," Weeks said without humor.

"They are. But I'll learn to live with 'em I reckon."

"Stuff some grass down into the toes of 'em, boy, and they'll set your feet better."

Cooper looked up in surprise. "I don't need," Weeks said in a surly tone, "a camp helper who's lamed up by ailin' feet."

Cooper nodded and stood. A few yards off there was some fresh, soft grass. Sitting next to it, Cooper took off a moccasin. He plucked several handfuls of the grass and stuffed them into the moccasins. He put the moccasin back on, stood, and tested it. He sat again and put more grass in. He did this several times before he was satisfied. Then he went through the procedure with the other one.

Finally he was done, knowing Weeks was growing more annoyed. But he took his time, not only because he wanted the moccasins as comfortable as possible, but also to aggravate Weeks.

Then he set about puttin up Weeks' tent and going about his other chores as darkness swept swiftly down on them. As it did, the wind kicked up considerably, whipping the smoke from the fire into small tornadoes, and scattering ashes. The temperature dropped, but Cooper was warm with his new buckskins and the work he was doing.

The next morning Weeks rode out to hunt. Tall Grass followed him, several of the new horses trailing behind her.

"Ain't I goin'?" Cooper had asked minutes before.

"No. Ye stay here with the goods and such. Somebody's got to watch over the possibles. And Tall Grass'll need plenty of meat racks when we get back."

"You'll be all right, Tall Grass?" Cooper asked, concerned.

"She'll be just fine, boy," Weeks retorted. "She's butchered meat by herself afore."

Cooper stared at Tall Grass for a few moments. The woman kept her eyes averted. Then Cooper shifted a cold gaze to Weeks. He nodded once and spun on his heel.

Cooper went right to work, chopping down some small cottonwoods and then stripping off the leaves and bark. He tied the poles together with strips of rawhide to make racks. Sweat was soon pouring off him, so he removed his hunting shirt and tossed it aside.

He began hearing steady gunfire in the distance and knew Weeks had found a stand. Then he heard another sound. Something different . . .

He glanced over his shoulder in alarm. Rushing at him was a good-sized grizzly, snuffling and roaring. Cooper knew he could not outrun the bear, but he could not stand and face its assault either. Despite his panic and fear, he concluded that his pistol would be useless. So he ran toward his rifle, which rested against a tree trunk not far away.

He snatched it up and dived, as the bear's claws raked shallow furrows down his back. He tumbled head over heels, swearing as his skin was abraded on dirt and stones. But he kept a grip on his rifle. He rolled to a stop against a tree trunk, and the bear roared past. Cooper was painfully aware of the big animal's powerful, musky odor.

The bear skidded and slipped on the grass as it tried to halt. When it did, it spun rapidly. Cooper, flat behind the tree, kept one eye on the bear as he pulled the stopper from his small priming powder horn. He snapped open the frizzen and poured powder into the pan without looking.

The bear was charging again but could not spot Cooper. So it stopped, and reared up, eyes blinking, nose quivering as it sought out the man scent. It growled, seemingly in frustration.

Cooper brought the rifle to his shoulder, figuring he had only one chance, and that while the bear was on its hind legs. He did not want to try shooting a rushing grizzly in the head.

He fired.

When the powder smoke cleared from in front of his eyes, he saw the bruin howling in rage, blood spouting from the severed neck artery. The animal's head lolled at an odd angle, and Cooper figured he had clipped the spine.

With the beast's roars in his ears, Cooper swiftly reloaded, spilling some powder as his hands shook. He primed it and cocked it, and then lay waiting. But the bear gave no signs of faltering, and after waiting a little while, Cooper put another ball in it.

As he reloaded, more calmly this time, Cooper watched the bear. After several minutes the grizzly fell and lay twitching.

For a long time Cooper lay there, watching, waiting, too wary to venture out to see if the bear was dead. He only hoped there was not another one in the area. But the bear did not move, and finally Cooper walked close to the beast. He jabbed at the animal with his rifle. The bear was dead.

Cooper wiped the perspiration off his face.

It was not sweat brought on by work, but by fear. His bladder spasmed, and Cooper relieved himself near a tree, eyes still on the bear. Done, he pulled his knife, and with a deep breath to steady himself, he moved in. It did not take long to skin the bear and remove the claws and teeth. He took some the meat, too, and hacked away some fat, to be melted into tallow both for their two lanterns and as grease for the guns.

He stretched the hide between some trees and began scraping off the clinging bits of meat and fat. Done, he rubbed in some brain matter, and then let it sit as he returned to building the meat scaffolds. Sweat running down his back stung the grooves ripped in his back by the bear.

Cooper was finished with several meat racks and had gathered plenty of wood when Weeks and Tall Grass rode back into camp. He was working on the bear skin again, and the sky was beginning to darken.

Weeks' eyes widened when he saw the hide. He dismounted and tossed the reins to Tall Grass. The woman dismounted and tied the pack horses to a tree while she led her horse and Weeks' away.

The trapper walked to where Cooper worked and appraised the hide critically. "Must've been a good size griz," he said noncommittally.

Cooper grunted but continued working.

"It'll be a nice addition to the other pelts we got."

"No," Cooper said, gasping from the exertion. He wiped a forearm across his perspiring brow.

Weeks seemed almost stunned. "What'd ye say, boy?"

"I said no. This here is my griz. I killed it myself, and I aim to keep the hide."

Weeks scrunched up an eye as he looked at the youth. "Ye forgettin' the deal we made, boy? Any pelts that're took is mine, till you've paid off your debts to me."

"You said nothin' about griz. Just beaver, wolf and buffalo." He stopped scraping and turned to face Weeks square. "But even if you meant bear, too, this one's mine. Winter'll be here soon, and this chil'," he was pleased at the expression, "don't cotton to freezin'. I want this as a sleepin' robe, or maybe even to make a coat of."

"What about that buffler robe ye took a while back and been usin'?" Weeks asked in irritation.

"Got no hair on it. You know that. It was a summer hide. It'll do for some things, but this bear pelt now . . ." Cooper went back to work, but he watched Weeks out of the corner of his eye. The trapper fingered his pistol. But then he turned and stalked away, shoving Tall Grass, who was unloading one of the horses, out of his way.

Thirteen

Hawley Cooper looked out over the Green River, which sparkled like a serpentine jewel under the warm sun of midafternoon. It had taken almost a week to get here, once they had left their camp on the unknown creek, where Cooper had shot the grizzly.

They had spent about five days there, making meat, and Josiah Weeks thought finally they might have enough to get them through the winter, or so he had said.

When they had left there, they followed the Sweetwater, then went southwest for several days before crossing the Big Sandy and spent the next night at a little spring in a wide, barren flat.

They were on the trail just after dawn, cutting across several creeks and streams without trouble, and by midafternoon had reached the Green River.

It took the rest of the day to get across the swift-moving Green, and it cost them. One of the mules packed with meat was torn from its rope and swept downriver, braying as it fought to make the bank. Then it was gone, drowned.

"Got-dammit," Weeks shouted, backhanding Tall Grass after they had climbed the far bank. "I told ye to keep a good grip on them animals, got-dammit, woman. Now we're out all that meat." He raised his hand to hit her again, but a shouted warning from Cooper stopped his hand in midair. Weeks looked at Cooper with hate and loathing. Then, with a smirk, Weeks smacked the Pawnee woman. Tall Grass winced but said nothing, and after the initial shock, her face resumed its normal placidness.

Cooper rode up until he was knee to knee with Weeks, staring into the trapper's eyes. "Don't ever let me catch you hittin' her again, boy," Cooper said. There was steel in his voice, and a glint in his eye that had not been there before.

"Or . . .?"

The answer was in Cooper's eyes, but Weeks did not want to believe it. After all, he had knocked this young pup down before, and killed his first man before Cooper was off his mother's teat.

Weeks swung a fist. But Cooper was ready for him this time. He was no longer the untested boy Weeks had flattened not long ago. Cooper's hand snaked out and caught Weeks' fist and held it firmly.

Both men struggled, sweat beading on their foreheads, seeping down into their beards. Their neck and arm muscles knotted with the strain. Weeks relaxed first, apprehension in his eyes.

Cooper held on a few seconds longer, then let Weeks' fist go. The warning was still clear in his eyes. Weeks turned in the saddle and spit tobacco juice on the ground. Then he jerked his head to the northwest. They started moving, and Weeks said, loudly enough for Cooper to hear, "Since ye lost that meat, woman, there'll be none for ye till I'm got-damned good and ready to let ye have some."

They were in prime beaver country now, and the going became slow. They stayed that night on LaBarge Creek, not far from where it entered the Green. And from then on, they stayed a few days at any likely spot to trap, before moving on.

Weeks waded into the pure, icy, fast-moving creeks and streams morning and night, often up to his thighs, to set his traps and to pull out the fat, early prime beaver. Weeks usually took Cooper with him. He would leave Cooper on the bank and toss the beaver carcasses to the youth. He would not let Cooper into the water with him, or even get too close, for fear Cooper would learn some of his secrets.

Within a few days Cooper could skin a beaver within seconds. A few deft slices with his sharp knife, a rip and a pull, and the skin was free. Most often he tossed the useless carcass into the cottonwoods, aspens or oaks, where in the night the coyotes, wolves and bears argued over the rotting flesh, their snarls and howls rending the night air. Occasionally he would keep a young beaver or two on which to feast that night. It was a tasty break from buffalo and helped conserve their meat supplies.

They swung north off LaBarge Creek to trap the various small forks of Piney Creek, before working their way northwestward to the branches of South Piney, Middle Piney, and then North Piney.

From there they set out westward, trapping, then crossing, Grey's River before moving onto Cottonwood Creek. There Cooper was surprised when Weeks sent him out to hunt. Cooper worried, thinking maybe Weeks was planning to ride out and leave him alone and without supplies.

He was much relieved, in a way, when he rode back into the camp to see Weeks sitting near the fire. Tall Grass had just given the trapper a bowl of stewed buffalo meat. Weeks grinned at Cooper, looking for all the world like the cat that had just swallowed the bird. It bothered Cooper, since he saw no reason for it.

Cooper shook his head and hauled the meat off the pack mule. There were cuts of a young buffalo cow, an elk, and a mule deer.

"That the whole of it, boy?" Weeks asked suspiciously.

"Damn near," Cooper said, surly.

"I want all of it, boy. Or have ye forgot our arrangement?"

"I ain't forgot."

"Then let's have it."

"You got all you're gonna get." He started leading the two animals away, ignoring Weeks' meager protests. A short way off, close to an aspen, he unloaded a small bundle of meat, and then took the animals over to the others, where he cared for them. When he went back to the aspen, he built himself a small fire and started cooking the meat. Soon after, Tall Grass, looking furtively behind her, arrived.

Cooper smiled at her, and she returned it. There was warmth in her smile, he realized, and it warmed him some. Since they had lost the meat-laden mule in the Green River, Weeks had not fed Tall Grass. So Cooper had taken it upon himself to give her about half what he took from the fire each night. Cooper suspected that Weeks knew, but the trapper had not said anything.

Tall Grass gave Cooper a gourd of fresh water and a handful of coffee beans. Cooper nodded and drank from the gourd. It was whiskey, which surprised him. Watered down considerably, but whiskey nonetheless. Tall Grass sat, shoulders sagging from tiredness.

"It'll be done soon," Cooper said, trying to get her to say something, anything to him. But she had not spoken a word to him in all the time they had traveled together. He shrugged.

Weeks bellowed for Tall Grass and she left. She was back soon after, though, tenseness etched on her face. Her face lightened, however, when she took the meat Cooper held out. She ate quickly, wiped her hands on some grass, and her mouth with the bottom of her buckskin dress. She stood and lightly touched Cooper's cheek. There was a longing in her eyes, Cooper thought, as she hurried away.

Cooper's thoughts were disturbed as he sat drinking the coffee brewed in his pewter cup. But he managed to push the thoughts aside as he curled into his blankets under a clear and cold sky.

The next morning, when Cooper was packing the mules and horses, he realized some supplies were gone. It seemed to him that a little of everything was gone: food, beaver plews, trade goods, whiskey, tobacco, lead and powder. Not enough to make a real difference, but enough to be noticed by Cooper, who did all the packing.

It seemed odd, but he shrugged it off. It was Weeks' plunder, and the trapper could do with it what he wished. There was still plenty.

Finished, he went back to his small fire, and began rolling up his blankets. The six-point one was gone. Anger welled up in Cooper, and he had to stand stock still for a few moments to let the worst of it subside. He figured Weeks had taken it, but he could not be certain.

Cursing, he stormed off to where Weeks still sat at his fire sipping coffee. "Where'n hell's my blanket, damn you?" Cooper shouted.

"How'n hell should I know, boy?" Weeks said in irritation.

"You took it didn't you?"

"Ye can't keep track of your things, boy,

don't come cryin' to me. You've seen fit of late to spend your time off away from me bein' unsociable, I can't keep track of your things for ye."

Cooper opened his mouth to say something, but he saw Tall Grass peering from Weeks' tent. She held a finger to her lips, asking him to be quiet. Cooper's eyes widened, and he was thankful Weeks had gone back to drinking his coffee and was no longer paying any attention to him. Head shaking in wonder, he turned and walked away. Perhaps Weeks had deprived her of that comfort, too, and so maybe she might have done it. Besides, Cooper still had the bear fur, well-tanned and warm, and the buffalo robe. He would be all right, but still, it rankled him.

The dying aspen leaves clacked and rattled as the two men and the woman rode. The nights were cold now, but the days still pleasantly warm. They headed mostly south now, toward Salt River Pass, and then onto Smith's Fork, where they trapped for several days. They followed Smith's Fork, trapping all the way, until they reached the Bear River, where they turned northwest, up that river.

It was early October, and the weather unpredictable. One day it would be sunny and quite warm; the next might find them fighting through a boiling thunderstorm punctuated with hail that sapped their strength and will. Three times they saw snow flurries.

Travel seemed to be more hazardous. Twice they had to plunge off the trail as landslides rumbled down at them, set off by some unseen hand, or the weather. Or maybe just bad spirits.

The days grew shorter, but the quality of beaver plews Weeks brought in got better, as the animals' fur thickened into plush coats in preparation for winter. Cooper learned well how to tan them, and the number of pelts piled up. Every few days they would fashion a crude press in their camp and flatten a pile of plews into a package tied with rawhide. Each weighed eighty to a hundred pounds.

Three more times Weeks sent Cooper off to hunt. After the second time, Cooper realized more supplies were gone, and he approached Weeks by the fire.

"There's some supplies missin'," Cooper said without preliminary.

"Cached 'em," Weeks said, looking over the rim of his tin mug.

"What's that?"

"Hid 'em." He put down his cup. "Dug

me a hole and put some plunder in. All good mountaineers do it."

"Why?"

"Got-damn, ye are dumb, ain't ye, boy?" He picked up his cup, took a sip and then tossed the dregs into the fire, where they sizzled briefly before dying. He dangled the cup from one finger. "That way we don't have to pack so much into the mountains. Won't wear out the animals. It also means we'll be certain to have some possibles once we start headin' to rendezvous."

"Oh." Cooper nodded, then realization hit him. "That why you sent me out huntin' yesterday and that other time? So I wouldn't know where your goddamned cache is?"

Weeks grinned insolently. "Maybe ye ain't so got-damn dumb after all, boy." He laughed when he saw Cooper glancing around. "Ye ain't ever gonna find one of my caches, boy. I can make a cache even a Crow couldn't root out. Ye certainly ain't gonna find it."

Angry, Cooper stalked away with Week's sickly laugh mocking him. He felt only slightly better the next day when, after relieving his bladder just after awakening, he went back to his small, separate fire and found his six-point blanket. It was on his bearskin sleeping robe and had been fashioned into a fine capote.

He picked up the capote, enjoying its thickness and potential warmth. The sky, which had been a leaden gray, suddenly opened and let forth its contents. Hurriedly, Cooper slipped the capote on and pulled the wide, generous hood over his head. He looked toward Weeks' tent and wondered at the Pawnee woman who lived so poorly within it. She was, Cooper knew, at least eating again, and she had not been beaten in a while, as far as he knew. Maybe he had done some good, after all, Cooper thought.

"Where'd ye get that capote, boy?" Weeks demanded later in the day when he saw Cooper for the first time.

"None of your business."

Weeks wheeled, face red, on Tall Grass. "Ye make that got-damned capote for him, woman?" he asked harshly.

She said nothing but stood looking down at her moccasins. Weeks swung at her, but missed, and slipped in the mud. Cooper suppressed a laugh, but a choking chuckle popped out for an instant before it, too, was smothered.

Weeks had heard the sound and spun on him, eyes bright with rage. He turned back toward the woman and charged her, knocking her down. He started punching her, howling in his rage.

Cooper raced over and barreled into Weeks, sending the trapper sprawling. As Weeks started to rise, Cooper kicked him in the face. "I told you to leave her alone, boy," Cooper screamed into the wind.

Weeks stared up at him, eyes and face engorged with blood, before his head fell back with a plop in the mud.

Cooper shook his head in disgust and left.

By morning the skies had cleared, and early in the day Weeks sent Cooper out hunting. The youth left like always, rifle across his saddle, and a stoic mule trailing on a rope behind. But a half-mile away, he doubled back, walking his horse through the thickets and aspens, which were rapidly losing their leaves. The air was fresh and clean here, scrubbed by the storm of the day before, and scented with pine and cedar. Aspen leaves clacked in the breezes before falling and then rattled as the wind drove them hustling along the ground.

Cooper's horse had fattened up considerably. She had responded well to his care and thoughtfulness, and she served him as well as she could. Though she would always be swaybacked and less than lightning on the run, she was a good horse, and Cooper was glad to have her.

The mare picked her way silently through the forest. Cooper was pleased. Then he heard a sound, and he reined up. He slid off the horse and tied her and the mule to a tree, where they could eat grass.

Cooper moved forward on foot, as quietly as he could. The noise he heard grew louder, and within minutes the sound of a shovel biting into dirt was clear. Then he could hear Weeks grunting with the effort of his chore and cursing the burden of it.

Cooper settled in behind a tree trunk. He watched as Weeks dug for more than two hours. Then the trapper laid a piece of canvas in the hole, onto which, with great gasping and heaving, he bundled two bales of beaver pelts and then some smaller parfleches and pouches of other supplies. Weeks pulled the ends of the canvas sheet over the goods and held them down with rocks

Wheezing some, Weeks collapsed into a sit. He drank deeply from a gourd canteen, and Cooper was sure it was not filled with water. After a short rest and much sipping Weeks stood. He sighed at the work still facing him but grabbed his shovel and started filling in the hole from the small mountain of dirt nearby.

It was boring watching, but Cooper stuck

it out. Weeks filled the hole, then tamped the dirt down with his feet. He dragged back bushes that had been carefully dug up, roots and all, and replanted them. He worked steadily, with only an occasional sip from the canteen.

Several hours later he was done, having arranged plants and even some grass carefully, then sweeping the remaining dirt with a broom of Indian paintbrush. He scattered aspen leaves and pine needles about, letting them fall in a natural way.

At last Weeks stepped back, pulling off his hat and wiping a ragged sleeve across his sweating forehead. With a smile of congratulations, he sat again and took up his gourd.

Cooper left as silently as he had come, but he carefully cut blazes in trees, making them unobtrusive. He did not know what good it would do him, but he thought it might pay off someday to know where this cache was. He marked trees all the way back to the buffalo trail he had followed out of camp. He felt certain that if he could find the trail again, he could find the cache.

Satisfied, he hurried on, and got lucky. He found two buffalo and a grizzly in a clearing not far away. He shot all three, the grizzly first and at close quarters. Then he butchered them and sat.

He loved it here with the quiet solitude. The wind blew steadily, though not often strongly, and he took off his cap to let the breeze ruffle through his long hair. Birds chirped their varying tunes, and he could hear a coyote off in the brush. The sky was bright blue and there seemed to be no end to it. There were but few clouds this day, mere balls of puffy white that drifted lazily across the azure.

Cooper stuck a blade of grass between his teeth, chewed on it lightly, and began humming *Old Dan Tucker.*

He dozed and awoke with a start. Looking up, he realized he had napped for less than an hour. But at this time of year it would be getting dark soon. He loaded the meat on the pack mule and started walking back to camp, singing.

He wished it could be always so. Alone and with plenty of meat. With a blue sky and few cares. Then he thought of Corn Flower and Falling Leaf. One of them would make his life complete. He would have to do something about that soon. Very soon.

FOURTEEN

Hawley Cooper came to with his face in the snow. His head throbbed unmercifully, and he was chilled to the bone. He just lay a while, trying to remember what had happened, but the pain in his head made it impossible.

He shoved himself up, groaning, until he was on hands and knees. He rested, panting, letting the raging inside his skull lessen. Then, with a deep breath, he pushed all the way to his feet. He clamped his eyes shut, feeling as if someone was jabbing them with hot pokers. He finally opened them cautiously, but the world twisted and spun before him. He swayed, and felt his gorge rising.

He fought off the sickness and, with great care, looked around. Where there had been a fairly comfortable winter camp, there was nothing but a few odds and ends that would signify only that a man had passed this way once. Josiah Weeks and Tall Grass were gone, as was the tipi the Pawnee woman had made not long ago. The furs, equipment, horses, mules. Everything was gone.

Cooper realized with a stab of fear that his rifle, pistol, capote, belt and possible bag were gone, too. "No!" he screamed into the depths of the canyon, the single, drawn-out word coming back with diminishing volume to mock him. He was utterly alone, in winter, without warm clothing, food, blankets or weapons. He was several hundred miles, at best, from any fort or town; and in the heart of Indian country, surrounded by wind-torn, snow-covered, dangerous mountains. He did not even really know where he was.

He slumped down, the pain in his head almost forgotten for the moment in his grief and fear. And he remembered how he came to be in such a state.

He, Weeks and Tall Grass had trapped their way slowly up the Bear River, past its giant U-turn, where it doubled around to head southward again. And they had entered a high-walled, heavily forested canyon. The cliffs kept the wind down some, and the thick clots of lodgepole pines, aspens and sturdy cottonwoods would provide plenty of firewood, and even feed for the animals.

Game was adequate, if not abundant, with a few buffalo, and small herds of elk and mule deer. An occasional moose ambled through, and once in a while a bighorn sheep or mountain goat could be spotted bounding amongst the craggy spires.

Surprisingly no one was there. Weeks had mumbled something about expecting to see other mountain men, or perhaps a band of Flatheads or even Nez Perce. But he had been happy no one was there.

"Got-damn, this'll do," Weeks said, stopping about a quarter of the way into the canyon from the northern end. He dismounted in a stand of trees that ran up to the sheer wall. A creek gurgled nearby.

Wearily Cooper set about making camp, helping Tall Grass put up the tent. He would spend most nights outside, at least until the weather turned really bad, maybe in another month or so.

It did not take that long, however. Two days after they arrived, a severe rainstorm lashed them, with a biting wind laced with hailstones as big as chicken eggs. It lasted three days, leaving a morass of mud. The storm also seemed to have finally and decisively broken the back of autumn, for within a few days they were getting regular snow flurries. And a week after the rainstorm ended, a blizzard shrieked through the canyon, nearly burying their still-burgeoning camp.

Weeks would not let Cooper inside the tent, despite the wickedness of the storm, and Cooper seethed. As soon as the blizzard abated, he set about making himself a crude, though functional, lean-to, well protected by trees and brush.

Cooper's work kept him busy, however. While Weeks spent his days on the trap lines, occasionally hunting, and often lazing about the camp, Cooper worked on his shelter; helped Tall Grass with the beaver plews; cooked his meals; hunted some; chopped cord after cord of firewood, enough for the winter; cared for the animals; reshoeing many; repaired other equipment; gathered shoots or stripped bark off trees as forage for the horses for when things got really bad, and more.

Cooper was tired all the time. His work never seemed to end, and it made him irritable. Weeks paid it no mind, often and with glee, Cooper thought finding him more chores to do. He watched longingly as Tall Grass put up the tipi she had made after arriving in the canyon, piecing together huge buffalo skins. It was, Cooper thought, a much better way to live than in a lean-to or even a tent, which threatened to fall over every time a strong wind blew. And a tipi did not collect snow on the roof. You could build a fire inside one, too.

Cooper wished he had such a lodge, but he had no skins of his own with which to make one, and he would be damned and dead before he would go into further debt to Weeks to buy the precious hides from him. His lean-to would have to serve. But it didn't make him feel any better.

Soon after the lodge was up, Weeks asked Cooper to drop what he was doing and help repair several traps.

"I'll get to it tomorrow," Cooper said more civilly than he felt. "First thing."

"I need 'em now, boy."

Cooper shrugged and went on with his work.

"Got-dammit, boy, I'm talkin' to ye," Weeks yelled, grabbing Cooper by the shoulder.

Cooper was too tired, hungry, cold and testy to put up with such behavior. And he was no longer afraid. As he let himself be hauled around, he came up hard with a fist, catching the older man under the chin. Weeks staggered back a few steps, shock in his eyes. He started to go for his pistol, but Cooper had his out first.

"Go on," Cooper said, wincing as fear knotted in his belly.

"I want ye out of my got-damn camp," Weeks said, anger making his eyes bulge. But he relaxed a little and straightened.

"Soon's I get my money, old man."

"What money, boy?"

"I been with you four months or so, by my reckoning. You owe me wages for all that. Plus I get to keep my horse, blankets, rifle and other such possibles as I might need. And some grub, of course."

Weeks laughed that old hoarse laugh of his, wheezing and sputtering. "Ye got gall, boy, ye sure do," he said around the choking guffaws. "What with all the supplies I gave ye already, ye owe me."

"The hell you say. You want me gone, you pay me and give me enough possibles to make my way to safety somewhere."

"Waste of good plunder, boy," Weeks said, no longer laughing. "You'll not be gone a week afore you're gone under. If'n the redskin bastards don't get ye, a griz will. Or the weather. Naw," he shook his head, "was I to give ye any plunder, it'd only be wasted. Reckon I'll just keep what I got."

"Then I'll be hangin' around a spell," Cooper said, angry eyes mirroring Weeks'. He put away his pistol. Weeks stared at him with eyes as cold as the mountain mornings. Then he turned and walked away.

Three days later Cooper strode back into camp with another load of firewood in his arms just in time to see Tall Grass fly out of the lodge. Weeks, angry and at least half drunk, followed her, poised to strike again.

Cooper dropped the wood and grabbed up a branch about as thick around as a man's arm and about three feet long. Then he ran. "Stop!" he yelled as he neared the couple.

Weeks craned his head around, pausing in his beating of Tall Grass. "This ain't your concern, boy," he snarled, turning blood-tinged eyes on the youth.

"You hit that woman again, you goddamn scoundrel, and I'll flatten your skull for you." Cooper could feel the fear inside as almost something tangible. But he was also aware of an exhilaration, and excitement. He had always been a strong youth, what with so many years of his young life working on his father's farm before becoming apprenticed to the blacksmith, no easy job either. And since they had made their winter camp, he had been working steadily and hard. He had faith now, and confidence, in his strength.

Weeks whirled and came up with a knife

in his hand. With a single fluid motion, he completed his turn and threw the knife. The blade made a thunking sound as it bit deep into the branch Cooper held in his right hand.

Cooper gasped and almost lost control of his bladder. He might have confidence in his strength and know he could best Weeks in a fair fight, but knives and guns were other matters. He was not well-versed with either knife or pistol, though he was a good shot with a rifle. He doubted that would be a factor.

He also realized Weeks could have killed him with the knife if he so desired. Cooper looked at the knife, still quivering in the wood, giving himself time to calm. He knew Weeks had seen the momentary look of fear that had splashed across his face, but when he spoke, his voice was steady, "Nice throw."

"I thought you'd like it." Weeks laughed a little, but felt suddenly unsettled, wondering if he shouldn't have killed the youth when he had the chance.

Cooper pulled the knife out of the wood with his left hand and dropped the branch. He hefted the knife, as if to test its balance. He flipped it up. It twirled a few times, and he deftly caught it in his right hand by the elk-horn hilt. He did it again, not watching the blade, but keeping his eyes on Weeks.

The trapper licked his lips, while his small Adam's apple bobbled beneath the grizzled beard. Cooper flipped the knife a few more times before tossing it so that it landed, blade first, in the frozen ground between Weeks' feet. Cooper was surprised at his accuracy.

"Leave the woman alone," Cooper said coldly before picking up the branch and walking away, shoulders hunched against the ball he expected from Weeks' pistol.

It never came, but Cooper worked in fear the rest of the day. Finally, disgusted with himself, he shoved the fear away, and set to his own small fire. He concluded that since Weeks had never done anything before after such incidents, he would do nothing now. So he stretched out in his robes and fell asleep.

He had always been a light sleeper, and his time in the wilds had strengthened that trait. So the rustling nearby woke him instantly. As panic burst through him, he scrambled for his pistol.

Suddenly a calloused, though soft hand, was over his lips. In the moonlight filtering through the trees and vaguely illuminating the small lean-to, Cooper could see Tall Grass remove her hand and stand. She slipped out of her capote, and then let her buckskin dress fall. Shivering in the bitter night, she slipped into Cooper's bed.

"What . . . ?" Cooper began.

"No talk," she said in English, and Cooper realized this was the first time she had ever spoken to him.

She slid her body over his, and her lips pounced on his. He relaxed and gave himself to her, willingly and with an ardor he had not known he possessed. There was something different about this than the other times, he thought vaguely as his numbed brain tried to function. He gave up the attempt and surrendered to his passions.

It was only later, when they were done and he had time to relax, that he realized the difference was that Tall Grass was a woman, experienced in life and love. Those others had been girls, and while Tall Grass might not be as beautiful as Falling Leaf or as well-endowed as Corn Flower, she was more of a woman than those two others.

With that knowledge, he relaxed even more, and asked, "Why?"

She shrugged. With her limited command of English, she would never be able to explain that she had wanted him for a long time. That she respected him, maybe even loved him. That she found his concern for her touching. That she had done nothing in the past because she feared Weeks. And she feared what Weeks might do to Cooper.

Nor could she explain that the latest incident in which Cooper had saved her from a beating again had made her determined to reward Cooper for his caring.

She shrugged again, and Cooper nodded, thinking he might understand even though she had said nothing. He stroked her cheek, and she winced. He pulled her head up to look at the discoloration. He kissed her lightly, then whispered, "We got to hang on, Tall Grass. For a little longer at least. Once spring comes, I'll get you away from here and him."

Tall Grass nodded. "Good," she said, before offering herself to him again.

Fifteen

Hawley Cooper shivered in the cold, and a dense gloom settled over him as he sat in the biting wind. The throbbing in his head did not go away, but he forced himself to move. Though each step jarred his skull, he continued on until he was in the cover of some barren aspens and oaks. Here, with the wind cut at least a bit, it seemed a little warmer.

Mostly unwillingly, Cooper remembered what had happened after Tall Grass had visited his robes that night.

They had fallen asleep then, without talking more. They awoke once in their shifting during the night, and sleepily clung together until they made love again.

When Cooper awoke with the dawn, Tall Grass was gone. He had been almost euphoric, but his spirits plummeted as he realized she had gone back to Weeks' lodge. He stood in the cold, gray light of morning, his emotions chaotic. He was filled with what he thought was love for Tall Grass and a silently screaming desire to confront Weeks, to end for all time his torment.

But he knew he was no cold-blooded killer, and that is what he would have to be if he wanted to face Weeks and free both himself and the woman from the trapper's bondage.

He ate without thinking and then set about on the day's chores. While Tall Grass was foremost in his mind that day, he did not let on, and did not go near Weeks' lodge. However, he did stay within the rough, small confines of the camp throughout the day, worried that Tall Grass might need his help.

All day he wrestled with the problem of what to do. Until finally, out of exasperation, he decided that he would do nothing, except try to keep an eye on Tall Grass' safety. Let time handle it, he told himself sternly as he set deer meat to cooking for his evening meal.

He did find, though, that when he turned in that night, it was with racing heart and trembling hand, as he anticipated another overnight visit from Tall Grass.

He was painfully disappointed when she did not come to him that night, nor the next. He resigned himself to thinking she might really care for Weeks, despite all the man's flaws, and had only given herself to Cooper because he had protected her several times.

He suddenly thought with growing dread that Weeks might have discovered their secret. Perhaps Tall Grass had even told him herself, either out of desires for revenge, or to anger Weeks into getting rid of her. Was the trapper sitting in his lodge now plotting some kind of vengeance? Cooper wondered, shivering. He did not stop to decide whether the shiver came from the fear or from the cold.

But the next night she showed up again, and after a hurried, almost uncomfortable lovemaking session, Cooper asked, "Why didn't you come to me last night? Or the night before?"

"Gray Beard don't trust me. You neither. Last time I see you, he had too much firewater. Sleep like winter bear."

"Can't you get him drunk every night?" Cooper asked somewhat peevishly.

She smiled, and there was real warmth in it. Cooper was amazed at how the small action brightened her face, making her look much younger. "Not enough firewater. And last two nights snow would give away tracks."

Cooper nodded, accepting the wisdom, but still uncomfortable. "He drunk again tonight?" Cooper asked hopefully.

"Yes." Again the brilliant smile. Tall Grass arched her back, stretching. The movement rubbed her naked flesh on Cooper's, and the lust rose in him again.

"Then we got all the night?" he asked hoarsely.

"Yes," she murmured into his ear.

The next morning, Cooper's mind was in turmoil again. The two nights Tall Grass had not come to see him had allowed him time to think. He had decided that he did not really love Tall Grass and he could not picture having her around permanently. He did know that he savored the pleasures of her body, and he was fairly certain she also enjoyed those nights with him. But was that enough reason to confront the vicious and unpredictable Weeks?

Worse, he was not even sure how she felt about him. Other than those two nights, she had never indicated any affection for him; indeed, until that first night she came to him, she had never uttered a word to him.

Still, he somehow felt responsible for her safety. He did not know why; it just seemed to have happened. Tall Grass seemed incapable of taking care of herself, and she had to be protected against Weeks.

Maybe he should try to buy Tall Grass from Weeks? He could keep her with him for the winter, enjoying her comforts. In the spring he could take her back to her village.

That might be the best, he thought. He figured Tall Grass would be grateful to him for getting her out of Weeks' clutches. And that might help him establish a trade with the Pawnees for when he headed back out here next season alone looking for beaver.

Besides, he could not live like this any longer, not only knowing that Tall Grass was in Weeks' lodge most of the time, suffering God only knew what indignities, but also Weeks' treatment of him all these months. It ate at him, cut through to his manhood to have someone lord it over him like this. It was why he had run away from the blacksmith in the first place.

The tumultuous thoughts about his position, and the confusion over what he should do to solve the untenable situation made eating a real task for Cooper that morning. But he forced himself to sit quietly and have his fill. He finally snorted at himself in aggravation. Damn fool, he thought.

In disgust, he pulled out his folding knife

and began whittling a green stick to a point at one end. The ones he had been using to cook meat were singed and worn.

He heard Weeks' off-key singing and knew the trapper was coming back into camp, most likely with a load of pelts for Cooper and Tall Grass to work on. Cooper was of no mind for such work, and outrage bubbled up again at his plight. In anger, he flipped the jackknife hard and it stuck, quivering into a nearby tree stump. "Dammit all," he snapped.

He stood, forcing himself to relax. There were plenty of other chores to be done, and by doing them, he could avoid helping Weeks with his plews. He did not want to face Weeks now, or anytime soon.

Cooper knew a confrontation was inevitable, but now, he thought, was not the time for it. He knew full well that if he went to help Weeks now, the showdown would come. He did not think he could take Weeks' smug smile as Tall Grass warmed his feet after the trapper had spent the early part of the morning in the icy water, or his possessiveness. Even if Cooper did not love Tall Grass, he could not stand by doing nothing when he saw any human treated so.

He picked up his rifle and headed off. He attacked his duties with a vigor born of anger. The work helped to ease his mind at least a little. Not long after midday he took a short rest. He was cold, though he was sweating from the work, and his face ached with the chill. And he was hungry. He made coffee in his mug and drank it while eating some deer meat. Both warmed him and gave him a slightly better outlook.

Feeling better, he went back to work. He was gathering more firewood, a job he learned long ago was never ending. As he toiled, he hummed *Landlord, Fill the Flowing Bowl,* almost enjoying himself.

Cooper was bending over, picking up a piece of wood when there was an explosion in his head. A bright light burst before his eyes, and he half turned, seeing Weeks standing over him with a log in his hand. He was still conscious as he fell, but the pain in his head was so great that he did not feel his nose break when it hit the frozen ground.

Before the blackness overwhelmed him, Cooper heard Weeks mutter, "Piss on ye, boy. There's a time for words, and a time for doin', boy. The time for words is long past. It's time I was doin'. I know all about your rendezvousin' with Tall Grass." Sparks of fury flickered in his eyes.

Cooper was aware of Weeks pawing at

him, but he was too stunned to know exactly what the trapper was doing. Then he was jerked around, and almost turned over.

"Try'n take my woman from me, will ye?" Weeks grumbled. "Got-damned Injun-humpin', no-good son of a bitch. Ye got some gall, boy, I'll say that for ye. Try'n to take my woman. Got-damn, thinkin' ye could do such to ol' Josiah Weeks."

Cooper tried to speak, but he was barely conscious. Still Weeks babbled on, "I'm in no tolerable mood for dealin' with the likes of ye anymore, boy. We'll just see how ye do after I'm through with ye." He laughed and almost giggled. There was more mumbling, but Cooper could no longer hear it.

Then Weeks was gone, and Cooper gratefully let the blackness smother him.

Now he sat, unable to stand any longer, holding his throbbing head in both hands, sucking in deep breaths to keep from vomiting. The pain was incredible.

How long he sat there, he did not know, but finally he could bear inaction no longer. He pushed himself unsteadily back up, realizing it was nearly dark. He stood weaving for a few moments before regaining his equilibrium.

Thinking still came hard, but he knew he

had to make some decisions fast or he would be dead very soon.

Cold. He was so cold. Those hours laying on the ground seemed to have sucked all life's warmth from his body, until even his bones ached.

Fire. Yes, that was it, his benumbed mind concluded at long last. He needed fire. For warmth. And light. He would feel better then. If he had a fire.

And food. Food would be good, too. It would help warm him from the inside, as the fire would warm him from the outside. He would be able to cope then.

But where to start? Wood was scattered all over, but his small fire pit made of stones he had painstakingly dragged up from the stream was gone, as were the fire pits where the lodge had stood. His lean-to had disappeared, shredded almost into dust under the hooves of horses and mules.

Cooper groaned. It was almost overwhelming. There was nothing left of the camp. Nothing. He closed his eyes and said a silent prayer, something he had not done since he was maybe ten. When he opened his eyes, his mind was made up. There was work to be done. Much work. First he would need a fire and then food. Everything else could wait.

He bent and picked up several pieces of wood he had been gathering when Weeks had cracked him on the head. It was a start. But for a moment he thought it might be the end. As he bent, dizziness splashed over him in sickening waves. The ground reeled before him, and small dots swam in his vision.

Cooper sat heavily, suddenly, breathing hard. But he had several pieces of wood clutched tightly in hand. After some long, deep breaths to calm himself, he leaned forward until he was on his hands and knees. He walked across the old campsite that way like a dog, he thought bitterly picking up sticks as he went, and shoving them ahead of him on the ice-covered snow. He returned to where his separate little camp had been, and without bothering to rebuild the fire ring, dropped the sticks. Shaking from the pain and the cold, he laboriously gathered tinder. With a thong torn from his shirt and a stick, he made a small bow.

With a monumental effort, he worked the bow until fire sprang forth in the tinder. He built it up until a pleasant little blaze was going. He leaned his back against a log. His face was beaded with sweat, though he estimated the temperature was near zero, and the pounding of his head threatened to overwhelm him again. He gulped frigid air, fighting the bile surging up his gullet seeking escape.

Whether he fell asleep or blacked out again, he did not know. All he knew was that one minute he was watching the cheery flames; the next he awoke with a start, the fire considerably lower. The pain had lessened fractionally, and he realized for the first time that his nose hurt considerably, too.

"Dammit all," he mumbled. He hated losing control; of being so vulnerable. Since that night Weeks had killed Iron Bow because Cooper was paralyzed by fear, Cooper had worried about losing his control again. It was a discomfiting thought.

Unsteady on his feet, he slowly gathered more wood, biting back the moans that tried to burst forth, and built up the fire again. The warmth soaked through him like a gentle spring rain, and his spirits rose a little.

Now he needed food, he thought. Good, rich meat laced through with fat to give him strength and more warmth.

Sixteen

Hawley Cooper smiled fractionally. There was bitterness in the grin, but also triumph. It was a small victory, to be sure, but a victory, nonetheless.

Josiah Weeks had left him nothing. But Cooper was not as stupid as Weeks had thought. Walking gingerly to the base of a nearby tree, Cooper knelt and carefully pulled away a bare grouse berry bush, roots and all. Then he dug with his hands. A foot or so down, he encountered buckskin. He smiled and dug faster, until he uncovered a package.

He pulled the bundle out and unwrapped the buckskin covering. Inside was the small supply of meat he had been hoarding: a pilfered block of pemmican, maybe eight inches by eight inches by two inches deep, wrapped in another piece of buckskin and sealed with beeswax; four dozen strips of jerky, taken a piece or two at a time from

Weeks' stores; and several hunks of fresh deer meat, placed there just the day before yesterday after a hunt. It wasn't much, he realized, but it would last several days, at least; more if he watched himself.

He took out the largest hunk of deer meat, which was frozen nearly all the way through, and laid it on a hot rock. When the meat had softened, he was able to force a sharp stick the one he had been whittling just yesterday through it. He hung the meat over the fire, propping the stick up on several other rocks.

The sizzling of the meat made his mouth water and his stomach rumble with anticipation. Eagerly he brought out the small pouch of coffee beans he had stockpiled. He reached for his pewter mug and realized, with horror, that it was gone.

"Goddamn that bastard to hell and gone!" he screamed into the growing night. "Sneakin', mean-spirited, connivin', flea-ridden, dog-eatin' son of a bitch. May you roast forever in the fires of hell, you black-hearted bastard!"

He ran out of steam, and his head was pounding again. He could understand why Weeks had stolen his horse, his gun, even his capote and bear robe; he could understand that Weeks had wrecked the camp and left him with nothing useful. But to steal the pewter mug was beyond him. There was no reason for it, other than pure meanness. Weeks knew how much it had cost Cooper, and how hard the youth had had to work for the sum. He also knew that Cooper was quite proud of his only real possession. Stealing the mug could have been done only out of simple, deep-seated cruelty.

Cooper sat, fuming, a slow rage warming him, though it was night now, and a bitter one at that. Reluctantly Cooper choked back the anger. It would do him little good and would only sap his strength. He pulled the hunk of meat from the fire and ate hungrily, wolfing down large baits of the mostly raw flesh that was barely warm inside. He washed it down with handfuls of snow he let melt in his mouth.

After some deliberation, he cooked another piece of meat. This he ate more slowly, savoring the richness of it. He licked the juices off his fingers when he was done. He felt like a new man after the sparse meal, though a gust of wind wrapped around him, swirling the snow particles on the ground so that they stung his face. It would be a long, cold night, he knew.

With a sigh, he wrapped up the rest of the meat and put the package back into the hole and covered it, both to keep it away from any animals that might be around, and in case Weeks should come back. Then, working as swiftly as he could in the dark, he dragged up some poles and branches and built a rough shelter almost atop the fire.

Done with that, he gathered up a good supply of firewood. It was hard work, doing it as he was with one hand while the other held a burning branch as a torch. His head still ached, as did his nose, and the cold seeped back into him.

Lastly he gathered up as many pine needles and leaves as he could find, and made a bed of them. Finally he lay on the frozen ground, barely two feet from the fire, and fell asleep.

It was an uncomfortable night. The wind blew steadily, punctuated with sharp, biting gusts that scattered ashes and sparks from the fire. It snowed off and on, interspersed with cutting sleet that stung his exposed flesh. The screeching wind or the cold woke Cooper numerous times. He would roll over, grab a handful of wood and feed the voracious fire before drifting back to sleep.

It was hard to tell exactly when dawn came, since the day was a leaden, dull gray. When he stood, pain shot through his head, and his vision bobbed and weaved. His body ached from the cold, and he figured the temperature was barely above zero.

The snow had stopped, and he built the fire into a roaring blaze that quickly warmed him through. He dug up his supplies and cooked the last of the fresh meat. It was a more substantial portion by far than he would have had normally at one sitting, but he figured he needed the warmth and strength it would provide.

Hunger mostly appeased, he walked stiffly around the campsite, wanting to see if anything that might help him survive had been left. The exercise also helped work some of the kinks out of his muscles.

He found that he could not make the circuit of the camp in one try. More than a few minutes away from the fire and he began to feel the cold biting deep into him. But he made it at last, and slumped back at his fire, feeling sorry for himself. Despair gripped him, and he fought back tears.

"Stop it, dammit," he told himself sternly. All was not lost. Though Weeks had left him nothing, Cooper did have some small supplies in his little cache. He pulled up the grouse berry bush and took inventory. He had two shards of flint, some sinew, two bone needles, a fair-size piece of deerskin, and several smaller scraps of it, and the rest of his meat. He smiled bitterly when he found the Kaw scalp, and the teeth and claws of the grizzly he had killed so long ago. He had wanted to make a necklace of the bear's remains but had never gotten to it. They were useless to him now, he thought.

It was pitifully little, he realized, but better than nothing. Still, he was worried and despondent. He had no coat, no blanket, and no transportation. It was December, and cold all the time. January would be worse, and February possibly even more so. Most likely he would freeze to death before long.

Beyond that, he had no means of hunting, or even trapping. Not that they had seen many animals in the canyon these last weeks anyway. The deer Cooper had killed two days ago had been the first one in the vicinity in at least a fortnight.

He sank back against the log near the fire, and found his folding knife stuck there. He shook his head in despair. Depression threatened to crush him under its unwieldy weight. It was no use, he thought resentfully. He would be dead by nightfall; tomorrow maybe. He might last a week or two at the longest. Why not just give himself up to it? Maybe even take the small pocketknife and cut his throat? Go out fast, effortlessly.

With trembling hand he grasped the knife. Almost as if he was someone else watching from a few feet above, he gazed at the blade, which glinted with a seemingly unnatural light. He could see his hand, gleaming knife clutched tightly, rise, ever closer to his neck. He stopped with the blade brushing the throbbing carotid artery. Just a jerk of the wrist and it would be all over. So easy. So simple. So . . .

"No!" he screamed, flinging the knife away as if it was a rattlesnake. He leaped up, screeching again, "No!" It was a wail of anguish and rebellion that trailed off into the mountain canyon, ringing back at him off the towering cliffs.

He sat again, trembling with the reaction. After some minutes, he regained his composure. "No, goddamn it," he said aloud, his breath pluming in the air. "No, I will not sit here and die."

He had no plan yet, but he would not give up. He had no warm clothing, and his too-big moccasins were wearing through in several spots. Should he try to find his way back to St. Louis? Should he stay where he was? Should he try to find a winter camp of some other mountain men? Or maybe a village of friendly Indians?

He wrestled with the problem. Perhaps staying here would be best, he thought. There was plenty of wood, and water, if he should need it. The high walls would help break some of the wind, and the dense groves of pines, cedars, aspens, oaks and cottonwoods would offer some protection from the snow, hail and sleet.

But there was little game left, and that presented the biggest problem. He would need food, and plenty of it.

That, and the fact that staying here seemed too much like sitting and waiting for death, made up his mind for him.

He would leave, he thought fiercely, taking his meager supplies, and try to make his way somewhere, anywhere. There had to be other trappers somewhere in these mountains. No, he decided, he would not sit here waiting to die. He would move on, fighting it out with Mother Nature, Indians, animals, whoever or whatever stood in his way. It was the closest thing to a warrior's death he could hope for now.

Mind made up, he set about making preparations. He retrieved his knife and made another circuit of the campsite. His heart pounded when he discovered a pouch under a huckleberry bush near his little camp. In wonder, he picked it up and looked inside. Nestled there were several kernels of corn, a tiny tuft of buffalo hair, a bit of bone and a small owl feather.

A smile curled Cooper's lips, and he crowed briefly. It was a medicine bundle, and of no practical use to him. But it made him feel better, especially since he knew, just knew, without understanding why that Tall Grass had made it for him. It gave him strength.

He found a stout branch and whittled a crude spear. It would do for now. Then he sewed, with great difficulty, a possible sack out of the deerskin. In it he placed his few possessions. He considered leaving the grizzly teeth and claws, and the scalp behind, but decided they might be useful in trading if he did find some Indians.

He placed his paltry supply of meat in its buckskin package, and with several thongs cut from the wrapping, he fashioned a crude backpack for the meat.

It was nearly midday when he finished. He stood near his fire, taking a last look around. Melancholy began to settle in on him again, but he refused to let it overwhelm him. There was only one good memory of this place.

"I'll come and find you, Tall Grass, and take you home," he said softly. "I'll not leave you in the hands of that son of a bitch."

He growled in irritation at his sentimentality and kicked snow over the fire. Without another thought of the place, he moved out, northward.

Iron gray clouds hung overhead, but the snow fell only intermittently. He kept his spirits up by singing tunes remembered from his childhood, and wished he still had his jaw-harp. He played it well, and the odd sound often soothed him.

After an hour or so, his feet began hurting, and his legs started to ache. Walking was difficult on the icy ground. In places the snow had drifted deep and was coated with ice. Each time a foot broke through the coating, it caused a sharp pain, and the effort of it strained his legs. His head still thumped with annoying regularity and intensity, and his broken nose made breathing difficult.

The frost crunched as he strode along purposefully. But beyond that and his singing, there was silence. Even the birds seemed to have left, gone southward, maybe, seeking what warmth they could. Cooper felt a twinge of jealousy at their freedom.

Hunger began to grip him by late afternoon, just after he passed the mouth of the canyon, and his mouth watered at the thought of the fat-rich block of pemmican nestled on his back. But he battled the feeling. If he ate now, his small supply of meat would be gone much too soon. He must persevere.

So he walked along with his belly grumbling in protest. He ignored the noises it produced, as he did the pain in his head, face, and legs, trying to keep alert for any game that might venture nearby. Maybe, and he touched the pouch under his hunting shirt, he would find a deer or elk, maybe even a buffalo, mired in the snow, just waiting for a fatal thrust of his homemade lance.

Seventeen

Hawley Cooper stumbled and lurched along, mind not really on what he was doing. Then he became aware of the gathering darkness. It had taken him by surprise, though once he thought about it, it was understandable since the gloom of the day merely faded until he was surrounded by darkness.

He muttered a curse, knowing he would have to find firewood in the dark again. He hurried about, eyes searching through the darkness, looking for enough wood to support a sizable fire throughout the night lest he freeze to death. It was difficult, but he kept at it, swearing at himself the whole while. He finally got lucky when he stumbled on a large pine log that lightning and cold had splintered into manageable chunks. He wrestled a few of the larger pieces to the spot he had chosen for his camp.

Heaving and blowing from the exertion,

though welcoming the warmth it had produced, he scraped up some tinder and kindling and then laid out his fire makings. Fortunately the cracker-dry tinder caught quickly, and before long Cooper had his small fire going. With a small smile of tired exultation, he placed his bow and tinder away.

With deliberation, he opened his makeshift backpack and cut off a goodly portion of pemmican. He set it on a flat rock to warm. He placed three strips of jerky next to it, also to heat, though it would do little to soften the hardness of the dried meat.

He ate happily, though depression began to set in again when he realized how pitifully small his dinner had been and how long it might be before he could have a good meal.

The cold made it worse. Without the wind, this night was not as bad as the last had been. But it was still bitter, and without blankets or robes, he suffered.

He awoke, his body stiff from the cold, his muscles aching from all the walking. He sat up, shivering, and rubbed his face gingerly. He gasped when he hit his throbbing nose. "Damn," he moaned through the pain. He sat still, letting the agony recede. The day was a little warmer, he noticed, and the sun was shining palely. He welcomed both.

Cooper thought of doing without food until evening but decided it would be better if he ate at least something in the mornings. He chewed down two strips of jerky and put another strip of the dried meat in his possible sack. He would, as he walked, cut off small pieces of it and work it around in his mouth, hoping the slow salivating on the meat would keep the hunger pangs to a minimum.

It helped some, he found as he walked, but not enough. That night he was ravenous but limited himself to a small chunk of the fast-dwindling pemmican, and one strip of jerky.

Each day was a repeat of the last, with a piece of jerky or two for breakfast; another piece eaten slowly through the day; and a small hunk of pemmican until it ran out four days after he left and one strip of jerked meat for a supper.

Within a few days he was constantly hungry and always cold. His muscles were sore, and his feet hurt. The cold stung his cheeks and slowly mending nose, making his eyes water. However, the pounding headaches were gone, helping keep his spirits up, though hopelessness often was his only companion.

He constantly searched for food: an old, weakened elk or buffalo; a deer struggling in the snow; a rabbit, anything he could kill with his crude spear. But no animal passed in his sight, and he saw no sign of any.

Two weeks out, on the calendar he kept with charcoal markings on the buckskin, he was gaunted down considerably, and filled with dejection. His food was gone, and he had been without anything to eat for the best part of two days. His legs trembled with each step, and there were sharp pains in his abdomen almost continually.

He found it hard to focus attention, and his eyesight sometimes blurred from the hunger. With his lack of concentration he had walked far on into the darkness the night before, oblivious to it. When he realized it, he stopped, muttering, "Dammit," and searched around on hands and knees, bumping into trees and rocks, for firewood.

He found some, but knew it was not enough. However, he could not think properly. Instead of making a fire and warming himself, then using the light to find more wood, he simply gave up and lay down under an evergreen's low boughs, on a bed of pine needles. And slept.

Demons of all sorts haunted his sleep. There were grizzly bears as tall as trees;

packs of wolves numbering in the hundreds, each wolf as big as a bear; mountain lions with fangs a foot long . . . And all guarding a mountain of food — fresh buffalo hump meat and tongues and ribs, sizzling with juices; beaver tail cooked over tantalizingly slow fires, rotating in aromatic smoke; johnny cakes; marrow oozing from cracked buffalo bones; roasts of succulent deer haunch; tender birds basted with marrow and fat, cooking on spits; bread, baked golden, teasing him with the smells of home and hearth . . .

He snapped awake with a startled shake of his head. He tried to move and found it difficult, and he realized with terror that he was coated with frost. A few more minutes asleep and he would have frozen to death. Had it been as cold as the night before, he would have been dead already.

Cooper started crying, tears of rage and despair. Hope seemingly had been frozen out of his heart. But something inside would not let him quit. It nagged at him, until the tears stopped, and he moved. It was slow and awkward going at first, and he did not even try to think of why he was doing it. He moved on impulse, without thought, until he had tinder and kindling, and wood gathered. With a concerted effort, he got a fire going. It took longer than usual, since he was working at far less than full efficiency, and he shook steadily from the cold.

A screaming wind blew up, making his job all the more precarious. But he kept on, hardly knowing what he was doing. Shortly after he got the fire going, and the warmth had edged into his body, he realized it had started to snow hard. Big wet flakes fell in a curtain. He shook his head. Another obstacle to overcome, he thought wearily. But the warmth of the fire helped, and he was dry under the tree.

He pushed himself up, exhaustion sitting heavily on him. He picked up a burning branch and sought more firewood. He winced when melted snow snaked icily down his neck as he worked. He kept at it until he had a huge blaze. Then he curled up near it and slept again.

In the morning, eyes glazed from hunger, he looked with disgust at the piece of buckskin that had held his meat supply. He took out his pocketknife, opened it, and then cut several strips. He carefully cut the leather into bite-size pieces. He gulped, not really wanting to do this, but knowing he had no choice. Then he took a deep breath and popped one of the bits into his mouth.

It was horrible, tasting of rancid fat, smoke, grease and dirt. And he thought his jaws would crack with all the chewing it necessitated. But he finally managed to swallow it. He started right on the next, forcing his thoughts away from what he was doing.

While chewing the second morsel, the first started to rebel in his stomach. He grimaced, trying desperately to keep the repulsive piece of leather from coming back up, all the while trying to chew the other.

He succeeded, but only with great effort. After that they went down a slightly easier, though the taste never improved, nor did the effort required for chewing lessen. He wished again that he had his cup. Boiling the repugnant meal might have helped.

He shrugged. Wishing would not make it so. He had to make do with what he had. It took him more than two hours, but he finally forced down two full strips of the buckskin, one bite at a time. But he felt better after it, and with slightly renewed life, he moved on.

The piece of buckskin lasted more than a week, though eating it never became easier. But it kept him alive and gave him the strength to continue walking from dawn to nearly dusk every day.

Snow came more frequently, and often with increased ferocity. During one storm, which started just after dawn one day, he stayed put for three days, letting the tempest blow itself out. It finally did, leaving several feet of new snow, making Cooper's walking much harder. But, Cooper thought hopefully, it could have been worse.

Walking through the deep snow, which often was crusted over with ice, strained his weakened constitution. But still Cooper fought on, often not even knowing why any longer. He just put one foot in the deep snow ahead of him, punched it through the rime, and followed it with the other, step after trembling step, mile after hard-fought mile.

He crossed innumerable streams, often not knowing it since many were frozen over and coated with snow. Some still ran, but fortunately were not wide. He jumped across these, the effort taxing his already strained muscles. Though he tried to remain vigilant, he saw no sign of game.

Cooper ran out of buckskin and was considering starting either on his possible sack or his moccasins when he suddenly plunged through the ice into a creek. The frigid water felt like fire on his legs.

He screamed in the shock of pain. Gasping, he surged forward, crunching through the inch-thick shell of ice. Then he slipped on a rock in the stream bed and fell, face first, into the water.

The shock almost knocked him unconscious. But he fought the blackness off, not really aware that he was doing so. He shoved himself up in one quick motion, drawing in a huge lungful of air to steady him. With short, quick gasps of pain, he drove ahead. It was only five more steps to the bank; then four; two . . .

He scrambled up the short, snowy bank, slipping and sliding, his bare, frozen hands clawing for a hold. His crude lance was gone somewhere, lost in the water. His breath came in jerks as the wind bit into his wet clothes, freezing him through as they frosted over. The cold was like a knife slicing repeatedly into his flesh.

"Dear Lord . . ." he gasped, unable to finish. Eyes not really seeing, brain not thinking, he stumbled on some yards, and found firewood, kindling and tinder. He was amazed as he watched himself from above while he drew out his bow and small block. Shaking violently he crumpled tinder into the hole in the block. His body was wracked with shivers as he jammed a stick into the hole and wrapped the bow's buckskin thong around it. Furiously he whipped the bow back and forth, gritting his teeth as his body spasmed.

With a surge of relief, he saw a wisp of smoke curl up from the tinder, with a finger of flame at its base. Still working reflexively, Cooper poured the tinder onto the ground and added kindling, nursing the fire into bloom. The pain gripped him so that he could hardly breathe, and his body jerked as if he suffered from St. Vitus' Dance. He had only minutes he figured, as his muscles convulsed from the coldness that had sunk deep into his bones.

A long tongue of flame shot up, sucking around a twig; then another, and another. Cooper hurried, almost unbearable pain cutting into him. He added larger twigs, and then a small log. Heat began to seep into him. Smoke from the evaporating water on his clothes wreathed him, making him look like a demon.

The warmth crept into his body far more slowly than the cold had charged in. But it got there nonetheless, and none too soon. He began to shiver more violently in reaction to the heat. But he knew it would help him. He turned after a few minutes so his back was to the fire. He repeated the process frequently.

He continued to shake for a long time, and his teeth chattered annoyingly. So much so that he clamped his teeth shut as hard as he could. Even then he could not control it, so he relaxed.

Shards of pain lanced deep into his warming hands and feet. He noticed an itching, burning feeling in his hands, particularly the left one, but it was a lesser pain, and he ignored it.

Darkness crept in, but still he did not move from the fire, other than brief excursions for more wood. He slept but minutes at a time, often while standing.

The temperature the next morning plunged, and he figured it was well below zero. Again he did not leave the fire other than to gather more wood and then only in brief trips. Hunger was almost forgotten as his body fought off the ravages of the frigid dunking.

He stayed there several days, hardly moving more than a few feet from the flames. Gradually the pain in his body eased, until the worst was his left pinkie, which was bright red and swollen, and it hurt when touched. But at least his nose seemed to have mended.

He ate some tree bark and pine needles for lack of anything else. It stayed down but did little to appease his hunger. And, while a blizzard stormed about him for two days, he whittled a new spear.

The storm snowed itself out, and the next day came a little warmer. The sun, behind a thin coating of clouds, was feebly bright. In a daze of exhaustion, fear, hopelessness and hunger, Cooper doused his fire and walked away.

Eighteen

Hawley Cooper struggled on through the driving snow and thundering wind. He was cold right through to the bone, and every muscle screamed with pain at each step. But still he pushed on, barely conscious, it seemed, hardly knowing where he was, where he was going, or how long it had been since he had left the canyon near the Bear River. It was almost funny, he thought at one point of near lucidness, that he did not even know the name of that canyon.

He was certain death was very near. Between the frigid air and lack of food, he could not have much time left. But he refused to give up. He would walk until his legs gave out. And then he would crawl, until the angry growling of his emptiness and the clawing fangs of the snow and cold killed him.

It had been a week maybe more, he was not certain, since he eaten the last putrid bits of buckskin. He had eaten more bark, and even some tree shoots, but it had done little for him. His cheeks were sunken and his stomach shriveled. And even when he warmed himself of a night by the fire, he still trembled and shook.

He was a little surprised that he did not feel more dejected, until he realized that it was because his mind was numb, unthinking. His body ran of its own accord, with little connection to the brain. It just ran on, pushing him, driving him.

What little thinking he did do usually centered on food, or on the delights of Corn Flower, or Falling Leaf, or Tall Grass. He would be swept away in his ravenous or carnal thoughts, transported to a world where the sun shone constantly and it was always warm and pleasant; where there was always fresh buffalo meat roasting, just waiting for him to pluck from a green stick over the fire and pop into his mouth. And one, sometimes all three, of the women would be there to wait on him, in a large skin lodge with a cheery fire . . .

It would, he thought once, almost rousing himself from his stupor, be near Christmas. In his mind's eye he could see his old home back in Maine. There would be candies for the children. His mother would have on her best cotton dress, and her soft bonnet, simple and warm, in preparation for going to services at the uncomfortable, intimidating at least to a boy, church. His father would have on his one good shirt, and the clean, homespun linsey-woolsey pants; and his boots would be shined.

It would be good, Cooper thought with a smile. His mother would be in a tolerant mood; and his father almost jovial, especially after he and some of his friends, who would congregate after the services, would toast each other and the season several times from a jug of corn squeezings made in the still nestled in old man Farrell's barn.

It would be a pleasant time, with the children able to get away with a lot more mischief than usual. And there would be the food for the big dinner. The whole house would smell of it: loaves of fresh-baked bread; a roast goose, big and brown, snuggled in its juices, and packed with spiced cornmeal stuffing dotted with walnuts; probably some pork from a recently butchered hog, the meat surrounded by warm apples; butter churned up just that morning by his sisters; and milk from the two cows; large, steaming mugs of tea, some flavored with cinnamon sticks; or coffee.

The daydream was so real that he thought

he could smell the blood from the butchering lingering on the snow outside the house; and the aroma of fresh meat; and hear the sounds of revelry; of family dogs fighting for a dropped morsel of meat. It was almost . . .

He was sent flying as a coyote pounced on his chest and slid off. Cooper swung his arms wildly to frighten the animal as he scrambled to get back up, slipping on the snow and ice. When he did, he saw four of the snarling beasts in a semicircle in front of him. They eyed him with hunger in their greenish eyes.

Cooper snapped to full consciousness and swiftly took in the scene before him. So dazed had he been or so involved in his daydream that he noticed neither that it had stopped snowing nor that he had wandered off the trail, if indeed he had been on a trail.

He had entered a small meadow, and there, ahead of him, beyond the coyotes, two mountain lions, a large, tawny one, and a smaller, dun-colored one, tore chunks of flesh from an elk that was but minutes ago downed. Steam still rose from the carcass. The coyotes, Cooper guessed, had been waiting out of reach of the cats for their turn when he stumbled on them, and they thought perhaps another meal was in the offing.

But first they would have to get Cooper down. The man did not seem to pose much of a threat, but still the coyotes hung back, fangs bared, snarls curling their pointed snouts.

Cooper backed slowly away until he had a tree behind him, reassuring him. The coyotes eyed him as he hefted the puny spear. He showed the animals none of the fear he felt. The beasts stood stiff-legged, prepared to hold their ground.

A coyote charged, and Cooper grinned viciously. He jabbed out with the lance, impaling the animal on the point and using the same motion to fling the yelping beast onto the snow some feet to his side.

He managed to get the butt end of the spear up enough to deflect the charge of another coyote. Cooper whirled, surprising himself with his speed and dexterity, and lanced a third coyote, pinning it to the snowy ground. He yanked the weapon free and retreated back to the tree. Two coyotes were dead, and the other two including the one he had hit with the lance watched him balefully.

Suddenly Cooper attacked, waving his lance wildly. The two coyotes held ground for a moment before racing away, their soft pads making little indentation in the snow. Cooper laughed, the first time he had done so in months. Then he started coughing from it, and it made him think of Josiah Weeks. Hate welled up in his chest, and his fists clenched. He took a deep breath and forced himself to relax. Hate would do him no good now. There were more important matters at hand.

With his mind almost fevered by the thought of food being so close, yet so unattainable as yet, Cooper hurriedly gathered wood. When he had enough, he cleared some snow from the base of a pine and laboriously built a blaze, trembling with hunger and anticipation.

Done, he took his lance in his right hand and a burning branch in the other. Then he set off toward the food. His food, as he began to think of it. He would take it with intimidation, if he could; with force if need be. He gave no thought to the fact that the animals could tear him to shreds. He would have this meat! Even his blistered, painful left pinkie and his weakened condition would not stop him.

He moved toward the two pumas. Both glared at him, muzzles coated with gore. Then they went back to tearing at the elk flesh, casting occasional sidelong glances at him.

"That meat is mine, boys," Cooper said aloud, voice cracking from hunger and disuse. "I reckon you've had your share. Now it's my turn." The cougars eyed him ominously. "Now I ain't an unreasonable man," Cooper said as he began to shake from the adrenaline coursing through his body. "There's other food available here. But I want to fill my belly, and some old ornery coyote meat ain't gonna do it. No, sir. And I want that hide you boys is so busy tryin' to tear to shreds."

Still the cougars continued to feed, casting doleful looks at him between mouthfuls of elk flesh.

Cooper was in a quandary. He wanted that meat. No, he needed that meat. And the hide. He was desperate for both. But attacking two mountain lions, even if one was but a cub, was a far different matter than taking on four coyotes. These large, well-fanged beasts would not take lightly to being rousted from their meal, and they were not likely to feel very threatened by a thinned down, weakened man, even if he did have a handmade spear and carried fire.

"Hell," Cooper mumbled, shifting his grip on the torch, and edging closer. The large cat growled. Cooper took a few more steps and the younger one snarled. Cooper retreated, and then had an idea. He went back and got the two coyote carcasses after slipping the spear down the back of his shirt. He carried both in one hand back toward the pumas, struggling as he walked.

"Look what I got for you boys," he said, feigning cheerfulness. The cold was getting to him again, and he was faint with weariness. The food that lay before him almost made him mad with anxiety. He dropped one carcass at his feet and then threw the other as far as he could. He was pleased to see that the younger puma raced after it.

But the big one remained where it was. "Goddammit, you son of a bitch," Cooper yelled. In anger he tossed the other coyote. The cougar stayed where it was. He drew in a deep breath and let it out harshly. He pulled out his lance. There was nothing else he could think of to do except . . .

With an explosive bellow, Cooper charged at the mother cougar. He waved the torch and the lance, and he screamed madly as he ran. He slipped, going down to one knee, and with fear exploding through him, shoved himself back up and attacked with renewed vigor.

The panther, weighing maybe one hundred and fifty pounds, faced him, black-tipped tail swishing angrily, fangs bared, small ears laid back.

Cooper slid to a stop right in front of the cat, dropped the torch and swung the lance up in both hands and lashed out with it. But the puma was no longer there. It had scooted sideways a few steps away from the elk. Then it leaped at Cooper, snarling and snapping.

Fear shot from Cooper's stomach into his extremities at the sight of the enraged animal's charge. He managed to half turn out of the way, but the animal hit his shoulder, knocking him on his face.

Cooper's terror was palpable as he scrambled desperately to get turned around and to rise. He knew the panther would be after him again in moments. Just as he turned, the puma charged again, and Cooper could not bring his lance into play.

Without thinking, he dropped the useless lance and grabbed the fur and thick muscles of the cougar's neck. He hung on for his life, the puma's snarling, saliva-coated muzzle inches from his own. He knew he could not hold on for long; and he knew that if the cat decided to end it he would have no chance. But Cooper was helpless.

The cougar's front claws raked paths in

Cooper's chest, tearing his buckskin shirt and the skin beneath. Cooper could barely feel it.

With a quick move, and again without thinking, Cooper lurched his head up and clamped his teeth onto the animal's nose. He bit as hard as he could, almost gagging. The puma roared and tried frantically to back away. But Cooper held fast, being dragged along the ground, but not giving up his grip on the animal's nose or neck.

Suddenly he let go, and the cougar slid backward a few steps. Before it could get its hindquarters bunched up under it for a charge, Cooper had snatched up his lance and leaped up, plunging the weapon into the cat's chest. The beast screamed and scratched the air savagely with its claws, snout wrinkled into a frightful mask.

Cooper pulled the lance out and lunged with it again, burying half its length into the cougar. The cat choked and sputtered before its life drained away.

Cooper wrenched his weapon free. His breath came in fits and starts. As he turned, the smaller cat slammed into his side, knocking him down. "Dammit," Cooper roared as he scrambled up. The young cougar sat on its haunches, growling. Cooper yelled and charged. The puma ran off and up a tree, where it perched, alternately growling and mewing.

With a wary eye on the young cat, Cooper hauled the older puma carcass over to that of the elk. He stuck his still-burning torch into the melting snow near the two animals, praying it would protect his plunder from predators. He walked off a short way, hoping to find enough wood nearby so that he would not have to leave his meat for long. To do so might mean having to fight for it again.

He found enough for the time being, and using his torch, started several small fires surrounding the two carcasses. Eagerness washed over him, and he could wait no longer. He finally cut some chunks of elk meat and punched a green stick through them. He propped the stick up so the meat was over one of the fires, and plunked wearily down. Weariness flooded over him, and he had to keep jerking himself awake.

Shuddering from exhaustion, cold and the easing of tension, he at last took the meat from the fire and began to eat. It was an old elk, and the meat stringy and tough. But Cooper did not care. He swallowed large chunks whole, barely giving them the once over with his teeth. He was reaching over to cut more meat when what he had just eaten revolted and spilled violently back out.

"Oh, goddamn," he mumbled when he was done retching. He sat, sucking in breaths. After a short while, he felt better, so he cut more meat, cooked it a little longer, and ate more slowly, giving his stomach time to adjust. The meat stuck and filled him with warmth.

It was starting to snow again, so he hurried about, laying in a supply of wood. As he did, he noticed that the young cat left its perch and skulked off, screeching its ill fortune.

Cooper grinned, watching. He found a spot amongst some pines where the low limbs would protect him. He built a good fire. Then he pulled the cougar and elk carcasses to his campsite. Once again, he built a ring of fires, carrying burning wood from the other fires on a piece of thick bark.

He rested again, ate more meat and then skinned both animals. Just before dark, he managed to get the panther hide stretched and partially scraped. He built up all his fires, wrapped himself in the bloody elk skin with pieces of meat and fat still clinging to it and fell into a deep sleep.

Nineteen

Hawley Cooper set off again with renewed vigor and a jaunty step, engulfed in confidence. He was warmly dressed and shod, and carried a supply of food, and life looked good to him again.

He had spent more than three weeks where he had won the battle with the coyotes and the pumas. He rested his trail-weary bones and muscles. He ate prodigious amounts of stringy elk meat, building back his strength. He worked long and hard during the days to tan the elk, cougar and two coyote pelts.

Physically he felt well. His head had stopped hurting long ago, and his nose was completely healed, though it would forever after be a little off center. His chest mended quickly, but his left pinkie seemed to be getting worse. He ignored that as much as possible, though it began to impede his work a little.

One of the first things he had done was to butcher the elk. He cut most of the meat into thin, narrow strips, which would be easy for him to handle, even after they froze.

He also took everything else he thought he could use from the elk carcass: some of the brains to be used for tanning hides, though he did not know if they would be as effective as those from a buffalo; several bones for marrow, and maybe to fashion another needle or two; the hooves, should he need to melt them down for glue; and as much sinew as he could.

After some second thoughts, he also butchered the cougar carcass. With some reluctance, he tried the meat. It had a musky, offensive taste, but it was meat, and would do in a pinch. It was, he told himself, better than the old buckskin and the tree bark he had eaten.

When he had all the hides tanned, he took one of the coyote pelts and cut it. Then he carefully cut apart his moccasins. He trimmed the hard soles so the moccasins would fit his feet this time. Then he lined the worn footgear with the coyote hide, fur side in. He folded the moccasins back up and re-sewed them tightly. He was quite pleased with his handiwork.

Before he put the finished moccasins back

on, though, he carefully checked both feet for signs of frostbite. He was surprised, but greatly relieved, when he found none. He knew what was wrong with his pinkie, though, and it troubled him considerably.

With his feet warm and dry, and with food in his belly, his outlook improved considerably. So he set about making himself a hat with the other coyote pelt. He cut and painstakingly stitched, swearing each of the many times he stuck himself with a bone needle. But eventually it was done, and he perched the hat debonairly on his head.

He laughed, knowing it must look ridiculous, but it was warm and serviceable, and that was all that mattered. The head of the coyote hide came down over his forehead, with the snout covering his nose. Cooper could look through the eye sockets in the hide, if he chose. The pelt covered his shoulders and hung halfway down his back.

With the remnants of the first coyote hide, he fashioned a crude pair of mittens. With the three articles of clothing and, using both the cougar and elk hides as blankets, he was quite comfortable, and he considered wintering here. It had snowed several times since he had arrived, but there had been little new accumulation, and the smaller cat had not returned.

The coyotes had returned just that morning, but they kept their distance. There were three of them. Evidently another had found its way into the pack, if it was the same pack. Cooper could not be certain. Still, it seemed a likely spot to stay.

He cut a strip from the puma hide to shorten it. Then he folded the skin in half and cut a circle at the folded end for his head.

He threw it on, poncho style, nodding. He had enough room inside it, and it was the right length just below the knees. It would keep him warm, worn hair side in, but still allow plenty of movement.

He took it off and laid it down, folded. He made a snowball and threw it at one of the coyotes, hitting the animal on the snout. "Go on, get out of here," he shouted good-naturedly, flapping his arms.

The coyotes backed off some more, and stood, snarling. Cooper laughed. Then he started the difficult and time-consuming task of sewing seams to make crude sleeves in his coat. Periodically he would rise, stretching his muscles and throw a snowball at the coyotes, just for the hell of it, or build up his fires, or gather more wood.

He finished one sleeve before allowing himself time to eat. By the time he finished the second, darkness was upon him.

In the morning he noticed the coyotes were gone. He was not sure whether he was happy or sad. He had to be wary when they were around, but at least they were company of a sort.

That day he sewed the side "seams" of his coat. He put the garment on, tied the strip he had cut off around his waist, pulled on his mittens, and slapped the cap on. He felt like a new man.

"I'll haunt your dreams, Josiah Weeks," he roared into the late morning sky. Then he laughed, not really caring if he ever saw Weeks again. Revenge did not burn deep in his soul, though he vowed again to try to rescue Tall Grass if he could. After all, it was the medicine pouch she had made that was keeping him alive. He was in her debt.

Feeling good, he began to bring up more firewood, and large branches that he could use to build a lean-to. Somehow in the past day, without thinking, he had decided to stay here. This was a good spot, he told himself. There were numerous trees offering some protection against the weather; plenty of wood. And there was game. Or was there?

As he worked, he began to worry again. The sky had turned a sullen gray and threatened snow; and the wind blew in shrieking gusts. The temperature had tumbled in the last several hours. Perhaps it was only the looming storm that had scared off the coyotes and kept the other animals away.

That must be it, he thought. But he could recall seeing no other game since the day he arrived here. No other elk had wandered through, nor other mountain lions, no buffalo, no wolves, not even a rabbit or a squirrel. In his frequent searches for wood, he had seen no sign other than that of the coyotes.

Snow began falling and the wind increased as he rushed to put up a shelter before the storm, which looked to be a bad one, hit. As he worked, he winced at the almost constant pain in his left pinkie.

Finally, in anger, he pulled off his mittens and looked at the digit. The blisters that had formed had broken several days ago, before the skin turned ghostly white. Now the tip of the pinkie was a strange, sickly color, almost black, and the skin looked dead.

Cooper had seen the results of frostbite before, and he knew the tip of his finger was dead. It had to come off or gangrene would set in and spread. He felt sick to his stomach. He did not think he was capable of doing what must be done; there was no whiskey to dull the pain, and the only sharp instrument he had was his pocketknife. He wondered if it and he would be strong enough for the job.

He worried, and the fear ate into him as he hurried to finish the lean-to. He did, at last, with the snow thick and blinding around him, swirling in the raging wind. With a sour taste in his mouth, knowing he could not put off the distasteful task of working on his finger any longer, he collected wood. He wanted to ring himself with blazes should the coyotes be drawn by the smell of blood. But in his searching, he almost got lost several times in the dense snowfall.

When he had several fires built in a semicircle around the opening of his lean-to, he sat and slowly began honing his knife with a rock he had found after a considerable search. Though it was a folding knife, it had a four-inch blade and was fairly heavy. He shrugged. It was all he had and would have to do.

At last, with his stomach churning in fear, he stuck the knife blade into the coals of the nearest fire. While it heated, he found an almost flat piece of wood. It would not roll and would give the blade something solid to cut against.

Cooper gulped as the enormity of what he was about to do gripped him. He felt his bowels tighten with fear, and the sour taste crept back into his mouth. He sat and stared into the fire for some time, listening to the shush of snow and the screech of the wind, before reaching for the knife, almost as if someone else was directing his hand. He seemed to himself to be in a daze, and again he had that feeling that he was floating above watching someone else.

He curled all his left-hand fingers except the pinkie and hung them off the edge of the wood, knuckles hard against it. The pinkie was flat on the wood, exposed. He placed the sharp edge of the blade on the pinkie. And yowled as the red-hot blade touched his skin.

He dropped the knife and jerked his hand up, sucking at the burn. He swore softly at his stupidity. How could he have thought he would saw through the finger with a hot blade? There was only one way to do this. Fast. Get it over with before shock overwhelmed him.

His stomach lurched, and his groin tightened, but he gamely stuck the knife back in the fire. He hoped the hot blade would make it all the way through on the first try and cauterize it. He hoped.

Cooper picked up the instrument and positioned his left hand on the wood again. Once more he had that disjointed feeling. He could see, as if he was far above looking down, the knife raised slowly up. It poised there for an instant, as if the blade was gathering its courage. Then it flashed down, glinting in the firelight.

Cooper screamed, the sound ringing hollow in the solitude. A black curtain began to fall over his eyes. He forced it away and looked at his hand. As if seeing with someone else's eyes, he noticed the blood pulsing slowly from the finger stump. And he was aware that he was holding the hand in the air, but the fingertip was still on the wood.

"I did it," he mumbled, jamming the wound into a small mound of snow nearby. The coldness sent another shock through him, and again he had to fight off the threatening blackness. He wrapped the hand in a piece of elk skin and cradled it close to his chest. Then he slumped over, unconscious before his head hit his hide bed.

Cooper awoke groggily, and his hand pulsated with pain. He pushed himself up, not knowing how long he had been out. It was dark, and the fires were down to mere dull coals. He had done the deed late in the afternoon. This was, he judged, the night of the day after.

Cooper spit dryly. He stood on shaky legs and built up all the fires. He put some frozen strips of meat over the fire in a "grill" of laced green twigs. Then he sat back, head swimming. When the world stopped spinning, he opened the bandage and looked at the hand.

The edge of the digit was coated with congealed blood, but the finger looked pink and healthy. Cooper wished he could remember what herbs and roots and such his mother had used in poultices and potions, but he could not. He sighed. He probably could not have found any of them anyway, he decided.

Well, he figured, either the hand would get better, or it wouldn't. There was little he could do for himself now. He washed the tender, oozing stump as gently as possible with fresh snow of which there was plenty wincing and sucking in his breath each time the cold hit the hand. Then he rewrapped it. He sat, sweating from fear and pain, his head light, his stomach churning.

He forced himself to eat, even though he did not want to. As he did, he watched the snow, which apparently had not stopped since it had started yesterday. It had not even eased. Then he curled up, pulling his elk skin blanket over him, and went to sleep.

As each day passed, his hand felt a little better. The weather, however, remained poor. The snow continued, sometimes heavily, and the wind moaned and shrieked unceasingly. Cooper began to wonder if maybe he would freeze to death here once his meat ran out. Perhaps this was not quite the wintry garden of Eden that he had at first thought.

As he made forays into the surrounding forest for wood, he watched for sign. But none was to be seen. Nothing could be seen in the blinding veil of the snow. Each venture out was more hazardous than the last, with the possibility of being lost increasing once he was more than a few feet from his shelter.

A week after performing the surgery on himself, the coyotes came back, howling into the night around him. Since he had seen no sign of other animals, Cooper began to suspect the coyotes were back to see if he had died or was weak enough to kill. The thought of becoming supper for a pack of coyotes was not a comforting one.

At least it had stopped snowing for the time being. It had stormed for four days before clearing for one. Another night of snow was followed by this day, which had been clear. But that night, though, with the coyotes' wailing splitting the night air, the snow began again. With it came the wind, which whistled mournfully around his camp.

This storm lasted the better part of three days, with the heaviest snow he had ever seen, until he began to think he would be buried in his lean-to, even under the protective covering of tree limbs. His supply of firewood was running low, but, he thought, at least the coyotes were gone again. He shoveled snow from his shelter by hand as best he could and stood outside.

It was cold. Bitter, unbelievably cold. Trees cracked and split from it, sounding like rifle shots, and Cooper jumped each time one did. His ring of fires had died, buried under the snow. Only the largest fire, the one almost inside his lean-to, still burned.

Fright licked at him again, but he controlled it. He managed to get out and find some dry wood hard up against tree trunks where the snow had not penetrated too deeply. But when he returned to his shelter, he had made up his mind. This was no place to winter. The weather here was harsher than any other place he had seen. And he needed to be up and moving, out on the trail, doing something. He could not just sit here waiting for the winter to kill him.

He took two more days to slowly smoke some of his dwindling supply of meat. The rest would stay frozen, but this way he would have some to eat while walking, as he had before.

It began snowing again that night, and he awoke to another blizzard. But he was determined. He could not — would not — sit through another raging storm in this hellacious pit. He packed the smoked meat in his possible sack and wrapped the frozen elk and cougar meat in the elk skin.

He tied his belt around his coat, hefted the elk skin package of meat onto his back; picked up his lance and shuffled off across the deep snow, into the howling wind and dense snowfall. The snowshoes he had made yesterday made soft soughing noises on the snow, sounds that were wiped out by the wind. But he was confident and warm.

Twenty

Hawley Cooper was almost happy. He had started keeping another calendar, and he knew he had been gone nine days from the meadow. It had snowed only twice in that time, though one storm had lasted more than three days, trapping him at first in a flat.

He had had to fight against the roaring wind, which battered him, knocking him down more times than he could recount. The snow sliced down on him, whipping at his face until he finally had enough sense to cut a piece of elk skin and tie it around the lower half of his face.

His breath came hard as he punched his way through the blizzard, looking for some sort of haven. But it was at least six hours of being rocked, buffeted and flattened by the storm before he found a copse of dead cottonwoods, their trunks twisted and deformed by the likes of the wind that ravaged Cooper.

Cooper sat behind one of the gnarled trunks, listening to it creak as the wind tried to rip it from its tired, dead old roots. But it was, for now at least, safety. He was panting from the exertion, slowly chewing a piece of smoked meat.

After an hour or so, he stood and moved, flapping his arms and stomping his snowshoes to keep his circulation going. He knew he could not sleep that night. With this storm and the temperature well below zero again and probably heading lower, he figured he would never awaken. Building a fire seemed out of the question in this shrieking white maelstrom, especially without tinder or much manageable wood available.

So he passed the night, and most of the next day, alternating between sitting, eating some of the jerked meat to retain his strength; and moving about to keep from freezing. His hand, which no longer gave him pain normally, throbbed in the bitter cold, and his muscles and bones seemed to ache from it.

The storm diminished until it had blustered its way out, leaving an aching silence and a knee-deep blanket of new snow in its wake. The wind was a mere whisper, and the snow fell only in soft, lazy flakes. Cooper stood with difficulty, stiff, and began trying to break branches from the dead tree. But it proved too tough. Hungry and nearly numb from cold and exhaustion, he moved on.

By nightfall he found a campsite and quickly had a fire going. The warmth of it cheered him, and he was soon eating heartily of elk and puma meat. He wished more than ever that he had a coffee pot or even his fine mug. He also wished for his small clay pipe and a plug of tobacco. He had never smoked often, but he thought it would be comforting now. And once more he wished for his jaw-harp, and . . . With a sigh he pushed the thoughts away. He had none of those things, and there was nothing he could do about it.

He resumed his lonely, arduous journey the next day refreshed from a comfortable sleep during a relatively warm night, and with a full stomach. He was as happy as could be expected under the circumstances.

He was heartened, too, by animal sign, though no creatures had passed within his vision. But at least there was game about, and when he ran out of meat, he might be able to track something down.

As he traveled, he hummed or sang, his slightly off-key voice sounding odd in the silence of this land of tall, stately pines;

thick, leafless cottonwoods; and bare, spidery aspens. He thought of home sometimes, and at others of Corn Flower or Falling Leaf or Tall Grass. He did not love any of those three women, but he would gladly be with any of them now. He still hoped to be able to rescue Tall Grass from Josiah Weeks. Then he would return her to her people. He owed her that much. He smiled a lonely smile and touched the pouch that still hung under his shirt on his chest.

He had no idea of how many miles he had traveled, but he estimated he was making perhaps ten miles a day. He felt strong and confident and was becoming more aware of the land around him. He followed the easiest path he could find, but since everything was covered with snow, he never knew if he was on a real trail or not. But it did not matter, he told himself frequently.

He no longer knew in which direction he was traveling, though he tried to use the sun when it appeared to keep on a southeasterly course. He just plodded along, figuring that as long as he was moving, he was all right. He was bound to stumble onto some people, whether red or white, some time. He just hoped they would be friendly. More than once he looked back on his trail, unsure whether to be happy or sad at the solitary line of footprints breaking the snow.

He had entered a narrow valley, or pass, he could never tell the difference, if there was any and was making his way toward a stand of aspens and oaks at the far side, maybe a mile away. He planned to camp there. He moved rapidly, shushing along on his snowshoes, whistling *Landlord, Fill the Flowing Bowl,* when they struck.

The first warning he had was when he heard snarling, yapping and growling. He spun, fear slicing icily through him. Racing across the tundra toward him were six, no, he thought, counting again without seeming to make the effort, seven wolves.

Cooper turned and started running, hoping he could make it to the trees. He knew it was foolish to think he could outrun these beasts over a mile, but he also knew he would not survive a fight in the open with these large, muscular beasts. He could hear them gaining, their padded paws making little noise on the deep carpet of snow. Cooper cursed at his snowshoes. His chest constricted as he sucked for air in the deep cold. Each inhalation brought a sharp pain to his lungs.

Knowing it was futile, he stopped running and turned. There was no conscious thought about it; it was just the now-ingrained determination to die fighting as the episode with Iron Bow continued to haunt him. He reached into his possible bag for the folding knife, and his hand encountered the jerky. He grabbed a handful and tossed the pieces. Two wolves veered off toward the meat, snapping at it and each other.

But the others did not slow. Cooper got his knife out and managed to open it after tearing off his mittens. He held it in his left hand and his spear in the right.

The first wolf, maybe one hundred and twenty-five pounds' worth, leaped at Cooper, smashing into his chest. Cooper stumbled backward two steps before falling on his back. The snarling wolf was astride him in an instant. Cooper had no time to think; he just reacted. He snapped the hand with the knife up, sinking the blade into the wolf's lower abdomen and then yanking it toward his own face. The blade tore a deep, bloody channel through the length of the wolf's underside, slicing open several vital organs.

The wolf yelped and tried to back away, aiding Cooper's effort. And then it died, quivering atop Cooper's legs. With a great effort, the youth shoved the beast off him and scrambled up, backing away from the carcass. The other wolves, including the two who had chased after the meat, circled him. Two finally darted in on the dead wolf, tearing at the dead animal's flesh.

Two more leapt for Cooper. The youth lashed out with lance and knife. But the wolf on his right sank his fangs into the youth's upper arm. Cooper bellowed and whipped around with his knife, stabbing the animal in the side. The wolf yipped and let go, running off to lick its wound. But the second, and another, attacked again.

It all became a blur to Cooper after that. He no longer felt the pain, although he knew his flesh was being torn regularly by fang and claw. His snowshoes were flung off to God knew where. Several times he was knocked down, but he always managed to regain his feet and fight on. He knew for certain he had killed at least one more wolf, running his lance through the beast. But as the wolf barked in agony, it whirled, yanking the spear still imbedded in its side from Cooper's hand.

Cooper was slammed to the snow again, and he lashed out desperately, frantically. He felt his knife sink into flesh and hit bone, and he heard a wolf howl. But Cooper was oblivious to the damage he suffered. He fought on blindly, yelling and swearing, kicking and punching, even biting.

Another wolf landed on Cooper's chest and tore a small chunk from his cheek. Cooper cursed and struck out savagely, driving his knife into the wolf's side three times before the yowling animal scooted off him.

Cooper staggered up, coated with blood, snow, ice and saliva. He could barely breathe, and he was soaked with sweat. His eyes were glazed with blood lust, but they began to focus when no attack came. He realized with wonder that the wolves were gone; the live ones, that is. Four of the animals lay dead in the gore-splattered valley. Cooper could see that two others, at least, had left a trail of blood behind, and he hoped they would die soon, too.

The pain was beginning to filter back into his consciousness, too, and he wanted to cry. But he would not allow himself that pleasure. He snapped his knife shut and put it away. Then he strapped his snowshoes back on and picked up his coyote fur cap. He put it on and then found his mittens. With a depressed shrug, he turned and started walking across the valley again, wondering, *Would it never end*?

Then he stopped and turned back. "Damn fool," he muttered. He had forgotten his lance.

He jerked it free of the wolf carcass, surprised to see that it was not broken. He was ready to leave again, but stood staring a few moments before saying, "What the hell."

He knelt and began skinning the wolf. Meat was meat, he decided, and he was getting low on elk. Besides, he would have the skins to trade if he found someone. Finished, he moved on to another, biting back the groans that sought to burst free.

Three of the four wolf hides were good enough to take, as was the meat. The other — the first he had killed — had been torn to shreds, and much had been eaten.

As he worked, he used the pains to take inventory of his wounds. He would wait until he made camp to check them more closely. His cheek throbbed and he could feel sticky blood on it. The elk skin cover he still wore over the lower half of his face had helped keep the injury from being too bad, but it still hurt. Though the puma-fur coat was not too badly torn, he knew the flesh beneath had been scored where the coat sleeves or body had ridden up. His right biceps ached intensely, and he could feel blood there, too.

In addition, he had trouble breathing and was certain something inside was broken.

With any luck it would only be a rib, he thought. Blood seeped down his belly, and his legs were torn. He had also pulled a muscle in his neck, causing extreme pain when he turned his head to the right.

He finished his work and hoisted the skins and meat over his shoulder, wincing. He shuffled off, and with each step the pains became more pronounced. Before he had gone a quarter of a mile, it felt like his entire body was on fire. He gritted his teeth and touched the pouch on his breast for strength. He moved on, agony dogging him.

Suddenly he realized he was disoriented. He did not know where he was. Nor was he even certain he knew who he was. He stopped, weaving, pain almost overpowering. He sank the point of the wood lance in the snow and leaned on the butt.

With a start he pushed himself straight. Using all his energy, he shouted, "Goddamn, I did it. Beat them goddamn wolves, I did. This chil' shines, he does!"

Then he pitched forward on his face, blessed unconsciousness covering him like a blanket.

He awoke to the sound of voices. They were strange voices, speaking an odd, guttural language. He thought he was dead and had gone to hell, to be punished for whatever sins he had committed; to suffer through all eternity with peoples he could never know nor understand.

It was dim, and many scents assailed his nostrils. He thought he smelled meat, and that was encouraging, and pine wood smoke. There were other earthy aromas. He could not place them, but they were somehow familiar.

He could see figures moving in the gloom. They had human forms, but he could discern nothing of their features. The chattering in the strange tongue continued. He sighed. At least he was warm and comfortable here.

He lay there, trying to sort it all out. But there seemed to be no answer. If he was dead, this did not fit his image of hell. Or heaven, for that matter. Maybe it was a waiting place where he would be judged on his worthiness to enter heaven.

Still, this place did not seem otherworldly. It was all too real: the smells, sounds, moving figures. Everything was familiar, but just beyond his reckoning.

Then it came to him: Yes! He was dreaming! That had to be it. He was still laying out in the snow, four wolves stretched out dead and skinned behind him, the cold seeping into his body, chilling him through, killing him.

He had to get up! He would die if he stayed here any longer. Panic gripped him, paralyzing him when he most needed to take action. He forced himself to calm down, let the panic drain away.

One of the manlike figures moved and headed for him. Terror gripped Cooper again, and he clamped his eyes shut, feigning death, or at least unconsciousness. It was a bear, he figured. Yes, that's what it was. He was still alive and laying helpless in the snow. And this was a bear. A hungry bear. Maybe if he pretended to be dead the animal would go away. He controlled his breathing as best he could. His heart fluttered occasionally as terror tightened its grip on him. But he would not let it show. He would not!

Finally he could stand it no longer. If the creature was still there, Cooper wanted to see it, wanted to see the face of his impending death.

He opened his lids the tiniest bit and rolled the eyeballs from side to side. The creature had moved away. But Cooper worried. He still could hear those odd voices, and it both frightened and perplexed him. Bears couldn't talk. But if this was a dream, his imagination was just turning bear grunt and growls into something that resembled a language.

He turned his head toward the sounds, wincing as pain wrenched him. That was real, at least, he thought as sweat coated his brow. But dimly he could see figures crouching. And there was a fire.

Steeling himself, knowing he had to do something, either to break the dream and move, or find out what manner of place he was in, he shoved with his hands. His back arched and his shoulders lifted fractionally.

Agony seared through him like a red-hot razor. He knew he screamed. Then he fell unconscious again.

TWENTY-ONE

Hawley Cooper awoke with a start and realized with horror that he was as naked as the day he was born. Granted, he was covered with a blanket or hide, and normally he might not have minded. But he did not know the young woman, dark-skinned and pretty, with deep eyes and strong fingers who hovered over him doing something to his chest.

He had no idea where he was. He remembered instantly the fight with the wolves, his skinning and butchering of the three animals, and walking away. Then nothing.

The young woman saw his eyes open, and she smiled at him, her bright teeth startlingly white against her dark face and the dimness of the room. Or was it a room? He smiled back, tentatively. She said something in a language he could not understand, though he was certain he had heard it before.

He shook his head. The movement gave him some pain, but it was manageable. He remembered the other pains, right after the fight, and he shuddered at the memory. He knew he had been grievously wounded in the ordeal, and he wondered if everything on his body still worked.

He blushed in embarrassment, as he realized that at least one part of his anatomy was in working order. The woman giggled, the sound delighting Cooper.

"Where am I?" he finally asked, fighting the lustful thoughts that rampaged in his mind.

"My father's lodge," she said.

"You speak English?" he asked in surprise.

"Yep. Damn good. I learned from trappers who come here."

"I'll be damned," he said in wonder.

"Damn right," she agreed cheerily, startling him once more. Then they both laughed.

"What am I doin' here?" he asked urgently. "How'd I get here? Where is here? How . . ?"

"Too many questions," the woman said, placing a work-calloused hand over his lips. The touch was exciting, and his body reacted again. "I'll tell you what I know. You hungry?"

"Yes," he said, realizing his stomach was very empty.

"I'll get food."

As she started to rise, Cooper lightly grabbed her arm. "Wait," he said urgently. "How long've I been here?"

"Four suns. No, five."

He nodded and let her go. She was gone less than a minute, returning with a bowl of buffalo flavored water in which chunks of meat floated. She helped him sit up against a willow backrest and started spooning broth and meat into his mouth.

He ate greedily, barely chewing the bits of meat. "Slow down," she laughed.

He nodded and opened his mouth for more. Between bites, he said, "Tell me."

She nodded. "My father, *Pah-Ka-Nah-Mah-Bake* — Cheyenne Killer — and some of the other men found you. The snow and the dead wolves told the tale. You're very brave. Damn brave, I'd say." She smiled, but he knew she was serious in what she had said.

"My brother was lost to wolves several moons ago, and my father figured you was sent from the spirits to take my brother's place. So he brought you here. My family's been takin' care of you since."

Terror flooded over Cooper, and he

stopped eating. He was a prisoner of Indians. "What people are you?" he asked, voice breaking.

"Shoshone. White eyes call us Snakes mostly."

"You gonna torture me?" he asked, voice squeaky with fear.

She laughed. "We ain't stinkin' Blackfeet, or Crows, you know. We ain't likely to do such."

Relief washed over Cooper like a cool waterfall on a summer's day, and his face regained the color it had lost. The woman saw it and grinned. "You ain't a captive, goddamn you," she said good-naturedly, and he realized she did not know she was blaspheming constantly. It was one of the stranger results of learning a language from wandering, uncouth mountaineers, he thought.

"Then what am I?"

"My brother."

"Huh?" he blurted, startled.

"I told you, my father said you was brought by the spirits to replace my brother, who was killed, goddamn him, some moons ago. So you will be my brother."

"I'd rather be someone else's brother."

It was her turn to be startled. "Why?"

He shot a glance toward his groin area,

and then looked away, embarrassed again.

She laughed, the sound still wonderful to his ears. "That does dampen the powder, don't it?" She paused and fed him. "Don't go frettin' on it now. Just fill your belly and then get some more sleep."

"All right," he said reluctantly. He didn't like it, but he was in no position to argue. "What's your name?" he finally asked.

"Pony Woman. You?"

"Hawley Cooper."

"I can't say that. You need another name, and goddamn quick."

He laughed and ate more before snuggling under the robes again and sleeping.

Two days later he got up for the first time, walking a few steps around the lodge under the watchful eyes of Pony Woman, Cheyenne Killer, and his two wives: Twisted Eye, so named because one eye looked off in a different direction than the rest of her; and Long Singer.

Each day he would walk a little more, a few steps added each day. And every day he would quietly suffer the indignity of having one of the three women coat his wounds with new poultices of God only knew what. They all took turns in their ministrations, and it had only been his good fortune, or was it bad?, that Pony Woman was with him when he had originally awoken. Since he was wounded all over, he had to be naked, or nearly so, during the ritual. It was not so bad with the two older women, since he had no desire for them, but Pony Woman was another matter.

She was a desirable, full-busted, plump young woman, and he wanted her badly. But he could not have her, and so he lived a life of inner strain and torment. He could not decide whether he wanted her to tend him, or if he preferred Long Singer or Twisted Eye. Pony Woman was infinitely more desirable for that task, or any other, but that only added to his anxiety.

Every day, too, would come The Raven, the village's medicine man. He would sing his songs, shake his pebble-filled gourd rattle, dance his dances, chant and spread his powders about Cooper. The youth was annoyed by it but knew better than to complain or make fun of it. Besides, maybe it would work.

Cooper began taking his meals with the family, wanting to be with people, and hoping it would help him learn.

Pony Woman spoke English quite well, if rather profanely. She had found it easy to pick up just by sitting outside the fires when trappers were around, which was often at times. She also spoke French and Spanish fairly well, and two other Indian tongues despite only being sixteen winters. Cheyenne Killer spoke English, French and Spanish moderately well, but with such a thick accent as to be unintelligible sometimes. His wives spoke hardly any language other than their own.

Cooper finally told them all to begin speaking more Shoshone to him. The regular hearing of it, combined with the irregular lessons given him by Pony Woman, would help him learn quickly, he hoped. He had much trouble with some of the odd sounds the language used, but he persevered.

Two weeks after he had come awake for real in the lodge, he stepped outside it. The day was bitter cold, and snow covered everything except the lodges and the trees. His breath plumed from nostrils and mouth as he breathed deeply of the frigid, fresh air. He was uneasy, he realized, when cooped up inside for too long a time.

He walked in new moccasins, made for him by Twisted Eye. Cooper did not know how she could do it with her eye the way it was, but her work was superb. The moccasins were wonderfully decorated with pony beads and dyed porcupine quills. An ermine tail followed each heel, and there was a small hawk bell on the top front of each.

Twisted Eye had also replaced his buckskin clothes and repaired his puma coat. His coyote-skin hat was on his head, and he was quite proud of the way he looked. As he walked along, slowly, he was aware that he was the center of the village's attention.

There were maybe twenty lodges, with an estimated population of ninety people. Of that number, perhaps twenty-five or thirty were warriors. They stared at him with curiosity, and he was somewhat surprised to see that there was no animosity or hate in their glances. Merely curiosity. He was to learn later that the Shoshones had been friendly with whites since the time of Lewis and Clark, and rarely was there trouble between the two peoples.

Cooper stared in return, wondering about them, surprised to see so many people outside on such a cold day. He asked about it, and Pony Woman told him that news of his impending walk had circulated and most of the people were outside just to see him. Usually they would remain in their lodges as much as possible during such weather.

He was not out long before he asked Pony Woman, "Can we go back to the lodge?"

"Yes," she said, looking at him in alarm.

He smiled. "I'm all right. Just cold and tired. I ain't used to such doin's, you know."

She grinned and led him back to the tipi. It was gaily painted on the outside in reds, ochers and browns, depicting the exploits of Cheyenne Killer, who, if the pictographs were to be believed, had earned his name.

That night visitors came. Two men, Eagle Claw and Black Beaver, arrived and sat at the fire with Cooper and Cheyenne Killer. When they did, Cooper pulled out the small pipe and twist of tobacco that Cheyenne Killer had given him. He cut off a piece of tobacco, stuffed it into his pipe, and then passed the tobacco around. The other men nodded, pleased that he had done the right thing. One never could be sure with these white eyes.

As the others filled their stone pipes, Cooper relaxed and looked them over. They were handsome men, for the most part, well-built, with large chests, substantial bellies, powerful, long arms and strong hands. Their skin was dark, and their cheekbones high. They were coated with grease under their plain buckskin hunting shirts, and probably would be crawling with lice in the summer. But they had dignity, and Cooper could see in them none of the depravity that Josiah Weeks had said infested all Indians.

No, Cooper thought, these were honorable men. They might be horse thieves and take scalps and mutilate their enemies, but it did not mean they were any less than white men. They might be savage in battle, and have ways that were foreign to white men, but they would not hit him on the back of the head and leave him to die. They were men, pure and simple, Cooper deduced, with all men's dreams, wishes and frailties.

He watched carefully after the three had filled their pipes. He noticed that Black Beaver had slipped the twist of tobacco into the pouch he wore at his side. Cooper grinned. He had more, and he would be more careful after this about how he dispensed it next time, though he did not begrudge the Shoshone for taking it. He observed carefully as the three other men lighted their pipes, then blew a mouthful of smoke at each of the four directions of the compass, then Father Sky and Mother earth before puffing normally. He followed suit.

They smoked in silence for a while, Cooper's eyes flickering from one Shoshone to the next. The silence dragged on and on, until Cooper realized they were waiting for him to speak. He did not know what to say; or what they wanted to hear.

At last Black Beaver said, "Tell how you

came here."

Cooper started with his arrival in St. Louis and told of how he had met Josiah Weeks. He held his breath when he mentioned the trapper's name, but the three warriors showed no sign of recognition of the name. Cooper sighed in relief and plunged ahead, telling of the rigors of the trip; of Weeks' treatment of Tall Grass; of his many and increasingly frequent arguments with the trapper. He left out the part about Iron Bow, and the fight with the Kaws. He did not know if the Shoshones were friends with either of those people and did not want to put himself in jeopardy.

The three Shoshones nodded frequently as Cooper spoke, as if knowing and understanding what he had gone through. From the corner of his eye, Cooper could see Pony Woman watching and listening. Cooper explained how Weeks had hit him on the head and left him with nothing after learning of his tryst with Tall Grass.

Black Beaver nodded vigorously. "One mean sumbitch, that one," he said. The others agreed.

"Pure mean," Cooper said, growing angry. He calmed himself and went on to tell of the rest: the hunger and cold; the snow and wind; the dousing in the icy stream; the fight for food.

Then he was done, and he knew he had won these men over. He would be accepted here, if he chose to stay. And right now that sounded like a good thing to him. He glanced at Pony Woman, who grinned at him. Manfully, he suppressed the desire to return it.

Twenty-Two

Hawley Cooper didn't think it possible, but the young woman before him was even prettier than Pony Woman. The two girls were about the same age and height, but Black Moon Woman, the one to whom he had just been introduced, had something special.

"Come," Pony Woman said, tugging him away. "You'll see her later. Goddamn yes. Can't stay here now. Come on."

Reluctantly he let himself be led away, his eyes still on Black Moon Woman, who watched him, though she kept her face averted.

Finally dragging his eyes away, Cooper asked, "What's going on anyway?" He waved his hand at all the activity in the village. The weather had warmed to above freezing, and it had not snowed in almost a week. Cooper felt good about it all.

"Big doin's tonight," Pony Woman said. "In the big lodge. Counsel fire."

"What's gonna happen?"

"Cheyenne Killer's gonna hold a fandango. Then everyone will know you're part of his family. Son of great war chief Cheyenne Killer. Brother of Pony Woman." She grinned.

He looked a little sick. Now that the great day was here, he was not so sure. "All this for me?" he asked, suddenly uncomfortable.

"Yep."

"Damn, I ain't sure I like all these doin's."

"You'll shine."

He found he was still a little surprised by her odd command of his language. "What'll happen tonight, exactly?" he asked, worried.

"Plenty of speechifyin', that's certain. Feastin'. Dancin' after. Shinin' times, all of it. You'll get a name, and . . ."

"I got a name," Cooper said grouchily.

"You need a Shoshone name. A real name."

"I got a real name, goddammit. It's been good enough all these nineteen years, it'll serve me the rest of my days."

"Well, you got to have a new one. That's that. Your war name. I hear tell some of the white eyes call it that. All the trappers got 'em, like Blanket Chief Bridger."

"Do I pick it?"

"No, your father'll do that for you."

"My father already . . ." He stopped, sheepish. Then he nodded in resignation. "You got any say in it?"

"No." She looked a little bitter, and for the first time he realized that she was angry about her lot in life. She was a woman, and that's all there was to it. She would not be able to take part in most of the ceremonies and counsels and such. Despite her usefulness as a translator, she was only a woman, and would never be considered as worthy as a man, any man. It rankled her. Cooper was rather shocked to see her anger at her fate, seeing as how it was God's will for men to be men and women to be women. But he would not say anything to her about it.

"He'll probably name me Foolish White Eyes, or somethin'," Cooper said, trying to cheer her.

Her face softened minutely. "No," she said in clipped tones.

"Maybe Fallin' Down Wolf Fighter, eh?" The smile started just a bit, and he was pleased. "Or maybe Goddamn Cold All the Time White Eyed Fool. Huh? That it?" She was smiling now, and on the verge of giggles. "Well, what is it?"

"I ain't tellin'." She laughed, releasing his hand. She had known it was wrong for her to be holding his hand that way. There were taboos against contact between brother and sister. It was best to start behaving like it now, since after tonight they would be such. She ran away, laughing.

Cooper trotted after her, still too weak to be able to catch her, but wanting to make the effort. Finally he stopped, puffing, and thought of Black Moon Woman. He did feel something for Pony Woman, and decided it was simply lust. But since she was off-limits to him now, he must cast his eyes about elsewhere. And Black Moon Woman was certainly pleasing to the eyes. Maybe, he thought, once he was a full member of the tribe, one of the People, he would be able to get close to her. In his mending body, his blood boiled, filling him with desire. In his mind's eye, he could picture Black Moon Woman, naked, her body thrusting under him . . .

"Best get your mind off that," he told himself firmly before heading back to the lodge.

It was by far the largest tipi Cooper ever saw when the women had succeeded in raising it late in the day. But even as large as it was, it would not hold everyone in the village. He learned that all the children would stay in their own lodges that night, watched over by the grandmothers. All the warriors, and most of the women managed to cram into the lodge, which, with the fire and the packed humanity, was stifling within minutes.

Cheyenne Killer stood, and after a time, had silence. Then he began his oration, of his life, of his son's short life, of their brave and many deeds. He told of how his son had died, and how the spirits had brought him a new son, in the guise of Cooper. And despite the pale color of Cooper's skin, Cheyenne Killer said the people should accept the young man as his son, since the spirits had spoken, and since Cooper had shown himself to be a brave and resourceful man.

There was much talking then, with other warriors having their say, as was right and proper for people. Until one finally asked, "How do we know this man has a brave heart?" He stood. "We have heard him tell of his bravery. But we have not seen it." He sat again.

Cheyenne Killer rose, and in his deep, gravelly voice, said in Shoshone, "This man, my son, brother to the Snake People, killed four wolves. *Oosh*. Yes. *Wat-so-wit itsup* — four wolves. He did this deed though the snow was very deep, and he was armed only with a small knife and a wooden lance."

He stopped and nodded, his wide face filled with passion. He was a big, blocky man, not much taller than Cooper, but considerably wider in shoulder and girth. He had a thick neck, big, fleshy arms, and a scarred chest. His skin was quite dark, and his nose wide and splayed. It was clear where his daughter had gotten her nose, though she had gotten her skin coloring from her lighter-hued mother.

"Wat-so-wit itsup!" Cheyenne Killer roared, making sure everyone knew of this wondrous deed. "He is brave, and strong. He has a *peyah nam-pe* — big heart — and I claim him as my *roo-et-se* — son. If any doubts his bravery, let them challenge me. Or challenge the eyes of Black Beaver and Eagle Claw, who saw him do these things."

He sat, face set, as if to brook no argument.

There was none, and the silence grew thickly. Then a broad, mean-visaged warrior whom Cooper would learn later was called Blue Bear stood. He spoke fast, his tongue making quick shifts and glottal stops, confusing Cooper some. But the youth caught the gist of it: "This young man might be *nah-re-ant* brave. Maybe not. He showed *peyah pe* against the *itsup.* But will he be so brave against the Crows or the Arapahos?" He almost sneered, but not quite.

Cheyenne Killer stood again and started to speak, but Cooper jumped to his feet. How dare this damned savage, and he regretted thinking the appellation instantly, talk about him as if he was a dog. He would not be argued over. He could defend himself. He started to speak several times, but he was so angry that all the words sputtered and died in his throat.

Blue Bear sat gloating, making rude remarks to his neighbors about Cooper's fumbling. It made the white youth all the angrier.

"*Him e-shem* — You lie!" he finally managed to sputter. Blue Bear stopped chattering and smirking immediately. His black eyes glittered, and he edged his hand toward the wood handle of the knife at his side.

Cheyenne Killer smiled gently and whispered to Cooper, "*Hobetah. Key toobook* — Go slow. Don't get mad."

Cooper took a deep breath and looked at Cheyenne Killer. *"Oosh,"* he said softly. He turned back to face Blue Bear, who sat as if ready to fight. Cooper grinned tightly, though he was very frightened. He reached into his possible bag, smiling when Blue Bear tensed. Then Cooper pulled out the

Kaw scalp he had kept with him all this time. He held it up for all to see.

There was a burst of excitement in the big, smoky lodge. Cooper said nothing, only stood as tall as he could, holding the scalp aloft.

Finally there was silence, and Cheyenne Killer's big voice filled it. "Is there any here who would deny me my son?"

There were no objections, and no more speeches. *"Shobegash,"* Cheyenne Killer said with certainty. "It is done." He surveyed the faces before him, then said, "I will give my son his true name."

Cooper winced, but he had enough sense not to say anything.

"I give to my son the name *Too-Shah-Itsup-Mah-Washay* — He Who is the White Wolf Killer. So he will be known to the People." He nodded with finality.

Cooper grinned and noticed that Blue Bear did not look displeased. He put away the scalp and sat. Cheyenne Killer sat next to him. Some women were bringing food around, and a whiskey jug started making the rounds. He thought he remembered hearing in St. Louis that giving whiskey to Indians was illegal, but he didn't see that it mattered much out here. He had also heard that giving whiskey to Indians was foolish, but he would have to see about that.

He drank some of the whiskey, but not too much, and partook freely of the food. He was surprised there was so much of it, and mostly fresh meat. Before long a drum had started outside, and a circle dance was going around the huge fire in the chill night. Cooper went outside and watched with interest as the blanket-wrapped people shuffled to the rhythm on the packed snow.

The music invaded his being, and he had trouble keeping his feet still. But he forced himself to do so. He had no idea of how to perform the dance, or whether he would be allowed to do so even if he wished. So he stood, chewing on some meat, sipping whiskey when the jug came around, watching. The fiery liquid spread through his system, warming him, making his heart swell with his importance.

Black Moon Woman walked over to him with Pony Woman at her side. The two giggled, and Pony Woman seemed to be pushing her friend forward. They stopped in front of Cooper, and after some more giggling and whispering, Black Moon Woman spoke in Shoshone.

He stared at her.

"She wants you to dance," Pony Woman said.

"I know that. But I don't know how."

"It ain't hard. Dammit no. Easy as pie."

Cooper shuffled his feet, looking uncomfortable.

"That's what this dance is for, dammit," Pony Woman said. "A woman can ask a man to dance here. It's all right. Goddamn all right."

"But I don't know how."

"Black Moon Woman'll teach you. Easy. Goddamn yes. *Meaie,*" she said, jerking her head at the dancers. "Go." She touched his arm, knowing her father would not like it if he saw. But the touch was brief and asexual. Then she said softly, "*Pabatse* — brother."

Cooper stood for a moment, thoughts awhirl. Then he nodded. "Hell, I'll give it a try." He took Black Moon Woman's tiny hands in his, and felt a shock run through his arm and speed through the rest of his body. He looked at her, excitement coursing through him.

She smiled, and to him it was summer again, with everything green and growing, filled with life, instead of shivering under the snow.

He was surprised at how quickly he picked up the simple shuffling, stutter steps to the dance, and after a time of biting his lips in concentration, he started to relax and enjoy himself. The others, he noted with relief, paid him little heed.

The dancing became easier, and he let the pounding of the drums and the hypnotic chanting of the singers drive his legs and arms. It sent him to another plane, though he was conscious — all too conscious — of the beautiful, lusty young woman at his side.

He did not know how long he danced, but suddenly Pony Woman was on his other side, whispering, "Take her back to our lodge."

"What?" he asked, still engrossed in the music.

"Take her back to our lodge. No one'll bother you. Not tonight. Goddamn no."

"Will she go?" he whispered back, eagerness in his voice.

"*Oosh.* Now go."

As they danced around the circle, Cooper looked at Black Moon Woman. Her face was flushed and bright. When they thought no one was looking, they dropped out of the circle, and without words, ran for Cheyenne Killer's lodge.

Inside they paused to catch their breath. Black Moon Woman had been tentative before, but now, seeing the look of lust and anticipation in Cooper's eyes, she was more certain of herself. She smiled and put her hands up on his shoulders. She kissed him and pulled him toward the buffalo robe he used as a bed.

He sank onto it, but she remained standing. With a knowing smile, she dropped her blanket, and then peeled off her buckskin dress. She stood before him, naked save for the moccasins on her small feet.

Cooper's mouth was dry. He tried to speak, and for the second time that night found himself incapable of that simple action.

"Ka tay-gwen," Black Moon Woman said softly to him, placing a hand to his lips. "No talking."

He nodded, and pulled her down on the robe with him, feeling her full, upturned breasts against his rough buckskin shirt. He kissed her deeply, oddly unsure of himself now, but trying not to show it. He cupped one breast as they stretched out on the robe.

Soon he was nude, too, and atop her. It was just as he had pictured as she groaned and ground against him. No, it was better, he thought.

Then he could think no more.

Twenty-Three

Hawley Cooper rolled over and realized he was alone. He snapped awake, remembering instantly that night's pleasures, the feel of Black Moon Woman's soft, hungry, compelling flesh on his own. But where was she?

Then he saw her standing, looking down on him, a smile making her face glow. She was holding her plain buckskin dress, ready to don it.

"In-e-shah onit?" he asked, worry creasing his brow. "What are you doing?"

"Ne aie kimahro," she said, trying to soften the blow with her smile. "I am going."

"Why?"

"I must," Black Moon Woman answered, struggling with his language. "The others return soon."

"Stay a while. Please?" his eyes implored her.

"I must go." She smiled again, but desire

lurked in her eyes.

"Once more," he said, looking at her boldly, but knowing he was blushing.

"*Kay* — no. It would not be good."

"Please."

Black Moon Woman stood thinking. It was true the others would be back soon. But maybe not too soon. She could still hear the drums, so the dancing was still in progress. It was well before dawn, and the night outside black. But there would be time yet, she decided. The others would be in the main lodge, sleeping off their drunk or the effects of the dancing. And what if someone did return early? She and this white man were doing nothing wrong, though her father might be angry that he had received no recompense.

She smiled brightly and dropped her dress. She came to him, arms and mouth reaching hungrily for his. He answered in kind.

When they were done, and laying wrapped in each other's arms, still panting, Cooper said softly, struggling with the Shoshone, *"Ne-tib-it-se cah-mah-gan o-yeant."* His feelings naked in his eyes. "I love the whole of you."

She looked at him dreamily but said nothing.

He looked a little worried. "Do you love me?" he asked, heart skipping several beats while he waited for the answer.

It came immediately: *"Ne seant nay sho-gan,"* she said in her melodious voice. "With all my heart."

He grinned, but she struggled out from his embrace. "I got to go," she said in English.

He nodded reluctantly, the smell of her still powerful in the lodge; the feel of her lingering on his skin, hands, lips; the taste of her fresh.

She slithered into her dress and knelt at his side. She kissed the tip of his nose, then slid a small hand down his thin, bearded cheek. She spun, gathering up her blanket and stood. Then she was gone.

Later, when Cheyenne Killer, his two wives and daughter returned, Pony Woman smiled knowingly at Cooper.

The days began to pass in a quick blur for Cooper. He spent much of his time trying to master the Shoshone language and the People's ways. Though he did not understand much, and he disagreed with some of their customs, he tried to live by their lights as best he could. One thing that meant was keeping away from Pony Woman, except in the most innocuous ways. That bothered him, since she was his main link to Black Moon Woman.

He wanted Black Moon Woman, more than he had ever wanted any of the others. He ached for her, and he spent much time in contriving ways to be alone with her. But he found few opportunities to do so, and it frustrated him.

Then he finally decided. He would make her his wife in the eyes of the People. He would do whatever was necessary to accomplish that. He asked his father, Cheyenne Killer, how he should go about it. The big, broad warrior laughed, and said in Shoshone, "So, you would become a man, eh? The winter is too cold for you alone in my lodge?"

Cooper grew angry, but he forced himself to keep it out of his voice and off his face. "All men have needs," he said in Shoshone, with dignity.

"So?" Cheyenne Killer said, looking at him, eyebrows raised. "And what will you give to her father to show you are worthy, eh?"

Cooper shrugged.

"You will have to wait, my son. When the spring comes, and the buffalo have returned, I will take you against the Crows. Or maybe the Cheyenne. We will steal many horses.

You will have many honors. Then you will have something to give to Blue Bear, to honor him."

"I can't wait that long, father."

"Then what will you do?"

"I will talk to Blue Bear. I will promise to bring him many horses when the grass is green and the world new again."

"A man cannot live on promises, or empty words." Cheyenne Killer looked at Cooper pointedly.

"You think he will doubt my words?" Cooper asked, letting some of the anger surface. "Do you doubt my words?"

"No. Neither will Blue Bear," Cheyenne Killer said evenly. "But you must give him something now."

"Why?"

"He has promised his daughter to *Coorah Tsekah* — Cuts Throat."

"Eh?" Cooper muttered, shocked. "When?"

"Several suns after the big dance when you became my son."

"Damn," Cooper breathed, falling back into English. "What'd he give Blue Bear? He ain't got many horses himself."

"Two ponies," the Shoshone said in his language. "And the promise of twenty more as soon as he raids the Crows."

Boiling with anger, Cooper stood and stalked away. He stewed most of the day, devising one scheme after another to spirit Black Moon Woman away. As he came up with each one, he immediately discarded it as impractical, or even stupid.

While in the throes of indecision, he saw Black Moon Woman heading for the frozen creek. In one hand she held a tomahawk; in the other a metal pot. She stopped at the edge of the creek, as Cooper started toward her. He watched her hack away enough ice to be able to dip the pot into the water. As she finished filling the pot and stood, Cooper arrived. She smiled. Her beauty took his breath away, and he was filled with thoughts and images of her. It blinded him to the tiredness that stretched her face.

"I have something to ask of you," he said in Shoshone. He waited until she nodded, then asked, "Do you love me?"

"Oosh."

His heart leaped. "Do you want me?"

"Oosh."

"Do you love Cuts Throat?"

She hesitated, then said, "*Kay* — No."

His spirits soared far above the leaden clouds. "But you are promised to him?"

"Oosh." Her voice was weary and resigned. Cuts Throat was a handsome warrior, very

brave, and had a good life facing him. She would have loved him easily and gone to his lodge willingly, had not this bearded young white man entered her village, and her life.

"Then I will talk to Blue Bear," Cooper said in determination.

"Kay!" she snapped, head coming up fast. He could see the concern and worry in her eyes.

"Oosh," he said firmly. He walked away, leaving her holding the heavy bucket of water and watching him. There were tears in her eyes, and behind them, love, mixed with fright. Her father had a fearsome temper and had his sights set on Cuts Throat as a son-in-law. However, if Cooper did not talk to Blue Bear, there was no chance she and the youth would ever be together. With a heart both heavy and light, she headed back to her lodge.

That night Cooper, with Cheyenne Killer at his side, called for entrance to Blue Bear's lodge. It was as large as Cheyenne Killer's and painted with the occupant's many deeds, a sparkling display of bravery and artistic talent.

They entered and took seats at the fire. Food was brought, but they ate but little, since a meal had been eaten not long ago. However, it would have been impolite to refuse entirely. Cheyenne Killer did not like being here; had not liked the whole plan when Cooper had brought it to him several hours earlier. But since Cooper had no one to act on his behalf in such matters, he had agreed to it.

Cheyenne Killer and Blue Bear made small talk, ignoring Cooper. The youth fidgeted and cast frequent glances at Black Moon Woman, who sat in the back of the lodge with her mother, grandmother and Blue Bear's second wife. They worked quietly, not talking much. Cooper thought Blue Bear knew of his looks, but he didn't really care if the older warrior knew or not.

Finally Cheyenne Killer came to the formality, saying in Shoshone, "My friend Blue Bear, there is something my son, White Wolf, wishes to ask of you."

"Ask," Blue Bear said, knowing what was coming. The single word was clipped, and he addressed Cheyenne Killer, not Cooper.

Cooper cleared his throat, then said in a strong voice, "I wish to marry your daughter, Black Moon Woman."

"Kay." There was no room for error in the voice.

"Might I ask why, father?" Cooper asked, using the term of respect he did not really feel.

Blue Bear turned hard eyes on him. Then he looked impassively back at Cheyenne Killer and said, "She will marry Cuts Throat. He is a brave warrior. He has honored me with ponies. And there will be more."

Cooper nodded, though Blue Bear still was not looking at him. "I can see as how you'd want Cuts Throat as part of your family, father," Cooper said, surprising everyone with his calm, measured tones. "But I am a brave warrior, too, and will have many horses soon. And many furs. Furs you can trade to other white-eyes for cloth or beads for your wives. Maybe even a gun for yourself."

There was a reaction deep in Blue Bear's eyes, but his face had not moved, and once again he spoke to Cheyenne Killer, "That might be true. You have a scalp. Maybe someone else took the scalp and gave it to you" — Cooper bit back an angry retort — "but you have not fought alongside the People to show your bravery."

"If it's presents you're lookin' for," Cooper said, reverting to English, both to express himself better, and to make Blue Bear struggle to understand, "I have some things that might interest you." He pulled out the scalp and laid it in front of him. "So?" he said, not really expecting a remark. He reached into the possible bag and came up with the bear-tooth-and-claw necklace he had finally finished. He laid it beside the scalp.

"With my bare hands I killed the *werah* — bear — and to you I give this necklace I made."

Cooper saw another spark of interest in Blue Bear's cold eyes. But all the warrior said was, "That is not enough."

"It should be," Cooper said with a hint of steel in his voice.

"Oh?" Blue Bear looked at him, eyebrows raised.

"To you," Cooper said carefully, "these things might not seem much. Perhaps you have killed many enemies and have their scalps. Maybe you have killed many bears and so have too many necklaces and other ornaments. Who knows? Maybe you have so many of these things that they mean little to you." He paused a heartbeat before continuing.

"But these things you see," he waved a hand at the scalp and necklace, "are all I have in the world. I have no food to call my own, though I will have more than I need soon. I have no gun, no horses, though these, too, I will have many of before two more moons have passed. I lay before you all I possess, with the promise of being welcome to share the riches I will gain in the moons to come."

Blue Bear almost smiled. "You speak well for a white-eye," he said seriously, casting a glance at Cheyenne Killer to see how his old friend would react to the depiction of his new son. "And you have a big heart. I would be honored to have you as the husband of my daughter" — Cooper's heart soared, then crashed — "if things were different. Black Moon Woman has been promised to Cuts Throat."

"But . . ." Cooper started to object, but an angry look from Cheyenne Killer silenced him.

Blue Bear continued. "I have spoken. I have given my word. It cannot be broken, even for one so brave and generous." He nodded with finality, signifying he was done.

Silence built, until it was almost palpable. The sounds of sinew being pulled through buckskin, soft breathing, the hissing of the fire grew until they were very loud. Cooper raged inside, though outwardly he remained calm. Then, knowing he had to tread carefully, he said in Shoshone, "It is good that my father-in-law" — there was a surprised look on Blue Bear's face — "is such an honorable man. I would not wish it otherwise."

He paused a bit, letting the words sink in. "But I desire Black Moon Woman above all others." He paused again, trying to formulate his ideas in English, then translate them in his head to Shoshone. It was difficult. He glanced at Cheyenne Killer, who sat impassively. But his father winked at him in encouragement without Blue Bear seeing it. Cooper almost smiled, but he caught himself. Then he looked at Black Moon Woman, and almost forgot everything he had been trying to say. She made his thinking muddy.

"Cuts Throat," Cooper said finally, tearing his eyes away from Black Moon Woman's, "does not love her. I do." It was said matter-of-factly.

"Sho-be gash," Blue Bear said firmly. "It is done. I cannot change it."

"I will change it," Cooper said, beginning to lose his temper at Blue Bear's stubbornness.

"Eh?" the warrior asked, seemingly amused.

"*Oosh.* I will challenge Cuts Throat for Black Moon Woman."

As Blue Bear, Cheyenne Killer and even Black Moon Woman sat with mouths agape, Cooper stalked out of the lodge, his heart pounding in his chest. *Oh, Lord,* he thought, *what have I done now?*

Twenty-Four

Hawley Cooper stood opposite Cuts Throat, the young Shoshone warrior. They were maybe twenty feet apart, and ringed by the people of the village. It was bitter cold, and the sky threatened snow, but no one seemed to mind. The snow on the ground was packed hard by hundreds of footsteps and would serve as the field of battle.

Cooper was aware that many of the men were wagering on the outcome of this fight, and that most of it was against him, though he had heard Cheyenne Killer taking some small bets that Cooper would be victorious. It gave Cooper a little confidence.

As did the frequent, loving glances of Black Moon Woman. As soon as Cooper had made the challenge, he had felt foolish, certain he had made a mistake. He was not sure he could beat Cuts Throat, and he had had doubts about Black Moon Woman's real affection for him. But it was done, and there was nothing he could do to get out of it.

He stood, facing his opponent. He was cold, with a deep loneliness settling over him. He looked at the sea of dark faces and knew he did not belong here. No matter what Cheyenne Killer had said or done, Cooper was still an outsider.

He looked up at the somber sky, which matched the gloominess he felt, as the first snowflakes began falling. He shrugged off his puma-skin coat. It was stained with grease and smoke, and his blood. He dropped it on the ground, along with his possible bag, fur cap and mittens. Around his waist was a thick leather belt, and attached to it was a beaded sheath housing a steel butcher knife that Cheyenne Killer had given him. It was the only weapon he had.

He watched his foe. Cuts Throat was a young, dark-skinned, cheerful youth, a few inches shorter than Cooper, but broader in the chest, shoulders and middle. He was slightly bowlegged, and his nose was long and wide. His thick black hair was greased and hung in two fur-wrapped braids.

Cuts Throat pulled off his blanket capote and dropped it. He stood in breechcloth, leggings, fur-lined moccasins and buckskin warshirt. The shirt was undecorated except for the one scalplock hanging from the left side of the breast. He took off his wolf-fur cap, too.

"Ready?" Cuts Throat called amiably.

Cooper nodded, uncertain of what his voice would be like if he tried to speak. He was quite bothered by all this. Cuts Throat seemed so friendly. Why, he thought, did he have to challenge the young Shoshone? He glanced at Black Moon Woman. The look in her sparkling dark eyes made all his doubts flee.

Cuts Throat pulled his knife and moved a few steps toward Cooper. The young white man stepped out, leaving his knife in its sheath. The Shoshone looked at him in surprise, stopping. Then he smiled and slid his own blade away.

Alert, each moved forward again, and a little to his own right. Cooper wiped his hands on his pants; the palms were sweaty despite the cold air. Dimly he could hear the yelling of the crowd, though it seemed far away.

Cuts Throat charged, head down, ramming his shoulder into Cooper, who grunted with the impact, and went down onto his back. Cuts Throat tried to crawl atop Cooper, who bucked and slid around on the ice, not letting the Indian get set.

Finally Cooper scooted free and stood, breathing hard, chest heaving. His whole body was sweating now. The Indian was fast, a lot faster than Cooper had expected with the bulk he carried. And he was deceptive. And Cooper was still a little weak after his ordeal. He tried to think of a way to defeat the wily young Shoshone.

Cuts Throat charged again, the same way, and Cooper stopped thinking and reacted more quickly than he thought he could. He slipped two steps to his right. He spun, bringing his right fist around with the move. His fist cracked into the Shoshone's cheek.

The Indian's feet slid as he tried to stop, and he finally slipped down onto one knee. Woozily he tried to shake off the effects of the blow.

Cooper lunged and grabbed Cuts Throat around the back in a bear hug. The Shoshone pushed himself up off the knee and jerked forward, head down, yanking at Cooper's hair with one hand and the white man's shirt with the other. He pulled with all his might, bringing Cooper flying over his head.

Cooper landed hard on his back and slid a few feet before coming to a stop, short of breath. He half turned, trying to shove himself up, fearing another imminent attack by Cuts Throat. But the Indian was back on one knee, wheezing, shaking his head groggily.

Both finally tottered up and regained their breath and balance. *"Him nah-te-bing sant,"* Cooper gasped. "You fight well."

Cuts Throat nodded, unmoving. Cooper was suspicious, watching Cuts Throat, but the Shoshone seemed worse off than he. He had given the Indian quite a punch, he thought. Maybe he had done more damage than he had first thought. He attacked, the way Cuts Throat had done earlier, head down, shoulders hunched up to drive into the young Shoshone's belly.

The Indian had been faking his weakness, Cooper realized at the last possible second. At least to some extent. The Shoshone rose up fast, just before Cooper reached him, swung up his leg, bent at the knee, sort of sideways to the charging white youth.

Cooper could not stop, and he plowed into the upraised, fast-moving leg, catching the full force of Cuts Throat's knee and thigh in the pit of his stomach. His breath whooshed out, and he stumbled on a few steps before falling, choking, body fighting to draw in breath.

I'm dead now, Cooper thought as he lay watching the world spin crazily before him.

Black dots did a war dance before his eyes. He clutched his abdomen and prayed to whatever god would listen, pleading desperately to be allowed to start breathing again soon.

He heard a crunching, and realized it was Cuts Throat's footsteps on the ice. They sounded surrealistically loud. The Shoshone was heading for the coup de grace. Surrounding, but not blocking the soft sound of the footsteps was the buzzing roar of the crowd.

Then he realized he was breathing. His breath came jerkily, but oxygen was getting to his system. He exalted, especially when he realized Cuts Throat was coming slowly, putting on a strutting show for his people, who nodded, yelled and whistled appreciatively.

Cooper lay as he had, but he sucked in breath for all he was worth, gathering his strength and wits, not giving away that he was no longer paralyzed. He knew surprise was his only weapon, and that he must time his move just right, for he would get only one opportunity. Besides, he was not all that certain he would be able to move once he struck. If he missed initially, he might be helpless.

Cuts Throat was very near now and had

pulled his knife. So, Cooper thought, not only was he to lose Black Moon Woman, he also was to lose his hair. Well, he told himself, smiling inwardly, we'll just see about that!

His legs lashed out, like a rattler striking. Both feet caught Cuts Throat on the left leg, one on the side of the knee, the other just below it. Cuts Throat yelled and went down as the knee buckled.

Cooper grinned and skittered away across the ice and snow. With a great effort, vaguely aware of the renewed gasp of excitement from the surrounding Indians, he managed to get up. He stood proudly, body still hungry for oxygen but recovering rapidly. He wiped a hand over his face, trying to calm himself. It was easier than he thought, and that surprised him. But he did not take the time to analyze it; he just welcomed it.

He should have gone right in after Cuts Throat, but he was not the type to kill a defenseless person. He had no desire to kill the young Shoshone under any circumstances. He would, if he had to, but he was hoping it would not be necessary. But after his treatment at the hands of Josiah Weeks, he was quite uneasy about taking unfair advantage of someone who was helpless. So he waited. He could use the time to let his system recover, anyway.

Cooper watched as Cuts Throat clutched at his knee. The Indian looked desperate at first, but relaxed when he saw that Cooper was not going to press his advantage. He tried more slowly to get up.

Cooper waited, oblivious to most of the crowd noise, though he did hear someone yell quite loudly, "Finish him." He supposed he should. He could go right on over and pound on Cuts Throat until he submitted, or until he was unconscious. Then Cooper would be declared the winner, and life could go on.

He walked forward, still a bit unsteady but improving with every step. He watched as Cuts Throat got to his good knee and tried to stand on the injured leg, without success. He knelt on the right knee and shin, left leg stretched out to the side. His left hand clutched the bad knee; the other rested on the ice, supporting most of his weight.

As Cooper approached, Cuts Throat's torso jerked upward, pivoting on the good leg. The hand on the ground came up fast, balled and hard, with all the power of the warrior's bunched shoulders behind it.

Cooper snapped his body backward, trying to avoid the blow. His feet slid out from under him, and he fell flat on his back, grunting at the impact. His face was as white as new snow when he realized how close the blow had come to smashing full force into his manhood. But there was no more time to think about that as Cuts Throat slid over him, trying to pin him.

Before the Shoshone could get set, Cooper smashed Cuts Throat with both fists wherever he could reach — side, face, hips.

Cuts Throat grunted with each punch but still managed to crawl atop Cooper. He reared his head back and then whipped it forward.

Cooper gasped as a starburst exploded inside his head. Great bursts of light shot in a dizzying pattern before his eyes, and Cuts Throat's dark face danced eerily over him. Tears leaked from his eyes.

But the blow had stunned its originator, too.

Cooper, still dazed, jerked his body as hard as he could, flinging Cuts Throat to the side. His head was clearing, and he became aware of the flood of blood from his nose. He swiped at it once, hoping it was not broken again, before leaping for Cuts Throat. The Shoshone, groggy, was on his hands and knees trying to get up. But his damaged knee made it difficult.

Cooper kicked Cuts Throat in the side, lifting him and rolling him over onto his back. The Indian collapsed with a soft grunt.

Cooper jumped on the Shoshone's chest. He hit Cuts Throat several quick, hard jabs to the face and head, hoping he would not break his hand on the youth's skull.

He watched Cuts Throat's eyes, and finally saw the light in them dim; the Shoshone was almost unconscious. Cooper grinned, making a grotesque mask, and leaned back to regain his breath. Then he pulled his knife and leaned forward. Brightness sprang into Cuts Throat's eyes for a moment, before resignation took over. There was no fear.

Cooper touched the blade to Cuts Throat's forehead, just at the hairline, and lingered there a moment before he pulled the blade away. "No," he said simply, grinning past the blood smeared across his face. He sheathed the knife and stood, holding out his hand.

With a questioning look, Cuts Throat took it and let Cooper pull him up. *"Hanse?"* Cooper asked, unafraid. "Friend?"

Cuts Throat stared at him for some moments, dark eyes searching the white youth's bearded face. Then he bobbed his head. *"Oosh,"* he said, trying to smile. "Yes."

Cooper let the Shoshone's hand go and turned away, experiencing a momentary shiver of fear as he turned his back on the young warrior. But it left as quickly as it had come. Cuts Throat was already known as a man of his word. He would try nothing.

Cooper smiled as Black Moon Woman raced toward him and swung her arms around him, much to the amusement of her gathered tribesmen. Cooper was aware of some of the more ribald comments from both men and women, but he chose to ignore them as he wrapped his arm around his woman and walked away.

The pain seeped into his consciousness. His nose and forehead were the worst, but his stomach, back and chest ached, and he grew more unsteady as he walked. He leaned on Black Moon Woman. She looked up, worried. "You all right?" she asked in English.

He nodded weakly. "Just need some rest is all." He grinned. "I'll have enough strength left for you tonight," he said boldly.

She matched his grin, lust naked in her eyes. "I'll make sure," she said in improved English. He wondered how she had bettered it, but the next statement explained: "God-damn yes." Pony Woman had been teaching her well.

Black Moon Woman tended to him that day as he rested on his robe in Cheyenne Killer's lodge. But that night, in a tipi given him by Cheyenne Killer, Cooper took his new wife the way a man should. The pain was forgotten in the heat of his passion; and Black Moon Woman was tender, though that did not hinder her enthusiastic display of love for her new husband.

And she made him forget his wounds several times during that sleepless, lust-filled night.

Twenty-Five

Hawley Cooper sat on one of Cheyenne Killer's war ponies. Slung across his back was a quiver of arrows and a bow case. His Shoshone father had been trying with great patience to teach him to use bow and arrow, but he could not seem to get the hang of it. He also carried his knife and a war club made of an oak branch, two and a half feet long, about four inches around, with three rusty knife blades sticking out one end, three inches apart.

Cooper was with five other Shoshones, including Cheyenne Killer, Blue Bear and Cuts Throat, forming a war party. Cheyenne Killer, tired of the winter, had called for warriors to go with him on a raid for horses against the Crows to the northeast. Cooper, feeling pressured by many of the Shoshones to prove his worth, volunteered.

It was early March, Cooper figured. Much snow remained, and the cold still kept a powerful grip on the land, though an occasional spring-like day snuck up on them. It was too early for the spring buffalo hunt. But Cheyenne Killer was itchy for something to do.

They were behind a screen of still-bare cottonwoods, looking over a small Crow village. They could see the quiet village, with few children playing or adults working outside because of the cold. Smoke drifted from lodges; dogs yapped; and scavenger birds flapped overhead looking for scraps. The large horse herd was to the Shoshones' right, being watched over lackadaisically by several warriors, aided by a few boys who were not quite ready for the war path or the hunt but were old enough for some responsibility. They moved among the horses on foot.

Cooper counted fifteen lodges, meaning no more than twenty-five warriors; perhaps only twenty. The tipis were scattered through the trees, but the horses were in a small meadow ringed by trees. It would not be easy to take them.

As Cooper looked over the village, thoughts of Falling Leaf nagged at his memory. It had been a pleasant interlude that afternoon he and Josiah Weeks stopped with the Crows. And Cooper wondered where Falling Leaf was, what she was doing. Had she married Gray Mountain, the young half-breed? Was she here in this village? Cooper wondered with a touch of dread. He had nothing against the Crows. They had treated him well. Yet here he was, ready to raid the village for horses, and possibly take scalps. He hoped this was a different village, since . . .

He shook off the feelings. The Shoshones had saved his life, and now he was one of them. As much so as if he had been born to the band. They were his people, and his people made war regularly with the Crows. And the Crows on the People. It was the way of things, and he could not harbor other thoughts, especially ones brought on by one carnally delightful afternoon a lifetime ago.

The other Shoshones began stringing their bows, and Cooper reluctantly did the same. Each man held several arrows in hand, ready for nocking. They began moving silently to their right, behind the cover of the trees. When they were about even with the horses, they stopped. Blue Bear and another warrior — Wolf's Ghost — stripped to breechcloth and moccasins. Cuts Throat and Red Leggings brought out pots of alabaster paint, thick like mud, and began coating Wolf's Ghost and Blue Bear with it.

Cooper watched with quiet interest. He had learned a lot about the ways of the People and their life. But there was so much more to learn.

When Blue Bear and Wolf's Ghost were coated with paint, they each took a small white blanket and moved to the edge of the trees. They got down on their bellies and began slinking off across the snow, virtually invisible with their white paint, toward the Crow horses.

To Cooper it was an agonizingly slow time. Cuts Throat and Red Leggings kept a close eye on the Crows. Cheyenne Killer watched the village. It was a tense time, but before long Wolf's Ghost and Blue Bear were at the nearest horses. So slowly and carefully had they moved that neither the Crow guards nor the animals suspected an enemy was in their midst. Cooper was amazed not only at his two friends' stealth, but also at their fortitude. He would have been shaking like an aspen limb in a storm if he had done what they were doing the way they were dressed or rather undressed.

Suddenly Blue Bear and Wolf's Ghost yipped war cries. They each jumped up and onto the back of a pony in a single motion. The horses they mounted snorted and tried to buck, but the Shoshones jabbed their heels hard into ponies' sides. The two warriors yelled and waved the small blankets they had carried, scaring the other horses into motion.

The herd began moving as Crow war cries split the air. The three warriors guarding the horses leaped onto their own ponies and began trying to turn the herd back. The boys who had been helping ran toward the village on foot, shouting an alarm. Several Crow warriors burst from the village on horseback, heading for the raiders. As they neared, Cheyenne Killer shouted "*Meaie*! Go!"

The Shoshone war leader shot out from the cover of the trees, trailed by his companions. Cooper's heart was in his mouth as he realized how outnumbered they were, only the four of them to protect the two running off the horses against at least a dozen angry Crows.

As they neared the Crows, Cooper could see that at least two of them had rifles. It made the fear set a little more firmly in his stomach. But then he thought if he could get close enough to either of the Crows, he might be able to get a rifle.

Each Shoshone headed for a Crow, hoping to create enough confusion to allow the others to get away with the horses. It was hoped that in the bedlam that followed they themselves could escape. Cooper picked out one of the Crows with a rifle and headed that way. The Crow saw him and raised the gun. Cooper gulped, but kept his head up as he rode, figuring that on horseback the Crow would not be able to hit him. He had seen some of the Shoshones shoot and he hoped the Crow was as poor a marksman.

The Crow fired, and Cooper had no idea where the ball went. He only knew that it had not hit him. He jammed his heels harder into the pony's side to get a little more speed. He closed in on the enemy rapidly. The Indian dropped his reins and shifted the rifle to his left hand. With his right he grabbed a stone-headed war club.

Cooper, the fear dissipated by the rush of adrenaline, slipped the bow over his shoulders, and dropped the three arrows he had been holding in his left hand. He pulled his own war club.

As they reached each other, the Crow yanked his horse hard to the side and swung his club at where Cooper should be. But Cheyenne Killer had trained this pony well. It followed the enemy horse, almost throwing Cooper, and plowed into it. The Crow pony, off balance from its rider's tug on the reins, slipped on the snow and went down.

Cooper, fear battling with exhilaration inside him, slipped off the war horse before it had stopped and jumped at the Crow. He slammed the three-blade war club down on the warrior's chest, using both hands to force the weapon through the thick blanket capote and into the chest cavity. The Indian gasped but uttered no words as he died. Cooper grabbed the rifle.

As he did, another Crow jumped off his horse, knocking Cooper rolling in the snow. His new rifle and the war club went flying.

"Shit," Cooper breathed. He came to a stop on his back, kicking, gouging and spitting, trying unsuccessfully to keep the Crow from lodging on his chest. The Crow grabbed Cooper's throat and squeezed. Cooper choked and pounded the Indian's sides. Cooper could not reach his knife, so he flailed away at any spot the Crow left unprotected. Then he felt the warrior's wood-handled knife. He snatched it from the sheath and plunged it into the Crow's side three times.

Above him, the warrior's eyes widened in shock and his mouth widened in silent agony. His grip on Cooper's throat diminished. Then he fell forward, not quite dead but only moments away from it. With an effort, Cooper shoved the Indian off and stood, chest pitching. His legs trembled as he looked around. The other Crows were some way off, in a running battle with the Shoshones. He glanced quickly at the village, but it was quiet.

The Crow horse herd was long gone. He looked down; the Crow was dead. With a sigh, but without feeling, Cooper cut off the Crow's very long hair, popping the scalp off. There was no excitement in it, but he was not disgusted at doing it the way he had been the first time. Cooper retrieved his war club and the captured rifle. Then he took the scalp from the first warrior he had killed. He stuffed both scalps in the front of his belt, and the war club in the back. He hefted the rifle and smiled. He yanked the bloody corpse up by the capote and took the Indian's powder horn and shooting pouch, which should contain all he would need. He glanced inside quickly. Yes, everything he would need including a ball mold was there.

With haste, he loaded the rifle. Feeling better, he jumped onto his horse and rode like hell away from the village, following the sign of the running battle. Among that sign were six Crow bodies. He scalped each one as he came to it. His Shoshone brothers had not had time to do so, but Cooper figured he could give them to whoever had earned them.

Then he came on the body of Red Leggings. The warrior had four Crow arrows in him, and his head had been smashed in by a club. "Damn it," he muttered. The Shoshones must be hard pressed, he thought, if they left a dead companion behind like this. Cooper was surprised that Red Leggings had not been scalped or mutilated, but he guessed the Crows planned on doing so on their way back to their lodges.

Red Leggings' pony wandered nearby, and Cooper caught it with little effort. With a growing sense of urgency, he put the warrior's body on the horse and rode out fast.

He finally caught up with his companions about two miles down the valley. They were still fighting a stop-and-go battle with the Crows and were in trouble.

Cooper shot a Crow with his new rifle from maybe a hundred yards. He reloaded quickly and, leaving Red Leggings' body behind, charged up to the Crow rear, slashing away with his war club.

Under this new and unexpected onslaught, the Crows broke off the fight and ran, howling in their anger as they did. The Shoshones counterattacked briefly, yelling war cries. As the Crows fled, the Shoshones loudly proclaimed their prowess.

"It is a good day, eh?" Cuts Throat said to Cheyenne Killer after the Crows had fled. Cheyenne Killer would gain much honor for leading this raid.

But Cooper's father was not as happy as he could be. It would have been a glorious raid, had he not lost a man. "We must not forget Red Leggings," he said somberly.

Cuts Throat nodded. "I will get his body."

"No need," Cooper said. He rode the short way to where he had left the body on the horse. He came back leading the animal.

Cheyenne Killer brightened some, pride in his son evident on his face. The radiance expanded when Cooper produced the Crow scalps, saying in English, "I thought you boys might want these."

Cuts Throat, who had become Cooper's closest companion and his confidante since their battle over Black Moon Woman, whooped. "You're some," he shouted in English, much to Cooper's delight.

"You did well?" Cheyenne Killer asked, nodding toward the rifle in Cooper's hands.

"Oosh. Wat pampay-tsah," he said proudly. "Yes. Two scalps. Plus the one here." Then he added, "And the gun." He puffed out his chest, but that hurt, and he quickly let it deflate.

Cuts Throat howled and yipped again. He, like Cooper, was too young to really realize death yet, though both had faced it many times. All they knew was that they were victorious; they had taken many horses, and scalps. Red Leggings' death was a black mark, but that was on Cheyenne Killer, since he led the raid. And the honors would probably be enough to counterbalance the loss of only one man when compared with the riches they brought home. No, Cuts Throat could see no gloom in this foray.

They rode out, and several miles later came upon Wolf's Ghost and Blue Bear with the Crow horses. The two grinned hugely, until they spotted Red Leggings' body. Wolf's Ghost was the most affected, since Red Leggings had been his closest friend. The warrior went off away from the others and began chanting and singing and howling in his grief for his lost friend.

Blue Bear tried to be solemn, but he could not contain his excitement. This was the most successful raid in which he had ever taken part. Perhaps the most successful in the band's history.

"How many horses?" Cheyenne Killer asked.

"Ni-vight she-maie-'o pit," Blue Bear said,

bursting with his own importance. "Sixty-three."

"Good," Cheyenne Killer said. He, too, felt Red Leggings' loss, but was happy with their success.

"How many scalps?" Blue Bear asked.

"She-mai-ro-win," Cheyenne Killer said. "Nine."

"Did he take any?" Blue Bear asked, pointing at Cooper, who bristled at the implication.

But it was Cuts Throat who answered, angry that Blue Bear should question his friend's abilities. "Three on his own," he said through tight lips in Shoshone. "And he brought back Red Leggings' body, which we others had had to leave behind." He smirked at the surprised look on Blue Bear's face.

"And," Cuts Throat said after a short pause, "he also brought back the scalps we had not been able to take."

"You did all that?" Blue Bear asked Cooper.

"Oosh." It was said simply. But there was something in the voice for all to hear. Cooper had proven himself in battle before these others. Never again would he have to listen to anyone question his honor, or his courage.

Blue Bear nodded, both at the word, and the strength behind it. He would say nothing, but he was proud the young white man was his son-in-law.

Twenty-Six

Hawley Cooper was tense. It had been impressed upon him for some time just how important the spring hunt was to the Shoshone band. The People were thin and hungry, and if the winter had lingered much longer, some might have suffered. But one morning a warm wind kissed the valley in which the village sat; and it seemed as if suddenly the world sprang back to life.

Blue Bear was chosen to lead this hunt, and he and his small, hand-picked contingent of warriors kept the others in line as the village moved toward where the buffalo had been spotted. This would, Cheyenne Killer had explained to Cooper, be a fall, in which the men would force the buffalo over a steep ridge, where they would pile atop one another. Later, after the village was assured of its first big feast, with meat plentiful and the winter famine behind them, Cooper would experience the freedom and joy of running the buffalo.

Cooper had nodded, excitement and curiosity spreading through his limbs. It would be good to hunt again, he thought. But even better, it would be good to have fresh meat. He was plumb, flat-out, all-fired sick of eating pemmican and jerky. He needed fresh tongue and hump meat and ribs and fleece and . . .

The anticipation had built up in him, and he noticed all the Shoshones were affected by it, too.

They moved up on the buffalo herd, a dozen chosen men who would start the herd running in the desired direction. Other warriors, some from other bands since this was a major undertaking, other villages had gathered together for it would keep the animals running through a funnel of human bodies, until the ground dropped out from under the beasts.

The day was superb, with the temperature in the mid-fifties and a slight breeze. The azure sky was limitless, unbroken by even the faintest wisp of cloud.

The herd was in sight, and Cooper was amazed anew at their numbers. The young white man sat proudly on one of his own ponies, granted him after the raid. He had received a dozen of the best ponies, and he tried to give all but one to Blue Bear in exchange for Black Moon Woman's hand. But the older warrior had gruffly refused, telling Cooper, "You have done enough for the People and me. You have shown your bravery and your skill in battle. I will take but half. I need no more. You must keep the others. You have a wife now, and," he added with a friendly leer, "maybe a family soon, eh? A man should not do without."

Cooper had nodded acceptance, pride welling up. But he kept a somber face.

He had, with the help of Blue Bear and Cheyenne Killer, worked with the already well-trained horse as often as he could in the cold months. But he had confidence in the pony's abilities.

Blue Bear gave the signal, and the line of men stopped. Evidently Blue Bear had detected a restlessness in the herd and wanted it to calm before moving on. Cooper could hear the snuffling grunts of the buffalo, and the pitiful wailing of the new calves. It was enough to lull him into daydreaming.

Just after the raid on the Crows, the winter had closed its fist on the valley again, squeezing the village in its icy grip. But it did not last long, and after a late blizzard blew itself out, the weather gradually improved. The ice on the creek cracked, as it did on the Wind River not far away.

Cheyenne Killer called for entrance to Cooper's lodge one morning. When Cooper told him to enter, the warrior did, and was greeted by his son and daughter-in-law. He sat, laying a clanking pile of traps at his side.

"Like most white-eyes," Cheyenne Killer said in English, "you came to mountains for beaver, eh?" When Cooper nodded, he went on. "The People catch many beavers. Make 'em come goddamn good. Beaver plentiful here in the land of the Wind River. You learn to take own *hanay enpue* beaver pelts, eh?"

"It's why I came out here, Father. Josiah Weeks promised me he'd commence to teach me how to make beaver come. I watched him some, so I know a little. But he never showed me nothin' really."

"You learn now. Come." Cheyenne Killer stood. Cooper donned his puma-hide coat and coyote-fur cap. It was not all that warm out yet, he thought, wondering how Cheyenne Killer could go about without a blanket or capote.

They spent the next several days in lessons. Cheyenne Killer showed Cooper the proper way to set a trap, how to daub castoreum on a stick overhanging the trap, and how to set the float stick. Much to his own annoyance, Cooper still gagged at the smell of the castoreum. He wondered how anyone got fully used to it, though Cheyenne Killer seemed oblivious to the stink. Cheyenne Killer also showed him how to spot beaver sign. The Shoshones had been trapping beaver for many years and they were experts at it. Cooper could have no better teacher.

They spent a good portion of each day in a stream, and each night Cooper staggered back to his lodge, his legs numb from the frigid water. As they warmed, both from the fire and from Black Moon Woman's loving ministrations, they would begin to tingle, and then ache, pain wrenching knee joints. He didn't know how other men could do this day in and day out for months on end without complaint.

Well, he would not complain either, he told himself the second night. He would bear it, as Cheyenne Killer did, as Weeks had.

In the evenings, while Black Moon Woman often with Pony Woman at her side worked carefully on the plews he had brought home that day, Cooper would sit and listen as Cheyenne Killer told him of other ways of the Shoshones, or of the mountains, or forest, or animals. Cheyenne Killer showed Cooper how to take the castor glands of the beaver and let them dry before making "medicine" from them — the castoreum that would draw beavers to his traps.

Within a week, Cooper was nearly as well-versed in finding and trapping beaver as Cheyenne Killer was. His father nodded, then, and left him alone after providing him with a half-dozen steel traps.

Black Moon Woman did her job well, too, and the plews Cooper accumulated were plush, thick with winter fur. They would bring top money either at St. Louis or at the rendezvous Weeks had mentioned several times.

Life was good for Cooper. His trapping went well, and he had won over the respect of the People in the village. He had a good friend in Cuts Throat, who had soon after his battle with Cooper, started playing his flute for Pony Woman, courting her. Those two shared a lodge now, too, usually not far from Cooper's. And Black Moon Woman was a solicitous wife, seeming most often to anticipate Cooper's wants and needs. She worked hard and was loving to him. She cared for him and showed the depths of her feelings in many small ways.

One such way was to make Cooper a new pair of pants. Though she was unfamiliar with pants as opposed to leggings, she figured them out and made a new pair for him. The tops of the trousers were of tough buffalo hide from a discarded tipi. The bottoms, from just above the knee, were from a colorfully stripped, four-point Hudson's Bay blanket.

He laughed a little at first, then felt his stomach wrench at the look of hurt in her eyes. "Well," he stammered, "they look funny."

"Use 'em," she said, anger and hurt mixing in her voice. It was only the second time he had hurt her. The first was when he tried to explain about the medicine bundle he carried from Tall Grass. She did not want him wearing it, since it was made by another woman, and offered to make him one of her own. He had refused, saying that it was a gift, and that by rights, he should make his own medicine bundles, which he would do when he found the time.

That hurt had lasted a few days, but he had talked soothingly and persuasively, until she understood that he had not loved Tall Grass, but that he owed her his life, because of the bundle, and when that debt was repaid, he would remove it. That mollified her.

She stayed angry overnight after he laughed at the new pants, but the next day he used them, and was wonderfully surprised at how much better they were than regular buckskins for trapping. Buckskins held the water and dried hard after being wet. The wool parts of the new pants were warmer, dried more quickly, and did not shrivel. When he got back to the lodge that night, he kissed Black Moon Woman and apologized profusely.

"Hell, I didn't know," he said lamely. "I'm just a damn fool."

"Goddamn right," she mumbled, still a little hurt and angry.

But his tenderness and consideration soon won her over again, and she was her usual cheerful self, turning to him in hunger and love.

Despite his growing pile of beaver plews, Cooper knew he needed buffalo. First, they needed food. But more than that, they needed many things that only the buffalo could provide: sleeping robes, hides to make into clothes and moccasins and parfleches; brains for tanning; sinew; horn from which to make cups, spoons and other small utensils; bone for needles.

Then came the call for the hunt. The village seemed to burst into a frenzy of activity. Cooper traded two beaver pelts to Wolf's Ghost for a bar of lead. He borrowed an old pot from Cheyenne Killer, melted the lead in it, and spent two nights casting balls for the rifle. Then he cleaned his rifle and made sure it was well-oiled with bear grease. With care, he chipped the rifle flint so the weapon would fire most every time.

Cooper got some old cloth from Twisted Eye and cut it into long strips. These he coated with bear grease and rolled up for convenience. They would be used to patch the rifle balls.

He cut back on trapping to work more with two of his captured ponies and to do all the other things needed to get ready.

At long last the village crier had come along shouting, "Time to go. Buffalo to eat. Time to go. Everyone get ready."

The next morning, the village began its migration. The People moved out slowly, strung along for some distance. Blue Bear and his family led the way; Cheyenne Killer and his following. Cooper and Black Moon Woman, with little to pack, were near the front, riding near Cuts Throat and Pony Woman. But there were always stragglers.

Only a few miles were made that first day, but by the second day the People had fallen back into the routine of traveling and made much better progress as they headed east and a little south. Midway through the third day, a blizzard screamed out of the mountains and pummeled them with thick, heavy snow, and winds that shrieked and pounded their hastily set up lodges.

As the storm howled into its third day, Cooper began to worry. All the Shoshones were strapped for food at this time of year, and he more than most. Black Moon Woman began showing some signs of strain.

"We'll make out," Cooper told his wife one night as they huddled, naked, in the thick buffalo robe. "Don't you worry none. It's just winter sayin' its final goodbyes before blowin' out, makin' way for spring."

She nodded, looking hungry, tired and miserable. She clung to him and was cheered by his warmth and presence.

Her spirits rose the next afternoon as the snow sifted to a stop and the massed dark clouds began splintering and racing off. "Hell," Cooper said cheerfully to her outside their lodge, making her smile, "ain't but knee deep."

She giggled, face tinged with rosiness from the cold. She bent and scooped up a handful of the new, wet snow and made a snowball. She threw it, and it plopped wetly on his cheek.

"Why you little . . ." He grinned and grabbed some snow. She saw it and started to run, legs lifting high in and out of the snow, her skirt flapping, baring her legs sometimes beyond the tops of her leggings, which went a little past her knees.

Cooper whooped and gave chase, racing after her through the makeshift village. Shoshones stopped and laughed and pointed, offering shouted words of advice or encouragement to one or the other. Cooper tossed the snowball and missed.

But with his longer legs, he soon caught up to his wife and tackled her. They rolled over and over in the deep, fresh snow, laughing. Cooper smothered her snow-wet face with hot kisses, and she returned them with ardor. Under the watchful, joyful, encouraging glances and shouts of the People, he scooped Black Moon Woman up and carried her back into their lodge . . .

They moved on the next morning with the sun shining brightly, if coldly, on them. And several days later, bolstered by the arrival of several other bands, they caught up with the herd.

There was a shout from Blue Bear, and Cooper snapped to alertness. The horsemen were moving forward slowly but gaining speed. Cooper's pony had not waited for him but had started with the others. Cooper joined the others in yelling and fired off his rifle.

The great shaggy brown mass of buffalo shifted and snorted, most of the animals lifting their heads to try to find the source of this disturbance. Then they began to run. The thunder of their hooves on the packed snow, torn up by beards and hooves in the animals' search for forage, rumbled up Cooper's pony's legs and into his belly. And the ground shook with the pounding race to death.

As the horsemen kept the herd running, other men popped up at intervals, shouting, waving blankets, occasionally firing a gun, keeping the herd moving in the desired direction. The first animals, bellowing and snorting in surprise, suddenly tumbled over the short, steep cliff. The ones just behind them, pressed by the thousands of bodies following, could not stop, until hundreds of buffalo had gone over the cliff.

Cooper was stunned at the orgy of killing that took place then. Warriors swarmed over the struggling, squirming mass of buffalo with lance and bow and arrow and club and knife, slaughtering those animals that had not been killed by the fall or by the tons of flesh that fell atop them.

Though he was amazed, Cooper was a

willing and agile participant in the carnage. He held before him not a vision of an abattoir, but rather one of fresh tongue and ribs and fleece and hump meat cooking juicy over a roaring fire in his comfortable lodge. A vision of him and Black Moon Woman feasting on the succulent flesh until they thought they would burst.

And so he killed with abandon, using his rifle sometimes, but more often using his lance.

And then the butchering began.

Twenty-Seven

Hawley Cooper missed Black Moon Woman, but this short trip was important, he kept telling himself. The idea had come to him a week or so earlier. One night he had been lounging in his lodge, talking with Black Moon Woman about how he had come to the Shoshone village. The more he talked, the more he thought he would like to get back at the old trapper somehow. It looked less and less likely that he would be able to help Tall Grass. But still, there had to be something he could do to irritate the old rogue.

Then he remembered Weeks' caches of beaver plews and other supplies. Cooper had only saw him making the one, but if he could find that cache again and remove the plews before Weeks started his trip out of the mountains . . .

He went to Cheyenne Killer the next day and told his father of it. Cheyenne Killer, who had a fine sense of humor, matched by his idea of justice, vowed to help him. "Where is this place?" he asked.

"I ain't sure," Cooper said with a rueful smile. "I don't know where I am in relation to that place. I thought when I left our winter camp that I was headin' east, and maybe north a little. That was the plan. But I reckon I got off the track real early."

"Anything you can remember?" Cheyenne Killer asked in Shoshone. "A mountain that looked different from the others? A ridge? A pass?"

Cooper looked thoughtful, and deep down he felt disgusted with himself for not being able to remember exactly where the place was. Then he brightened. "Wait. We was travelin' along the Bear River," he said, excited and lapsing back into English.

"It was on the *Coo-yah Paw*?"

"Yes. No, wait." He thought again. "No, it was on a creek leadin' into the Bear. Not long after he dug it, we traveled northeast, I think. I remember Weeks sayin' we come through . . . what the hell was that pass . . . Wait. Um . . ." His face screwed up in thought, then brightened. "Yeah, I think he called it Salt River Pass. You know of it?" When Cheyenne Killer nodded, Cooper said, "It was just a couple days after coming through the pass that he made the cache. That's about the best I can do," he said, embarrassed. "Weeks weren't the most talkative of boys. We went another few days before makin' our winter camp." He slapped his thigh in annoyance.

"We will look," his father told him.

Cooper was not placated. That night he dreamed of the place. It seemed so clear to him in the dream, and he was sure he would know the place when he found it. The trouble was getting there. Unfortunately there was nothing in the dream to help him. Mountains were mountains, passes were passes and creeks were creeks. They all looked much alike to him. He awoke angry and bitter.

But he rode out in the company of Cheyenne Killer, Blue Bear, and Cuts Throat. They headed southwest from their camp on the western slope of the Wind River Mountains. As they rode, Blue Bear and Cuts Throat sang songs Cooper did not understand, but their style and rhythm were infectious; and their voices quite compatible. Cuts Throat sang in a wavering, reedy voice that danced rings around Blue Bear's deeper, more solid baritone. It was a pleasant way to start the journey, and Cooper found himself cheered.

Without women and children and lodges to slow them, the men traveled easily and quickly. They made small but comfortable camps at night, with each man taking on duties without having to be told. Cooper usually tended to the fire and firewood; Cuts Throat to the animals; Cheyenne Killer, the best hunter, kept fresh meat in supply; and Blue Bear, an unsurpassed tracker, found their way each day and kept a constant vigil for sign of enemies.

The journey was uneventful, really. Unlike Cooper's solitary trek so long ago. The few incidents that occurred were barely worth mentioning even in their little circle. What matter was it to them that they were attacked by a grizzly sow protecting her young? What kind of men would they be to worry over fording a stream or river swollen by snowmelt? What importance would men attach to being followed for a time by a small pack of wolves starved lean by the long winter and looking for an easy meal? Who should find it worrisome at having to abandon two campsites because they were infested by rattlesnakes? No, warriors had more momentous things to occupy their minds.

Like missing their women. Cooper almost pined for Black Moon Woman, but he would not let the others see the depths of his loneliness. And his desolation was tinged with worry. It would be easy enough for Black Moon Woman to divorce him. Simply toss his things out of the lodge. But she wouldn't do that, he was sure. Would she?

Though neither said anything, Cooper knew Cuts Throat had the same yearnings and worries over Pony Woman. It was a small comfort to Cooper to know that.

He growled inwardly at himself. Such thoughts would get him nowhere, he told himself silently. Bah, he spat, better to spend the day learning tracking and hunting from two masters; or learning enemies, both man and animal; or learning which plants could be eaten in starving times, and which would kill him as quickly as a Crow arrow.

He was an avid student and learned quickly. He finally began to relax and to enjoy himself, and the loneliness of missing Black Moon Woman lessened some as they made their way from creek to creek, skirting high, snow-covered peaks and precipitous drop-offs. He loosened up and began joking more with Cuts Throat and Cheyenne Killer, and even Blue Bear, who, when he was feeling good, was not quite the ogre Cooper had imagined him.

They made their way though a pass, and

when they were through it, Cheyenne Killer asked, “Does this place seem familiar to you?”

“I’m not sure,” Cooper confessed sheepishly. “Why? Where are we?”

“We have come through Salt River Pass, as the white eyes call that place. In two suns, maybe three, we will be at the *Werah Paw.*”

“Sorry,” Cooper said, face burning with shame. He looked around, trying to place this spot, seeing if it registered. It was a nice site, with plenty of grass on the sloping variegated hills; interspersed with thick pines, and some aspens and cottonwoods, both of which were beginning to bloom. It was a pleasing place, Cooper thought, both to the eye and the spirit. But it was unfamiliar to him, and doubts began to cloud his mind.

“No matter,” Blue Bear said. He was jovial these days, enjoying the warmer weather. It was April, Cooper guessed, and pleasant under the sunlight, though the nights still were cold, and snow occasionally blew in. New grass was springing up, and the first of the spring flowers were poking their heads through the snow, which still lay thick where the sun did not heat the earth much. The trees were putting out new shoots, and Blue Bear could feel the earth awakening after its long, dreary sleep.

Cooper could feel it, too, and tried to enjoy it. But his annoyance at himself made it hard. Still, there was something almost intoxicating about the air and the awesome scenery, and Cooper allowed himself to drink it all in.

Early on the second day after coming through the pass, they saw the broad Bear River shining below them, and Cooper felt an excitement growing. "Yes," he muttered. "Yes, this is near the place. There," he pointed up the river to a craggy mountain spur with several boulders perched precariously at top, "I know that place."

Cheyenne Killer grinned and shook his head with Blue Bear over the foolishness of white men. But they turned their ponies north along the river. They were extra wary. The Bannocks, into whose lands they were heading, were friendly, but it always paid to be careful.

Besides, Blue Bear explained to Cooper, this was a land much crossed by many tribes, both friendly and not — the Utes from the south would always fight the Shoshones; the Crows and the Blackfoot, both warlike and far-ranging, would wander here, sometimes to trade, but most often looking to steal horses, count coup and raise hair; the Nez Perce, usually friendly, bringing their herds of Appaloosas from the northwest.

Cooper nodded, only half absorbing the lesson. He was busy watching their trail. It was becoming more and more familiar, with recognition coming in short, exciting bursts. Yes, there was the giant, lightning-shattered cottonwood where he had picked up firewood one night. And several miles up the trail was the strange formation of rock reminding Cooper of a dog baiting a bear.

They had been gone a week and a half or so, Cooper estimated, when he reined to a stop, letting the others, who were ahead of him, ride on. There was something terribly familiar about this spot, something that tantalized him . . .

He craned his neck slowly, pivoting his head from right to left. He smiled, liking it here. The others had gone around a curve in the path carved by thousands of buffalo and pony hooves, and human feet. It was perfectly quiet now, except for the shrill, piercing whistle of a hawk far off. The wind blew mildly, bringing with it the fragrance of spring. But it was tinged yet with winter.

Cooper took a few moments to enjoy the blissful quiet and the wonderful tang of the air before searching with his eyes some more. Something about this place tickled his mind. He dismounted, letting the rope reins dangle. With rifle in hand, he started looking around.

He went from tree to tree, searching for the marks he had made. He took his time, not wanting to rush and miss any blazes. It was slow and tedious work since he was not even sure this was the right area.

After looking for some time, he realized the others still had not returned, and that it was much colder. The mild breeze had turned into a savage wind. Thick, dark clouds clotted overhead. "Hell and damnation," he mumbled, looking up at the threatening sky, knowing it would rain soon, and probably snow.

He was sure this was the right spot, though he had not found any proof of that. He just had a nagging feeling. In the dream it had all been so close and so easy to see. But standing here in the midst of the clearing, his recollection was murky.

Cooper climbed on his horse and trotted off just as the first snowflakes and raindrops began falling. It took him nearly an hour to reach the others, who were heading slowly back along the trail.

The rain had stopped, and the snowfall had increased. The gusty wind roared, blowing the snow in their faces.

"I think I found the place," Cooper said, excitement tempered by the storm. He paused, suddenly feeling foolish. He had dragged his friends all these miles on a whim. Even if he could find the cache, Weeks most likely had already come by and picked up his supplies and such. He shrugged. What the hell, they had come this far.

"I'm not really sure it's the place, but there's a spot a little way back that looks powerful familiar. I was lookin' for the trees I marked when the storm blew up and I realized you boys was gone."

Cheyenne Killer nodded solemnly. Perhaps he really thought this a wild goose chase. But he would never let his son know if he did. This was important to Cooper, and so it was important to Cheyenne Killer. "We will go back there," he said with no sense of urgency. The others looked miserable, but Cheyenne Killer actually liked this weather. He pulled his blanket tighter around him and rode off.

They made their small camp quickly and sat to a hastily made meal of deer meat. The snow fell even harder, and the wind blew all the more. But they were not bad off, sheltered by trees, wrapped in blankets or capotes. By morning there was about a foot of new snow on the ground, and the flakes were still falling.

Cooper fretted. The day was dim because of the charcoal skies, but that did not stop him from moving slowly from tree to tree, peering up and around, looking for his marks.

His three friends sat and chatted or sang; even gambled a little. Cooper suspected at least a little of the wagering was on the outcome of his quest.

"Whooo-eee," Cooper suddenly shouted.

The others hurried up as he started following marks, moving rapidly from one to the other. Once he had found one mark, the others were easy to spot. Then Cooper stopped and pointed. "That's where it is," he said, beaming. "Right under that large huckleberry bush."

He slid down the small slope to the spot and searched for sign. But everything was covered with snow. "Don't look like anyone's been here," he said hopefully. He was not convinced. After seeing what kind of man Weeks was, Cooper suspected the trapper came back first thing after knocking Cooper on the head and destroying the camp.

Cooper started pushing snow off the spot

with his hands, wishing he had a shovel. But Cheyenne Killer stopped him. "Tomorrow," he said, tugging Cooper away. "When the snows have gone from the sky."

Cooper nodded reluctantly and let himself be led away. He was out at first light, shoving snow out of the way again. He had had little sleep in his excitement and was still amusing his friends with his antics.

A shovel was thrust in front of his nose. "Would this help?" Blue Bear asked, sarcasm heavy in his voice.

Cooper looked up and smiled, not noticing the sarcasm. He grabbed the implement and quickly scraped the snow away. Then he jabbed the small, pointed edge of the shovel, probably stolen from some trapper, no doubt, he thought, into the ground. "Damn," he growled. The ground was still frozen. His shoulders slumped.

But his friends had been busy gathering wood. They brought down some coals from their fire and started a widespread blaze, not high. Several hours later the ground was soft enough to dig, which Cooper did with a vengeance.

Then he whooped and let out a war cry.

Twenty-Eight

Hawley Cooper felt a growing excitement as he looked down over the great encampment along the sandy shores of Bear Lake. As far as his eyes could see, there were lodges and tipis of mountain men, Shoshones, Nez Perce, Flatheads and Crows; tents of varying sizes; and lean-tos of old buffalo hide strung to trees.

Cooper and Cheyenne Killer's band of Shoshones had come in across the ridgeback of the Prouse Mountains, and Bear Lake stretched out before them, sparkling in the sun. The mountains behind them framed the large camp, which was alive with activity. There a group of men, red and white, were throwing tomahawks at a propped up log; and over there men were firing rifles and pistols at targets of varying shapes and sizes, some of them living, at least for the moment. A whoop and a shout arose above the general clamor, and Cooper saw half a dozen horses racing around a pole stuck in the ground at the south end of the camp and racing back toward them. Men and women lined the temporary race-track, shouting for their favorites.

The smoke from hundreds of fires drifted lazily into the air, making the camp look like it was engulfed in a thin, filmy fog from the far-off ocean.

Cheyenne Killer grinned at Cooper. "Goddamn good, eh?" he said with a chuckle.

"Goddamn good," Cooper agreed, excitement filling him almost to bursting. His heart pounded with it, and all thoughts of the long, harsh winter, with its many travails left him. Almost. A vision of Josiah Weeks leapt into his mind, and Cooper wondered if he would see the scoundrel here. If he was here, would Tall Grass be with him? If she was, Cooper would see to it that she was freed, somehow.

But the festive nature of the rendezvous infected him even at this distance. He glanced at his marred left hand, and the gloom began to resettle in him. But his exuberance returned when Black Moon Woman sidled her pony up to his and smiled.

"Come on, let's go," Cooper said to Cheyenne Killer eagerly.

They moved on and soon were within the vast perimeters of the camp. Blue Bear had ridden ahead of the main group to find a site for the band to make its camp, and he trotted his horse up to lead them.

It took little time for the camp to be set up. It was spread among cottonwoods and willows near the lake, north of the main encampment. Several other camps of Shoshones were close by.

Before the camp was done, a buckskin-clad white man rode in to pay his respects to Cheyenne Killer, Blue Bear, Lame Elk, the aging civil chief of the band, and several other leaders. He registered some surprise when he saw Cooper. Then he shrugged and held out his hand. "Name's Bridger," he said in a deep voice. "Jim Bridger."

"Hawley Cooper," the youth said, shaking Bridger's hand, sizing up the newcomer. Bridger was a few inches taller than Cooper, and maybe five or six years older. He had broad, strong shoulders, a large neck, and powerful hands. He was somber-looking, and his eyes were calm and direct, missing nothing.

"First time here, boy?"

"Yes, sir," Cooper said, feeling the need to be respectful.

"Been out long?"

"Nope. Seems like a lifetime, though."

Bridger cracked a smile. He generally was not the smiling sort. "It'll get easier, I reckon." He paused and then asked, "That your woman there?" He nodded his head in Black Moon Woman's direction.

"Yes," Cooper said proudly.

"I'd keep her to my side most times, boy, was I you, while you're here," Bridger said roughly. "Most of these boys'd give an arm to spend a night in the robes with a looker like her." His voice dropped to a whisper. "And these folks sometimes ain't got no sense of chasteness bein' a virtue. You leave that little gal alone, she just might jump into the robes with the first man with a pile of foofaraw."

Cooper sputtered a few times before saying angrily, "You'd be wise to watch what you're sayin, lest someone takes exception to your jabberin'."

Bridger did grin then, unafraid. "I didn't mean nothin' by it, boy. Didn't mean no disrespect to you or your woman. Just friendly advice."

"I'll consider payin' it heed, then," Cooper said, somewhat mollified.

Bridger drifted off to counsel with the Shoshones, and Cooper took Black Moon Woman back into their lodge. He told her basically what Bridger had said, and then asked, anxiety in his voice, "That ain't true, is it? You ain't that kind, are you?"

Black Moon Woman looked at him blankly for a time, trying to ascertain what the trouble was. In fumbling fits and starts, Cooper finally made her understand. Then she said vehemently, "No, I ain't like that. Others maybe. Goddamn not me. I'm your woman."

Cooper felt relief, but for the most part, he tried to keep her near him. He smiled and said, "Come on, let's go look around."

With his captured trade rifle cradled in his left arm, and Black Moon Woman walking on his right side, hanging back a step or two as she thought she should, Cooper set out for the main doings of the rendezvous. He did little that day but observe, watching one thing for a little while before wandering off to see something new. All the while he kept his eyes open for any sign of Weeks.

It was a wild and raucous place, with a constant barrage of noise: people shouting and singing; horses running; arguments; guns being fired; and music. At various parts of the large encampment, he heard the wailing drone of bagpipes; the quick, high-pitched screech of fiddles; the plaintive tones of a dulcimer; jaw-harps; Indian drums, rattles and flutes; and a few other instruments he could not identify.

More than once he had to dance out of the way of a rough-and-tumble fight that seemed to erupt for no apparent reason, and each of which attracted a group of shouting, betting onlookers.

And such gambling there was. Everywhere he turned men were wagering on one thing or another — horse races, shooting, knife or tomahawk throwing, fights, foot races, wrestling matches, hand games, card games, dice games. If it could be bet on, Cooper quickly realized, these men, whether white or red, would put their money, furs, horses, sometimes even guns or women on it.

Cooper was stunned at the diversity of the rendezvous. He heard maybe a dozen Indian languages, as well as English, French, Spanish, Irish brogues, Scottish burrs, the guttural sounds of German and Dutch, and others he could not place.

He soon learned that many of the men worked under contract to the various fur companies. But others, and these could be picked out easily, were free trappers. They were strutting, swaggering men, dressed in colorfully decorated buckskins. They were, for the most part, long of hair, touchy and arrogant of demeanor, and covered with foofaraw. As were their women.

There were black men here, and quite a few half-breeds. There were chattering French-Canadians with their vivid cloth shirts and bright red wool caps, worn here even under the harsh July sun. And dark Spaniards, with their distinctive dress of short, tight-fitting jackets over flared buckskin pants with silver conchos down the sides, and wide-brimmed hats. Indians of various tribes abounded, each man dressed in his best finery.

And all of them got along for the most part. Granted, there were plenty of brawls. While some of those came because of long-held regional animosities, or because of women, or because of fur company rivalries, most could be blamed on the fact that the men liberally dosed themselves with burning alcohol. Cooper learned quickly that the alcohol was sold, cut considerably with river water and filled with various strange "ingredients" to spice it, at exorbitant prices.

Most of the men, and not a few of the Indian women, Cooper saw, were in some state of intoxication. Over the next several days it became apparent that the time of day made little difference to these men. They were almost never without a jug, bottle, tin cup, gourd or bucket of whiskey in hand. They would begin drinking when they awoke, whatever time that was, and would stop when they collapsed somewhere.

Cooper's mind was filled with wonder as he tried to sleep that night. All he had seen floated through his mind, thoughts whirling and bumping into each other. It was well past dark when he finally managed to block it all out and sleep.

He was checking on his plews the next day, preparing to sell them, when a Shoshone warrior from another band raced into their camp. He jerked his frothing mount to a stop and shouted, "*Oveant kim. Nah-beting. Ne Pike*! All come. There is a fight with the Blackfeet!"

"Shoshone?" Cheyenne Killer asked grimly.

"Oosh." The courier charged off to warn the other bands.

Cheyenne Killer shouted a few commands and ran for a horse. Cooper raced into his lodge to get his rifle, shooting pouch and powder horn. By the time he came out, Black Moon Woman had his favorite pony ready. The others were already speeding out of camp. "Come on, boy," he shouted to the horse, ramming it with his heels. The pony leaped forward and hit full stride in only a few steps.

Cooper caught up with the other warriors of his band. As they raced along, in the direction the courier had pointed, Cooper could see other bands of Shoshones forming and galloping after them.

Several miles from the rendezvous, a small band of Shoshones was engaged with a much larger troop of Blackfeet. Both forces were on foot, hidden behind trees or hastily formed bulwarks of logs, dead animals, saddles or bundles of pelts.

As Cooper's band neared the battlefield, five mounted Blackfeet, riding low over their horses' necks, burst from the trees on their side of the small meadow and ran hard for the Shoshones.

Cooper urged a burst of speed from his mount and raced ahead of the others. But Cheyenne Killer and Cuts Throat caught up with him. The three headed off the five Blackfeet. Cooper gunned one down, a lucky shot, he knew, at this distance. Within seconds another went down with one of Cuts Throat's arrows in his throat.

They closed on the enemy, who tried to turn their horses and head back for the protection of their comrades. But the three Shoshones were on them. Cooper, unable to reload in the short time, stuffed the rifle into a loop on his saddle and pulled his crude war club.

He headed for one of the Blackfeet, who realized he could not make safety, and so he whirled, firing three shafts from his bow in the blink of an eye. Cooper had no time to react but breathed a sigh of relief as all three missed. Cooper, who had not really had the time to feel fear, jumped off his racing pony onto the back of the Blackfoot horse, knocking the Indian off, tumbling after him. He landed with a knee in the Blackfoot's stomach, knocking the air out of the Indian.

It was but a moment's work before Cooper had imbedded the blades of his war club in the Blackfoot's forehead. It was but a few seconds more before he had the Indian's scalp in his hand. He was, he thought for a moment in ghastly pride, getting quite adept at taking scalps.

Cooper grabbed the rope rein for his horse and vaulted onto its back in one movement, feeling a twinge of pain in his left leg. He looked down and went white with fear as he saw an arrow sticking out of his left leg near the side. And for the first time he noticed blood on his left side. So the Blackfoot warrior's arrows had not missed. One had scraped his side. The other, he found, was barely stuck in his leg.

He smiled, as relief and fear fought for

dominance inside him. He plucked the arrow free easily. He started to throw it away but decided to keep it. With the shaft in hand, he roared defiance at the Blackfeet in the trees before turning his horse and heading toward safety. He saw Cuts Throat and Cheyenne Killer riding sedately a little distance ahead.

Cooper hurried a bit, reaction setting in. His mouth was dry and his hands wet. His stomach and groin were tight, and he found that his hands were shaking slightly.

Inside the cover of the trees, he saw that many of the mountain men had come to the aid of the Shoshones. He saw Bill Sublette, the acknowledged leader of the mountaineers. And the dour-looking Jed Smith, whose recent return from the dangers and privations encountered on the way back from California was much cause for celebration. Cooper spotted Bridger and nodded. Old Gabe returned it solemnly.

Screwing up his courage, Cooper rode his pony over to Bridger and asked, "What're you doin' here?"

Bridger shrugged and then said seriously, "It gives me a heap of pleasure to kill me Blackfeet whenever and wheresomever I can."

"Seems a likely thing," Cooper said before

riding off to tether his pony.

The battle lasted several hours, mostly at long distance, with each side sniping uselessly at the other. Half a dozen times the Blackfeet mounted charges of varying sizes. Each time they were beaten back by the combined force of mountaineers and Shoshones. Likewise, the Shoshones tried several mounted forays against the Blackfeet. These, too, met with no success.

Cooper, after giving his horse a chance to rest, joined in one of the charges, which had Sublette at its head. Cooper raced across the meadow low on his horse, his heart thumping just behind his Adam's apple. He fired his rifle once and then shoved it into the loop. He pounded into the trees, unhit, and suddenly realized he was behind the Blackfoot lines and alone.

Dread welled up in him. It grew when two Blackfeet jumped from behind trees, one on either side of him. Each was painted. One was armed with a bone war club, the other with a short lance.

With a shout, Cooper kicked his horse. The pony leaped forward and trampled one of the Blackfeet. The horse turned on its own, knowing its master would want to face the other enemy warriors. And it caught the second Blackfoot's lance in its chest.

The pony squealed and went down onto its forelegs. It tried to rise but did not have the strength. Cooper slid off his back, shouting, "You son of a bitch!" He grabbed his war club in both hands and went for the Blackfoot, who was still trying to pull his spear from the struggling horse's chest. He saw Cooper coming and let go of the lance, reaching for his knife in the same movement.

It was too late. Cooper swung the club wildly, fear overwhelmed by rage. He pulverized the Indian's head before he brought himself under control. He stood, breathing heavily, head bowed, war club dangling from his right hand. Slowly he became aware of the danger he was in. He was surrounded by hostile Blackfeet even if they might not know for the moment that he was there alone and on foot.

He fought to control the fear that built up in him, and won. He slid the war club away. He glanced around, making sure no other Blackfoot were lurking. With a shrug, he lifted the two Blackfoot scalps. When he retrieved his rifle, he saw that the horse was still alive. With a lump in his throat, he cut the animal's jugular, ending its misery. Then he calmly loaded his rifle.

Twenty-Nine

Hawley Cooper walked in the Shoshone camp at rendezvous looking rather jaunty, despite some scratches and blood. The trek from the Blackfoot battle had not been easy, but he had been through much worse.

When he strode into the camp, his friends, who had been wailing in their grief for him, raggedly stopped their howling, staring at him in disbelief. He put on a face of fearlessness. He was still shaken. He grabbed a dazed, unprotesting Black Moon Woman and dragged her into their lodge, where he made love to her violently, releasing his pent-up fear, rage and frustration.

She had said nothing throughout. She was still so stunned by his miraculous return that she could not really enjoy their lovemaking. And while her mind struggled with this marvelous good fortune, she remained detached and preoccupied. It was not every day that she was made love to by a ghost.

When it was over and Cooper had regained his breath, Black Moon Woman asked him with quivering voice what had happened. She found she was getting used to having him back already and was intensely pleased.

"It weren't shinin' times, I can tell you," Cooper said with feeling. He explained about the two Blackfeet and the pony. There was a note of regret in his voice. "I figure the rest of the Blackfoot thought those two had took care of me. Elsewise they would've sent others after me, I reckon. By the time they found out them two of their friends weren't comin' back, I was workin' my way back here."

"Goddamn good." She stroked his stubbled cheek. In deference to Black Moon Woman and the rest of the Shoshones, who did not like beards Cooper had been keeping himself shaven, or mostly so. He had found when he arrived at the rendezvous that many of the mountaineers did the same, and for the same reasons.

"Yeah," Cooper agreed, still stunned to be alive. "Goddamn good."

Right after he had killed the two Blackfeet and taken the scalps, he stood muttering, "Goddamn stinkin' Blackfeet." He was angry at the loss of his pony, which was an intelligent, fearless, well-trained beast. He looked out across the meadow toward safety, knowing he would be dead long before he got halfway across the wide expanse of grass.

He nodded, once again fighting back the fear that crawled through his blood, laying like a coiled snake in his belly. With a sigh, he got his bearings and plunged deeper into the woods. There was no path, and he had to fight his way through tangled brush. He stumbled over logs and roots, cursing softly each time. He moved slowly, though it seemed that inside he was racing. He tried making as little noise as possible, though he was sure he was not succeeding.

He heard horses, and his heart quickened in excitement and fear. It must be the Blackfoot herd, he thought. Perhaps he could steal a pony. Or better, he thought, having a vision of becoming a hero, scatter the animals, forcing the Blackfeet to abandon the battle to chase down their horses.

With renewed purpose, he picked his way carefully in the direction of the sounds. And walked right onto a Blackfoot warrior. The Indian had been lying on his stomach next to a blackberry bush, silent and still. He knew Cooper was coming, and had planned to wait until the white man had passed before leaping onto Cooper's back. It would be easy to kill whoever it was then.

But the Indian reacted immediately when Cooper's moccasin came down on his back. He bellowed a warning to the others even as he rolled, throwing Cooper off balance. Cooper fell, sitting, as the Blackfoot jumped up, knife in hand.

Without thinking, Cooper snapped up his rifle and fired. The explosion was loud in the dense thicket, and at this range it left powder burns on the Blackfoot's skin as the .50-caliber ball punched a hole through the Indian.

"Damn, that's done it now," Cooper mumbled. He jerked himself up and saw several other warriors heading in his direction. There was no time even to take the scalp. It surprised him that he even thought of it. Nor was there time to reload the trade rifle. He turned and rushed into the brush, away from the horses.

Cooper could hear at least two Blackfeet chasing him. His heart pounded, and he cursed at the branches that whipped his face and tore at his clothing.

He tripped over a root and fell, scraping his face on the dirt. "Goddamn it," he shouted. He scrambled up and plunged onward, not even certain in what direction he was running anymore. He had a sudden attack of panic when the thought for a moment that he might have gotten turned around and would soon run smack into the heart of the Blackfoot battle line.

He kept running, his chest burning with the effort. His breathing was labored, and his legs felt like they were being jabbed with hot knives. He tripped and fell again. For a few moments he hugged the ground, wishing he could be swallowed up in the earth so that he could rest his aching muscles.

There was a war cry behind him, and fear forced him to move. Without thought, he was running again, each step more painful than the last. There was a stitch in his side, and his stomach hurt from the struggle to breathe.

He thought that perhaps he had outrun his pursuers, or that they might have turned back. He could hear nothing but his own pounding heart and thumping feet, and an occasional jay squawking in protest at his passing. He slowed and then stopped. He bent over, head hanging down, and gulped air. Still there was silence in the forest around him. Even the sounds of the battle had faded.

After several minutes he straightened. He closed his eyes and leaned back against an aspen. Gradually his breathing became less strained, and he relaxed.

His eyes popped open at the war cry, and he saw a Blackfoot four feet away, war club in hand, charging. With no time for fear or thought, Cooper brought his empty rifle up in both hands, like a bat, and swung hard. The butt crashed against the Indian's hand and forearm, sending the war club sailing.

But the Blackfoot could not be slowed. He plowed into Cooper, slamming him back up against the tree. Cooper felt the rifle slip from his fingers. The two men grappled, straining.

Cooper was sweating and several muscles threatened to cramp. He could smell the rancid grease on the Blackfoot's hair and body, and he could see the Indian's deep brown eyes, rimmed with red-tinged white. There was no sympathy or compassion in them.

Over the Blackfoot's shoulder, Cooper could see another warrior coming from the trees. Instead of giving into the feeling of doom that arose, Cooper fought harder, turning vicious in his desperation.

That desperation gave him extra strength, and he wrestled the Indian to the side, throwing him down. He kicked the Blackfoot in the side and then in the face as the Indian fell. "Goddamn murderous savage," he screamed, wrenching out his war club. As the Blackfoot tried to rise, Cooper smashed his face with the club.

Cooper turned, gory war club in hand. "Come on, you mean-assed son of a bitch," he snarled at the other Blackfoot. He was stunned to realize he was no longer afraid. He was beyond that. He had faced death and pain too many times since Josiah Weeks had left him to die in that canyon those many months ago. He would not be afraid of one Blackfoot warrior.

He advanced a few steps toward the Indian, who stood unwavering, knife in his left hand, tomahawk in the other.

"Well, come on, goddamn it," Cooper snapped, his face a mask of determined rage. "You want to raise hair, boy? Well, come on, I'm waitin' for you."

A jay screeched overhead as the two men faced each other silently. Time seemed to stand still. Cooper was aware of the sunbeams filtering down through the trees, creating a patchwork of light and shadow. And he was conscious of the sweat trickling down his sides and stomach. It did not bother him — it was the perspiration of heat and exertion, not the unwelcome sweat of fear.

Cooper took a few more steps toward the

Blackfoot, who spun and disappeared into the foliage. Cooper stood a while, waiting to see if the Indian would return. But he could hear the Blackfoot making his way through the woods, heading back toward where the battle had been. Cooper put away his club and reloaded his rifle, checking to make sure it had not been damaged when he had hit the Indian with it.

Cooper knelt over the Blackfoot, knife in hand. As he started to take the scalp, he looked down on the Indian's shattered face. Without sympathy but without joy he took note of the blood and crushed bones, the vacant eyes staring at the treetops. It gave him an eerie feeling. But it soon passed, and he went on about his business.

Cooper got his bearings and stepped off. He was unhurried and made no effort at concealment. Hell, he thought, if the Blackfeet wanted him, let them find him!

Several hours of walking through tangled brush and scrambling over rocks brought him to the Shoshone camp, where Cheyenne Killer, Twisted Eye, Long Singer, Black Moon Woman, Cuts Throat, and some of his other friends were wailing in mourning at Cooper's passing. The battle had ended shortly after Cooper disappeared into the trees, he learned, and the men had drifted, victorious, back to the rendezvous as the Blackfeet fled northward.

After telling Black Moon Woman his story, she hugged him tightly, and made love to him. Then he slept, while Black Moon Woman went to tell the others of her brave, strong husband's adventures.

Cooper slept straight through until morning. He was awake before first light, laying quietly in his robes, enjoying the feel of Black Moon Woman's naked body next to his, and the smells of the lodge — fur and buckskin, food and smoke, the warmth of the summer morning.

Black Moon Woman sensed him awake and woke, too, smiling at him. "Food, my husband?" she asked.

"Later," he growled, taking her in his arms.

A little while after, she arose and cooked some buffalo and elk meat in a stew. Afterward, Black Moon Woman poulticed Cooper's small wounds. Then she gave him a new set of buckskins, finely decorated with patterns of glass beads, hawk bells and dyed porcupine quills. The buckskin had been tanned to a creamy, off-white color. The sleeves of the shirt hung with long fringes, and two Crow scalps dangled from the breast. The pants also had long fringes down each side, and a curlicue pattern of colored decorations adorned the front. A pair of moccasins, contoured to his feet, decorated in much the same way completed the package.

"When'd you do this?" Cooper asked, joy bright in his eyes.

"I been working on them," Black Moon Woman said in Shoshone, trying not to show the pride that threatened to burst her heart. She had started them two days after they were married and worked on them whenever she could. She had planned to give them to him in a few days, while still at rendezvous, because they were not as completely decorated as she would like. But his extraordinary return made her put those plans aside, and she give him the garments now.

"Goddamn, these're nice," Cooper said in hushed tones.

Black Moon Woman beamed, though she averted her face so he would not see it. It was not right that she reveal her pride to him, but later, when she was with Pony Woman and some of the other women . . .

When Cooper stepped out of the dim lodge into the bright hot sunshine of the July afternoon, he noticed a new respect for him in the eyes of the other Shoshones. And as he wandered around the rendezvous, he noticed it in the eyes of the other mountain men. He began to strut just a little, chest puffed with pride, both in his newfound self-assurance, and because he was so finely decked out.

Late that morning he brought his furs down to the trading tents. He talked with the agent of the American Fur Company but decided to sell his furs to Bill Sublette.

After pocketing his gold coins, he began looking around the trading tents. He wanted nearly everything he saw: pipes, tobacco, foodstuffs, knives, tomahawks, foofaraw of all sorts. But he put it off. Black Moon Woman was a good wife, and a good woman, but still, like the other women, she wanted her share of geegaws. He intended that she have plenty of it.

But first he needed supplies and such for the next season: traps, with spare parts; powder, lead and flints; a few cookpots; a coffee pot, coffee, tea, sugar; hardtack and a few other foodstuffs; some whiskey; tobacco; a new pipe; trade goods like awls, knives, blankets, mirrors, bolts of cloth and such.

He began to think the list would never end. Besides, he did not have that much money. With the prices that shocked him at their excessiveness, it would not last long.

He talked with Cheyenne Killer, and finally decided to get basically just what he needed for trapping. If he was sparing in his use of the supplies and wintered with the Shoshones, as was likely, he would not need much in the way of trade goods. The savings could be used for essentials.

He made his purchases as wisely as he could, though he bought more foofaraw for Black Moon Woman and her family than he should have. Whatever else he needed probably could wait. He took everything back to his lodge.

Then, with Black Moon Woman in tow, rifle cradled in his left arm and a bottle of whiskey swinging in his right hand, he set off to take part in the rendezvous. It was time.

He was happy for the first time since he had left the blacksmith's shop a little more than a year ago. Had it been only that long? He finally felt like he fit in somewhere, as men red and white greeted him as their equal. It was a pleasant feeling.

The bright, warm feeling vanished in an instant when he saw a familiar face. An icy rage gripped him. He spun, face set in stone, to Black Moon Woman. "Go on back to the lodge," he said more harshly than he had intended, shocking her with his vehemence.

"What . . . ?"

"Do it, woman." He turned away from her, took a few steps and shouted, "Josiah Weeks!"

THIRTY

Hawley Cooper dropped the bottle of whiskey, not caring in the least that it cost five dollars a pint here. He started bringing his rifle up. Fury roared through his veins. He had not really thought of revenge in the intervening months, despite all that had happened to him. But the sight of Josiah Weeks standing there, half-drunk, covered with filth, gore and festering hatred, sent Cooper's blood boiling.

Cooper checked himself, drawing in a ragged breath. He settled the rifle back in its cradle of an arm as he looked over Weeks. The man had not changed, really, though to Cooper he was an infinitely more pitiable man. His nose was redder than Cooper remembered, laced with a fine river system of veins, as were his eyes. There might have been another gap where a tooth had come out. But the wide, square shoulders and big hands still looked strong.

Weeks looked like he had just seen a spirit. He was shaken, and his face pasty white. He recovered quickly, as the noise around the two men faded with Cooper's shout. Many turned to stare, and wonder. Few had any liking for Josiah Weeks, and Cooper, with his actions in the battle against the Blackfeet, had gained much respect.

"Looks like you've done well, boy," Weeks said, trying to smile without much success.

"No thanks to you, you son of a bitch," Cooper snarled.

Weeks shrugged, seeming unconcerned. "Ye made it, boy. Seems to me like I done ye some good."

"By leavin' me stretched out cold and alone to die. It weren't bad enough you hit me from behind and then ran off, but you stole all my possibles to boot. Left me with nothin' but my wits and my will."

"It done ye all right."

"Dammit, you don't steal a man's plunder and leave him to die!"

"That don't shine with this coon," someone in the growing crowd shouted.

"Raise hair, boy," another roared.

"Never should've took my woman into your robes, boy."

Cooper felt a shock run through him, and he gulped. He was afraid the crowd would turn against him. But no man here had any liking for Weeks. And, knowing Weeks as some of them did, most would reckon that Cooper had done the woman, whoever she might be, a favor. Only a few grumbles trickled through the crowd. "I wouldn't have," Cooper said, trying to keep his voice calm, "if you hadn't of been whompin' on her regular."

Cooper relaxed, knowing from the sounds that the crowd was behind him. Any sympathy Weeks might have gotten by revealing that Cooper had stolen his woman was suddenly lost on these men. Most of the mountain men would lodgepole their women when they thought it necessary, or even trade them off. But for the most part they didn't hold with a man as big as Weeks beating on a woman regular.

Weeks spat and shifted the Dickert rifle in his hands.

"Where is Tall Grass anyway?" Cooper asked, suddenly feeling ice in his innards.

Weeks grinned sardonically but said nothing.

More men had drifted up. Cooper was conscious of it, but he ignored it. He suddenly felt the presence of Cheyenne Killer a step behind him on his left and Cuts Throat in the same position on his right.

"Whoo-ee, boy," Weeks rasped, swigging from a bottle. "Even brung along your pet Injuns, eh?"

Weeks was an incredibly stupid man, Cooper realized. The crowd was already against him for reasons too numerous to list, had someone asked. Now he was disparaging the Shoshones, who had been friends with the white man since Lewis and Clark visited them.

"I don't need no goddamn . . ." Cooper began, then abruptly stopped. He drew in a ragged breath to calm his temper. "They're here because they're my friends. But I reckon that's not somethin' you'd understand."

"I got friends," Weeks said, surly.

"Can you pick one out?" Cooper looked around and then shook his head. "I reckon you can't. Not here leastways."

"You're gettin' yourself in deep shit here, boy. Ye keep shootin' off your mouth, I might take exception to it."

"Makes no difference to me," Cooper said. "Only way you're gonna hurt me is if I turn my back to you. It's the only way you do things. But I ain't gonna do that. Not no more."

Weeks laughed the horrid, raspy sound that Cooper hated so much. "Ye sure are makin' me tremble, boy," he chuckled. "I've faced down Sioux and Crow and Blackfoot and other tribes too numerous to tell, and I come away from it all with my hair intact. I. . ."

"The hell with your tales, old man. I asked you where Tall Grass was." His heart skipped a beat as he waited.

Weeks smiled crookedly and shook his rifle, making the scalp attached there dance a little. "Right here, boy," Weeks laughed, wheezing some. "She were a good one, old Tall Grass were. Leastways till her usefulness run out. She were particularly appealin' just after ye left us. She knew how to treat a man right, then, she did." Weeks' laughter sickened Cooper.

But the young man managed to control his emotions. "It's time somebody commenced teaching you a thing or two, old man," Cooper said quietly, drawing an excited buzz from the crowd.

Weeks laughed again. "You?" he asked.

Cooper seethed but said nothing. Without taking his eyes off Weeks, he handed his rifle to Cheyenne Killer, pulled off his possible sack, powder horn and shooting bag, gave them to Cuts Throat, and then started peeling off his shirt.

Weeks grinned malevolently, and brought

his rifle up, the muzzle aiming for Cooper's chest.

Cooper saw a calico-sleeved arm shoot out and grab the barrel of Weeks' rifle and shove it skyward. There was an explosion as the rifle fired harmlessly into the air.

"We canna be havin' noon of that now, can we?" a Scottish burr said. "Nae. Now let's hae the rifle, and ye can commence fightin'."

Weeks sneered at the man holding his rifle, then spit at him.

"Now, laddie," the man said, nonplussed, but his voice was suddenly hard as stone, "ye do that again, and ye'll nae be livin' long enough to take the few steps o'er yonder to face young laddie boy who's awaitin' your pleasure."

Weeks tried staring the man down, but broke his gaze away quickly, not liking what he had seen in the other man's eyes. Scowling, he turned back toward Cooper and started walking.

Cooper smiled. He was not afraid, and he knew that he had grown up. He was no longer the young, untested boy who had bumped into Weeks on a squalid street in St. Louis. No, he was a man now, tried and tempered by the worst the mountains could throw at him. He was strong and sure, completely healed of his wounds from the past winter. Even the minor injuries from the battle with the Blackfeet would not hamper him.

He touched the pouch that still hung on his chest under his shirt. He said a silent farewell to the bland-faced Pawnee woman, and he hoped she had found a happier place. He crouched then, wary, as he neared Weeks.

Weeks suddenly fell to the side and swept both his legs at Cooper's. Cooper jumped up and over the sweep, but as he landed, Weeks's heels doubled back and caught Cooper behind both knees. Cooper went down to his knees as if jerked by a rope. In a flash Weeks was on his back, greasy-sleeved arm around his throat, squeezing.

"Think ye can take me, boy?" Weeks rasped in Cooper's ear. "Think I'm easy pickin's, eh, ye Injun-lovin' son of a bitch?"

Cooper said nothing, but clawed at Weeks's arm, trying to dislodge the painful vise that threatened his life. It did no good. He suddenly stopped and balled each hand into a fist, thumbs out. He jerked each arm backward over his shoulder as hard as he could.

He felt pain as one thumb slammed into Weeks' bony forehead. But the other sank into Weeks's eye. The trapper roared and loosened his grip enough for Cooper to get his hands on Weeks' forearm and wrench it from around his neck. He swiveled on his knees, digging his right shoulder into Weeks's armpit and yanking. Weeks sailed over Cooper's shoulder, flipping, to land on his back.

Cooper fell forward onto his hands, breathing harshly. Fire raged in his throat, and his eyesight was blurred. But with several gulps of air, he saw the world in a better light.

Weeks was a little slow getting up, but Cooper, who rocked back onto his heels, was still sitting when the trapper got to his feet. Weeks kicked at Cooper's head, but the youth ducked out of the way and fell to the side, rolling and coming up on his feet.

This was not going to be as easy as he had thought, Cooper realized, but he was not about to quit now. He wiped the sweat from his forehead, and then his damp hand on his pants. It was a boiling hot day, without a cloud in the sky, and barely a breeze.

Weeks charged him, and Cooper retreated systematically, swinging punches at Weeks as he moved slowly backward. Several caught Weeks on the head, making Cooper's knuckles hurt. Weeks tried to give back as good as he got, but he was swinging wildly. Then he ducked inside one of Cooper's punches and grabbed the young man in a bear hug. He tried to squeeze the life from the youth.

Cooper nearly gagged at Weeks's fetid breath and rancid body odor, but he kept his wits about him. Remembering his battle with Cuts Throat, Cooper reared back his head and then whipped it forward, ramming Weeks' forehead. Weeks grunted but relaxed his grip only fractionally. Cooper sucked in a great breath, expanding his chest. Then he flexed his shoulders and arms with all his might. His neck veins bulged, and his muscles seemed to crackle with the effort. Suddenly he popped out of Weeks' grip. He shoved Weeks away, then began pummeling him mercilessly.

Weeks staggered back and back. His nose burst in a small shower of blood, and cuts appeared over both eyes. His lips swelled. He brought up his arms, trying to fend off the shower of blows, but still the punches rained on him. There was a loud splat and a gash erupted on his cheekbone. He spit out a tooth.

Weeks stumbled and sank to one knee. Cooper loomed over him, hands aching from the punches. But his right fist was poised over Weeks. "I want," Cooper panted, "all my plunder back. Every last bit of it. Includin' my mug, damn you."

"Ain't nothin' left," Weeks said, voice barely audible.

Cooper was aware of an awesome silence, and he realized that all the shouting by the bystanders had stopped. They were all waiting eagerly for the coup de grace. "Where's your lodge?" Cooper asked.

Weeks nodded his head toward the south. "Near the creek thataway."

"You sold your plews yet?"

Weeks nodded, exhaustion and doom laying heavily on him as he awaited his execution.

"You spent it all yet?"

"Nope."

"I ought to kill you," Cooper said vehemently. "But I ain't gonna do that." There was an angry roar of the bystanders. They had gathered to see a killing, and now they thought they would be disappointed. Money changed hands as bets were paid.

Suddenly Cooper's fist smashed into the side of Weeks' face. A cheer exploded from the crowd as Weeks collapsed, groaning from the cracked bones of his cheek and jaw.

"No, I ain't gonna do that," Cooper said,

almost enjoying this. "But what I am gonna do, old man, is to leave you just the way you left me. With nothin'."

The crowd buzzed excitedly as the idea caught on.

Weeks moaned as Cooper went through his possible bag. He pulled out a small roll of paper dollars and a buckskin pouch of coins. Cooper stood and looked at the crowd. "Some of you boys know what this man done to me," he shouted for all to hear. "Others of you will know if you ask about. I aim to see Weeks gets the same as he give me. I find any of you has supplied him with so much as a handful of parched corn, I'll come lookin' for you."

Cooper stuffed the money back into the possible bag and then tore the sack off the groaning Weeks. Then he took Weeks' shooting pouch and powder horn. With the three items in his left hand, he walked to where Weeks had been when the fight started. He held out his right hand, and the burly, bearded Scot who had taken the Dickert flintlock from Weeks put it silently in his hands, nodding with a small smile curling his lips. Cooper strolled toward where Cheyenne Killer, Cuts Throat, Blue Bear, Black Moon Woman and Pony Woman stood, beaming with smiles, waiting for him.

He was almost to them when Black Moon Woman screamed, holding out her hand in horror.

Cooper froze in midstep as Weeks shouted, "I come to this here rendezvous with the hair of the bear on me, boy, and I aim to leave the same way. Ain't no young pup like ye gonna put me under slow like some got-damned redskin savage would."

The words were garbled, but understandable. Cooper turned. Weeks' face was a bloody mask, and his jaw would not work right. He stood, weaving, eyes clouded with hate and pain. But there was a pistol in his hand, pointed at Cooper.

"Come on ahead, then," Cooper said, voice calm though a sliver of fear wormed into his belly. "Fire, you Injin-killin' bastard. You ain't got the balls to shoot me face on, dammit." He stood facing Weeks, swelling hands balled into fists resting on his hips.

Weeks fired, surprising Cooper, who was knocked back by the power of the .54-caliber lead ball hitting him. He gasped at the fire of the pain, and wondered why he did not fall writhing in agony. The sudden burst of fear that had splashed over him was washed away by relief when he realized the rifle ball had only grazed his left shoulder.

"You're euchred out, Weeks," Cooper said

calmly. He started forward, pulling his knife.

Weeks turned and tried to run. But he hit a wall of flesh, as the angry mountain men shoved him back to meet his fate. Weeks turned, terror written all over the bloody, broken face, as he pulled his own knife and advanced woozily.

Within striking range, Weeks swung his blade. With hardly an effort, Cooper slapped it away. Then, feeling the rage boil over, he rammed the knife home. With some pleasure, Cooper watched the shock of it in Weeks' eyes. He ripped the knife upward, tearing through flesh, muscles and organs.

Weeks sagged against him, and Cooper shoved the man away, wrenching the knife free at the same time. Then, without thinking about it, he carved off Weeks' scalp. There was a cheer from the crowd, and more money passed hands.

"What was his is mine," Cooper shouted. "Whatever plunder this man's had comes to me now."

Cooper did not wait for arguments or approbation. He just nodded and tore off the medicine bundle from around his neck. He dropped it on Weeks' body and walked back to his friends and his woman.

ABOUT THE AUTHOR

John Legg has published more than 55 novels, all on Old West themes. Legg holds a B.A. in Communications and an M.S. in Journalism, and is a copy editor with The New York Times News Service.

Since his first two books, Legg has, under his own name, entertained the Western audience with many more tales of man's fight for independence on the Western frontier. In addition, he has had published several historical novels set in the Old West. Among those are *War at Bent's Fort* and *Blood at Fort Bridger.*

In addition, Legg has, under pseudonyms, contributed to the Rameses series, and was the sole author of the eight books in the Saddle Tramp series. He also was the sole author of Wildgun, an eight-book adult Western series.

The employees of Thorndike Press hope you have enjoyed this Large Print book. All our Thorndike Large Print titles are designed for easy reading, and all our books are made to last. Other Thorndike Press Large Print books are available at your library, through selected bookstores, or directly from us.

For information about titles, please call:
(800) 223-1244

or visit our website at:
gale.com/thorndike